ALONE TOGETHER

"Memory is a thing best held at bay this night. We have a future to cement," Quin said.

True to expectation, the color on Siannon's cheeks paled, but to her credit, his bride did not shrink from the idea, meeting his gaze with a steady look.

Quin sucked in his breath and admired her. Awash in the cool moonlight spilling in from the windows, the satin gown clung to her curves with an intimate caress, both hiding and revealing the enticing promise of her body. No longer was she little Siannon Rhodes.

His heartbeat pounded in his ears accompanied by long-ago echoes of Granny's tales. Who would ever have suspected he would find himself wed to little Siannon, let alone fired beyond all reason with the desire to make love to her?

Grasping her shoulders through the thin stuff of her gown, he pulled her from her chair. "You don't belong here, Siannon," he growled, wishing she didn't feel as if she belonged exactly where she was— in his arms, in his home, in his soul.

"No?" Her tone held softness, but nothing disguised the light of battle glowing in her eyes. "Where do I belong, Quin?"

Dear Romance Reader,

In July, we launched the Ballad line with four new series, and each month we'll present both new and continuing stories set everywhere from medieval England to the American West—the kind of passionate, romantic stories you love best, written by the most gifted authors. At the back of each book, we'll tell you when you can find subsequent books in the series that have captured your heart.

Debuting this month with a fabulous new series called *The Sword and the Ring*, Suzanne McMinn offers **My Lady Imposter.** The pageantry and adventure of medieval England come vividly to life in the rousing story of one incredible family in an age when men lived and died by the sword and a woman's life might be forever changed by a betrothal ring. Next, Alice Duncan continues *The Dream Maker* series with **Beauty and the Brain,** as an actress hiding her intelligence meets her match in a research assistant who knows everything . . . except about love.

Travel back to Regency England with Joy Reed's romantic *Wishing Well* trilogy. In **Anne's Wish,** a marriage of convenience promises unexpected love—unless a jealous rival comes between the newlyweds. Finally, the third book in Elizabeth Keys's charming *Irish Blessing* series reunites childhood companions, but will **Reilly's Pride** stand in the way of a love destined to unite two souls in matrimony?

Kate Duffy
Editorial Director

Irish Blessing

REILLY'S PRIDE

Elizabeth Keys

To Lillian
Pleasure meeting you
again! MaryAnn & Susan
AKA
Elizabeth Keys

ZEBRA BOOKS
KENSINGTON PUBLISHING CORP.
http://www.zebrabooks.com

ZEBRA BOOKS are published by

Kensington Publishing Corp.
850 Third Avenue
New York, NY 10022

All Kensington titles, imprints and distributed lines are available at special quantity discounts for bulk purchases for sales
promotion, premiums, fund-raising, educational or institutional
use.

Special book excerpts or customized printings can also be created to fit specific needs. For details, write or phone the office of
the Kensington Special Sales Manager: Kensington Publishing
Corp., 850 Third Avenue, New York, NY 10022. Attn. Special
Sales Department. Phone: 1-800-221-2647.

First Printing: May 2001
10 9 8 7 6 5 4 3 2 1

Printed in the United States of America

This book is dedicated to our sisters, Bonnie and Linda, for their support and caring; to our critique-sisters, Carolyn, Gwen, and Ruth Ellen, for loving our heroes almost as much as we do and forcing us to "specify"; to our husbands, Drew and Tom, for being the very special men they are; and to our children, Andy, Tommy, Brian, Corey, Kyle, Rachel, and Connor, the true *blessings* in our lives.

Prologue

Beannacht Island
Western Ireland
1842

The three Reilly brothers stood for a moment in the doorway to the too-silent bedchamber, loath to leave, as though that meant their granny truly was gone.

"Good night, Granny," Bryan, the middle one, offered. His words sounded hollow as they pushed across the hardwood floor.

"We love you," Devin, the youngest, sniffed.

"And we'll remember," Quin whispered firmly.

Quintin, the eldest of the boys, had been charged with the telling this night. Now that his duty had been discharged, he picked up the lamp and they all trudged out into the corridor.

The last glow from the fireplace died away, leaving the room awash in pallid moonlight and the lingering scent of Granny Reilly's lavender perfume.

Waiting a few moments more, the girl edged out of the wardrobe and shivered. She'd nearly been discovered.

The emotions ebbing from the room with the boys' departure still swirled through her—love and dreams, anger and grief. She shivered again and tried to rein in the feelings as her own gran had taught her.

Lacing her fingers together, she sat on the edge of Granny Reilly's rocker. There was too little warmth from the hearth to still her quaking. She scooted backward and hugged her knees, the comforting scent of lavender from the green wool shawl behind her finally quieting her shaking.

It was always thus with her, she felt what others felt—their fear, their joy, and every emotion in between. For her gran The Sight came as visions, both of what was at a distance or soon might be. Mama heard things whispering in her ear—warnings and predictions no others harkened.

For her, it came as waves of pure emotion, sometimes lifting her spirit, sometimes threatening to sweep her away and dash her against the rocks of another's despair.

She was too young to interpret all that she felt, so Gran explained—to filter through what was useful and block what would harm her. But she would learn, Gran said, and someday she would put to good use this talent she'd been given.

She wished she could use her Gift tonight, as she peeked through the door on the wardrobe, use it to find the words and tell her friends that soon the weight of their grief would pass. That the light of their granny's love would shine for them once more. But even without her special ability she could tell this was a solemn, private ritual. The Reilly brothers would not have welcomed her intrusion no matter her intentions.

Especially Quin. He always took things too seriously.

"Ye must be ready fer The Blessing at any time," he intoned. "And ye must heed it, fer a blessing missed is a curse indeed."

His words still seemed to echo reverently within Granny Reilly's room. The shivering started again with the thought she was not alone.

She wrapped the shawl around her shoulders and considered the import of what she'd heard. The Blessing. She liked the sound of that. And the explanation that had followed.

" 'Tis a sound once heard that lingers on. A sight once seen and never forgotten. A feeling once felt, always remembered. 'Tis in the blood of all Reillys," Quin had said.

Sight, sound, and feeling, just like the bounty given her own family. She'd never known anyone else, besides Mama and Gran, who had a gift that set them apart. Papa called them signs of the devil. The only emotion she ever felt from Papa was anger—black and suffocating.

Better to think of what the boys had said. To memorize the chant for later contemplation.

"Reillys take heed and Reillys beware, for unto ye is delivered a great gift. A token of esteem, a promise, a fearsome gratitude." The firelight had flickered over Quin's solemn face, the only one she could see through the crack. "For nine unto nine, ye must make the choice. Only ye can direct the course to joy or sorrow. Only ye decide if it is Blessing or Curse."

"I hope mine's not a curse," Devin, nearest in age to her and her playmate during her annual visits, whispered.

The older two ignored him.

"It can roll in with the thunder or seep in like the dew. It might fly past in a flash or dance by on a song. The knowin' is up to us. The doin' another part," Quin continued.

"Aye," Bryan agreed. "The joy of yer heart, the wish of yer soul, the direction of yer life, the path of yer choosing."

"The choice, once made, cannot be undone," Quintin intoned.

"The decision once forged cannot be altered," Bryan and Devin both returned.

"Blessing or Curse for all time," they all spoke as one.

"For all time," they repeated.

The three voices died away, leaving only the solemn tick of the clock on the fireplace mantel and the murmur of the adult voices from the parlor below.

Devin sighed. "I still wish Gran was here to do the telling. I especially like the way she talked of the first Blessing. And the Druids."

"Aye. We all wish Gran were still here." Quintin's agreement held equal sorrow.

She thought of them as they'd stood earlier in the day on a windswept hill, dressed in their Sunday best. Three pairs of mirthless green eyes so like their da's. A row of dark heads bowed with grief in a sea of mourners. Granny Reilly would be missed by many this night and in the lifetimes to come.

The boys spoke for a bit more as the fire in Granny Reilly's hearth died, discussing the funeral and debating whether their baby sister had a chance at her own Blessing. Anything to put off leaving the room and bringing to a close this day's events and the good-bye they all dreaded facing in its finality. She'd almost given herself away then, so cramped was she in the wardrobe.

"Come on, we'd best get to bed before they discover we're not there." Quintin took charge finally, as he usually did to Bryan's unease and Devin's awe. "It will be a long time till any of us experience The Blessing."

But experience it they would, each in their own way. She was certain. Sights, sounds, and feelings they'd yet to explore.

"The joy of their hearts, the wish of their souls," she repeated. The Blessing added a luster to the future for each Reilly. Wistful envy twined through her, followed by a soothing hum that blocked all of the emotions from the wake below and all her fears for her own life. Curled under the green shawl, she rested her head on the arm of the rocker and found the refuge she had sought here.

A questing rippled the air, waking her before she ever heard the call.

"Siannon. Siannon. It's time to go." Her gran's voice sounded from below, searching for her in the crowded parlor.

She scrambled up, dazed from the momentary peace she had been granted. She scooped the shawl that had fallen to the floor into her arms and hugged it, inhaling the lavender as its rough texture rubbed her cheeks.

Chapter One

Limerick, Ireland
1858

"Diabhal."

Moderating his onshore language to include only the mildest curses was yet one more concession grating like sand against Quintin Reilly's soul. The Gaelic version of "devil" didn't come close to expressing his true level of frustration. His sigh barely echoed back to him from across the paper-shrouded office before the door sprang open.

Again.

"They are ready for you, Captain Reilly." The eager expression on the young English clerk's face served only to sharpen the misgivings gnawing with such jagged persistence at Quin's gut.

This was all happening much too quickly.

"Aye," he answered, not bothering to tamp back the growl that came from deep inside him. Guilt floated too near his surface for a nicety of manners.

The clerk's eyes widened. "Shall I say you are on your way?"

"Aye." Irritation flared anew, prodded more by memory than by present circumstances, though the fellow's clipped English tones did little to commend him to Quin's good graces.

If Bryan were there, he'd make sure everything was shipshape and deal with this paper-poker to boot. Quin knew his brother would either agree with the logic leading to this choice or provide a check for a grave personal error looming on the horizon. But Bryan had asked for a leave from his firm and left town aboard the *Caithream* earlier in the week without apprising anyone of his destination. What sort of trouble could have caused his brother to leave without so much as a word or a stop at the island?

"Diabhal." Quin swore again as this new worry joined the cargo he already freighted. He'd let Bryan down once and vowed never to let it happen again. But how could he be of any use if his taciturn brother failed to enlighten him?

"Oh, dear." The young clerk's eyes bulged at the expletive before he disappeared back the way he had come, rattling the glass panes in the door with his efforts to quit the vicinity with all due haste.

Quin snorted. Such a meek soul would not survive even one night at sea. Not even with a barrel of Granny's special ginger tea to bolster him. A short bark of laughter escaped him as he pushed to his feet, though the shot of humor did little to improve his mood or to lighten the worries that had become a perpetual part of him over the last months.

Even if he mustered all the financing necessary to complete the Ship Works' latest contract, could he find the suppliers for the materials in time? They could not afford the penalties for failure to deliver the goods on schedule. These endless snags must have driven Da into the poor health even a trip to Italy's warm climes had yet to improve.

Thinking of his parents and their possible reactions to his current course unsettled him further. He touched the most recent missive from his mother, which he'd shoved into his pocket. What would they have to say about the events now unfolding within the prestigious depths of Limerick's history-laden courthouse? And what would the rest of Beannacht Island have to say as well?

Too late to change his heading now. He pushed his doubts aside with an impatient shift of his shoulders, shoving them down along with the rest of the questions circling relentlessly through his mind. He'd already spent more time away from the Ship Works and the mounting pressure of his responsibilities than he intended. He'd no more time to waste.

He grasped the cold brass doorknob in his fingers and gave it a resolute turn. What he wouldn't give to have the solid feel of a Reilly deck beneath his feet and the invigorating whip of the wind in his face as it filled the sails over his head. Such had been his life and breath for the past eight years.

But his time was no longer his own, his course no longer his to chart to suit himself. Reilly Ship Works was his command now. Her destiny, and that of all the people who depended on her for their livelihood, rested with him. As it should. The Ship Works was part of him, bone and blood and sinew, Reilly born and Reilly bred, just as he was.

The needs summoning him from his ship took precedence despite his continued longing for the open sea and the scent of adventure waiting at every crisp snap of a sail. The responsibility for the family fell to the eldest son. He'd always known it would someday. The time had just arrived much more quickly than he'd anticipated.

Now his duty would be divided still further, surrendered in part to a woman he barely remembered. A woman he hadn't seen since she was a child scrambling over the rocks with his little brother. A woman to whom he owed the very life of that brother.

The fact that she came with a ready-made anchor of her own served to further complicate their tangled situation. What kind of seaman allows himself to be snagged so thoroughly on such ragged shoals?

A desperate one. The truth mocked him for his attempted arrogance in claiming this course was set to smooth the passage for his wife-to-be alone. Benefits rested in these waters for both of them.

"Best to have done with it." Standing there like a fearful landsman chafed his already raw nerves.

His boots rang hollow against the floorboards as he strode into the hallway and crossed the massive corridor to the magistrate's private chambers.

The low hum of conversation ceased as he entered and shut the solid oaken portal behind him.

"He has arrived, my lord." The clerk's high-pitched tone carried toward him. The clerk glanced at the paper he clutched. "May I present Captain Quintin

Reilly of Beannacht Island and the Widow Crofton, Si-Sian—"

"Her name is said like the river that runs not far from here." Though his gaze remained transfixed by the woman seated on a low bench across the chamber, Quintin growled at the English clerk, who betrayed his ignorance of the land he now sought to claim for his home. "The River Shannon. If you plan to live in our land, you could at least attempt to learn how to pronounce our names as they were meant to be said. Siannon Rhodes Crofton."

Siannon stood as the cerk stammered an apology, her skirts rustling to the floor in a hasty whisper of silvery gray silk, a perfect match for the darkened depths of her eyes as she turned to face him. She had come to him still garbed in the half-mourning widow's hues society demanded of her.

How oddly appropriate.

The gown's subdued color served only to highlight the lush golden red of her hair and the smooth porcelain fineness of her skin. The gangly girl she had once been had definitely retreated into the past, recognizable only in the hesitation still lurking in her eyes. Quin tamped down a wisp of regret for the time lost to them both. He was far from the boy he had been as well.

How would they deal together? Surely the solution of the present would cause rough water in the future. How would they face the storms?

Questions far too late to ask, too daunting to answer.

"Hello, Quin." Prim and soft, she greeted him, holding out her hand as though they were meeting on the street or at a casual gathering for tea in a

Limerick drawing room. The determination with which she had addressed him the previous day seemed to have disappeared.

He touched her fingers briefly—they were soft and cool against his own.

"We'd best hurry; my father—"

"Aye." He cut off her worries before she could finish them. Best not to further muddy the legal waters until after the deed was truly done. The thought startled another errant twinge of humor from him. Apparently he had absorbed a small portion of legal wariness from all those conversations with Bryan.

How interesting.

Would Bryan get a chuckle out of the predicament Quin now found himself in; voluntarily anchoring himself to port in such a permanent fashion? Bryan had made the adjustment when he'd given up his hopes for a life at sea for his legal studies. His elder brother would learn to adjust as well.

"Captain. Madam." The magistrate addressed them directly.

Quin straightened to attention as Siannon stood at his side. The soft scents of lavender and lilac drifted from her hair, unleashing an odd and unwanted tenderness in his chest.

He'd have sworn he hadn't once thought of Siannon Rhodes since she left the island nearly ten summers before, or at least since he heard her father had successfully married her to Percival Crofton. Eustace Rhodes gained connections and a hefty bride-price for his daughter. What had Siannon gained?

When Quin received her letter, he'd known he couldn't ignore her plight. Outside the offices of

O'Brien and Mallory just the day before, the fear and desperation haunting those deep gray eyes had forced him to realize she had never been far from his thoughts.

Her resolute proposal, delivered in cool, short bursts, had shown how precarious her situation had grown, how hard she'd pinned her hopes to her offer. Despite the awkwardness of her position, there had been no embarrassment, no display of weakness in the gaze she'd locked with his. His admiration had twined with his own determination that this was their most expedient course. Relief that their thoughts were so compatible had sealed the bargain right there on Limerick's main thoroughfare. The capital she offered only sweetened the deal.

Doubts flooded him now as they had not then. Did they plague her as well? She had not been happy in her first marriage despite the much-heralded birth of her son. At least this time she would be safe. He owed her that much. The Reillys owed her grandparents that much and more.

"Join hands," the magistrate intoned.

Quin took Siannon's cool fingers in his own again. Her gaze met his as the magistrate cleared his throat.

"Thank you, Quintin." Her whisper tore through him.

Her gratitude chafed against raw wounds he'd striven to forget for too long. The certainty he was selling his name for the opportunity to help Reilly Ship Works out of its present debacle seared his soul.

Still, this marriage provided protection for Siannon and the boy by the most sure and expedient means. He would have to swallow the fact that in doing this he obligated himself in the one manner he had sworn never to experience again. This action would settle old debts owed her family that money would never touch—the only balm he could use to salve his pride. He broke the invisible bonds she held on his gaze as the magistrate droned the words that would tie them irrevocably together.

A vivid image of Granny frowning her disappointment hovered in his thoughts and tightened his throat. *The Blessing.* Of all of them, he had been charged with the telling, and somehow with that charge had come the ability to still believe for the stretch of many years. Though his brothers had long ago ceased to carry the trust, Quintin accepted the truth deep in the most private depths of himself, where no one could touch him.

He believed in The Blessing, and the terrible responsibility that went along with it. Only his own neglect had forced him to finally leave that ancient tale behind him. To turn his back on generations of ingrained teachings, on history and the fearsome gratitude awaiting him. He did not deserve such.

Memories churned acid in his stomach.

He slid his signet ring on Siannon's finger, noticing again how slim and soft and white her hands were. The gold Celtic knot flanking the *R* dangled awkwardly from her finger as the magistrate finished his recitation. It was done now; there would be no going back. Whatever the outcome from this, he would have to deal with it as best he could and hope that his years of experience as a ship's captain would help them avoid the shallows sure to lie ahead.

"You may kiss your bride."

Quin turned to Siannon, waiting quietly by his side. His wife.

He leaned toward her, intent on giving her a brief public caress to seal the bargain they had just wrought. He'd had no intention of taking a wife before her letter arrived. But she was his now and that was that. Their bargain was about to be signed and sealed.

He cupped her chin. Her turbulent, storm-tossed gaze locked with his as he bent toward her. Impossibly, he could hear the crash of waves against solid timber in the distance, smell the fresh salt of white water, a strange and seductive siren call pulling him toward her. He brushed his lips across hers. A sudden blinding wave of heat rolled through him, carrying the pitch and toss of an unseen sea, demanding everything he had to give and more.

The Blessing.

" *'Tis a sound once heard that lingers on. A sight once seen and never forgotten. A feeling once felt, always remembered.* "

Granny Reilly's teachings roared across the years, rocking him from the mores he'd grown accustomed to, promising the formidable appreciation that was his right. No, more than that. His duty. What portent could The Blessing carry at this time? The deed was already done. The choice made. Still, he felt powerless to resist the maelstrom exploding within him.

He pulled Siannon to him, unable to stop himself, swallowing the soft gasp his sudden demands startled from her. He could not pull back no matter the distant alarm ringing in his mind. He could not keep from ravishing her mouth, molding her body thoroughly against his. She was so incredibly, bewitchingly soft. Her hands clutched his shoulders as he anchored his fingers in the shiny coppery depths of her hair gathered at her nape.

He tilted her head to more openly accommodate him. The pungently sweet smell of sun-warmed lavender and lilacs rose from her to envelop him. Surely no woman had ever felt so in his arms, never threatened to tear his soul from him with the touch of her lips or rend to shreds any measure of self-possession he laid claim to.

His tongue slid against hers, tasting her. Sunshine and deep summer grass.

Sweet heaven, the fiery heat would surely burn them both to cinders. He had never wanted a woman more swiftly or completely than he now wanted Siannon Crofton.

No, Siannon *Reilly*.

Fierce possession exploded through him. Certainty pierced his thoughts that regardless of their present circumstances or who looked on, he could make love to her right there and damn the consequences.

He shuddered, unable to reconcile the passion raging inside him with the pain that had been his constant companion for five long years. He forced himself to release her as The Blessing echoed down to his toes in all its raw power. With a silent groan, he reached desperately for any tattered shreds of sanity he might yet possess. Her cheeks and lips were flushed, her gaze wide and filled with a sultry mix of confusion and lingering passion that stabbed fresh desire through his gut.

Everything Granny had crooned proved truer than he could ever have guessed and more overwhelming than anything he had ever anticipated. But what did it mean?

"The knowin' is up to us. The doin' another part. Capture The Blessing or suffer The Curse."

"Well, I'd say that about seals the vows as best as I've ever seen it done." The magistrate's chuckle joined his clerk's high titter.

The court officials' amusement grated on Quin's nerves, still raw from what he had just shared with his wife. He didn't have time to dwell on this muddle. Even now his ship made ready in the harbor to sail back at first light to Beannacht and the duties awaiting him there.

Quin turned his regard toward the magistrate and the snickering clerk, gratified to watch the lad's amusement die away on his lips with a nervous flutter. The magistrate scowled.

"Is the deed completed?" Quin clipped the words off in an effort to hide the rough desire still raging inside him. He refused to look back into Siannon's eyes and risk being snared by the swirl of emotions he'd glimpsed there already.

"Aye." The magistrate ruffled his thick white mustache with his fingers, as though wiping the last vestiges of humor away. "You've only to sign the register."

They accomplished the signing in relative silence, sealing his fate with that of Eustace Rhodes's daughter and forever binding their futures together. The finality of the act dragged against his shoulders like weighted stone, Blessing or no.

For a moment he felt tempted to obliterate the two entwined names from the register page and demand his freedom. And hers. He ground his teeth together and turned away from the register. He could not forsake the ancient ties that bound the Reilly and McManus families. The Blessing served only to tighten those bonds. A curse in fact as well as in deed.

"Quin?" Siannon's voice cut through his thoughts, and he turned from the register to face the questions shining in her eyes. "Are you all right?"

Somehow all right didn't begin to describe his current state of mind. Mary McManus, Siannon's mother, had been an islander. Maternal and fraternal grandfathers on both sides had worked at the shipyard for generations. He would not allow Siannon to be lost, as her mother had been. He could not.

"Aye." He managed to answer beyond the tightness in his throat. Suddenly he could bear the confines of the musty courthouse not one moment longer. He nodded to the magistrate and cupped Siannon's elbow, directing their course toward the street and the open air.

The shouts of the street vendors and rumble of carriage wheels passing below them barely registered for Siannon as Quin guided her down the courthouse steps toward the waiting hackney. Looped over her wrist, her bonnet fluttered behind them along with her reticule. Her husband had not even allowed her the time to pull on her gloves, so eager did he appear to flee the ceremony that had sealed their fates together for eternity.

The late afternoon sun glinting on the windows across the street, passersby in a harlequin of colors and dress, the pungent scent of the nearby harbor— everything seemed to swirl and eddy in the distance while the hammering of her heart pounded through her with the inescapable knowledge her long-held fantasy had just come true.

She was Mrs. Quintin Reilly.

A bubble of laughter, burned by tears, battled for release within her. She swallowed hard, refusing to give in to a hysteria that might very well overwhelm her with no hope of regaining control.

For the moment, she was safe. And more importantly, Timothy was safe too. Just one look at Quintin Reilly assured her this was so. For now that would have to be enough.

Little else of her childhood dreams had survived the cold reality of the bargain they had struck, yet for the moment she could cling to the illusion of destiny fulfilled that Quin had flared to life within her when he'd swept her into his embrace in the magistrate's office. The kiss they'd shared to seal their vows still burned on her lips, melting through her fears—past, present, and future. Kissing Quin was more than she'd ever dared to hope for, far more than she'd ever imagined—a wild surge of sea and wind flaming into passion such as she had never even guessed was possible. Not for her.

The hackney driver tipped his cap and opened the door for them as they approached. She stopped at the base of the steps and looked up to meet her new husband's dark gaze, searching for the boy she had idolized in the man he had become. Her eyes flicked over the small scar by his brow, a long-ago trophy from a mock sword battle with Bryan. How she'd cried when she'd seen the blood pouring from his wound that afternoon. Now it was visible only to the discerning eye.

Despite her inability to read this man before her,

he must still be the same person, the same Quin whose every emotion had been so clear to her so long ago. And yet he was a stranger. She caught back the urge to stroke her finger over his small imperfection.

"Quin." She swallowed around the sudden lump in her throat. He was so very handsome in his gray worsted suit and brushed bowler. A tailored gentleman of business, so very unlike the sea captain he'd been until recently. Or the boy she'd once worshiped.

"I hope you know . . . how"—the unblinking green of his eyes seemed to look straight through her as she stumbled over what she wanted to say—"how deeply . . . that if there had been less urgency . . . or another . . ."

He halted her by gripping her shoulders. "What's done is done, Mrs. Reilly. No use in regrets and no need for pointless gratitude. There'll be no turning back for either of us."

Mrs. Reilly.

Her new name seemed to hang in the air between them along with echoes of the kiss they had just shared. And the shadowy possibilities lurking in their future together. His fingers bore into her. Familiar fears hovered, ready to pounce and obliterate the veneer of peace she grasped with this bargain. She had just bound herself, and her son, to another man. How would they deal with one another?

The pressure of Quin's fingers eased a little but not the determined set of his face. Had she made the right choice or merely set herself up for further subjugation with a new piper calling the tune? It had to be the right choice. She clutched back her fears with an effort.

"We both know what we have to gain from this bargain, Siannon." The ice in Quin's gaze did little to ease the rising tide of her doubt. "We'll face the rest together."

He clamped his lips shut and studied her intently. She should have waited. She should have stammered out her appreciation later, in private. He looked so grim, she regretted having spoken at all. Some truths were best left unspoken, so her gran had told her on more than one occasion. The boldness of her desperate proposal to him yesterday still shook her almost as deeply as the swiftness with which he had agreed. Was Reilly Ship Works really in such desperate straits? What else did he have to gain from this match? She scarcely dared to think he'd harbored secret longings like her own all these years.

She reached out with her Gift, trying to sense the feelings hidden behind Quin's stoic mask. Anger? Resignation? Happiness?

Her temples began to throb, but she ignored the pain as she pushed forward tentatively. Concentrating, she peeled away the protective layers she'd learned to wrap around herself and stretched with a question that met only thick gray fog. Barren.

Too soon. Too close.

Whatever abilities she had harbored to read the boy he had been seemed to have disappeared when faced with the man he had become. Panic and a strange emptiness swirled through her, carrying a loneliness so absolute, she grew dizzy. She hadn't realized just how much she had counted on their old connection to carry them through the future. She pressed her icy fingers against her forehead, trying to chase the pain away.

What now? She had so hoped for more. The tension along his jawline did little to lighten the worries tugging at her heart. How could she expect anything more from him beyond the huge concession he had already made? In the span of one short day she had changed his life with no regard for his own plans and whatever hopes he had harbored for the future.

Guilt twinged inside her. She forced it back. What she had proposed had not been solely for herself. Timothy had been her prime concern. And she had not come to this marriage solely beholden. She brought with her the only thing she thought Quin might value and the only positive result of her marriage to Percival Crofton—her ability to help Reilly Ship Works with some of its present financial difficulties.

She offered Quin a tentative smile. Her heart twisted with the soft curving of his own lips, an answer that would have to do for now. At least he seemed willing to try. He released her shoulders and took her arm in his. His warmth and strength seemed to flow through her; a ray of hope streaked through her middle.

"We'd best be on our way and make certain your lad and his nurse are settled." The husky timbre of his voice resonated within her. "We'll be casting off for the island at daybreak."

They turned to proceed to the hackney's still-open door. She hoped the introduction between her son and his new father would go well and that the deed they had just accomplished would be enough to hold her father at bay.

Familiar rough hands snatched her away from

Quin's side as though her thoughts had conjured forth the very man she sought to escape.

"Here now, you feebleminded little strumpet. It seems I've arrived in time to halt this folly after all. Where is my grandson?" The cold fury in her father's voice cut through her almost as painfully as his tight grip on her arm.

"Papa!" With her defenses still lowered from her efforts to feel Quin, she had no protection from the blackness of her father's bitterness and anger. Nausea roiled in her stomach. She pressed a hand to her mouth as her father's icy disgust tore through her, jagged and determined. And so very cold. She tried to pull back from the snarling frown he fixed on her as he dragged her closer.

"I'll ask you to release my wife immediately, Mr. Rhodes." Quin clamped a restraining hand on her father's shoulder. "But I'll ask only once."

Danger glistened in the depths of Quin's green gaze and rumbled in his tone. An air of capable hostility shrouded his muscular frame, making him even more a stranger to her yet underscoring the very reasons she had turned to him for help.

Papa narrowed his eyes as he assessed Quin's threat for a heart-pounding moment, then eased his hold on her arm. "So the deed is done, is it? You'll get no joy from this luckless union."

His gaze shot back to Siannon. "Percy's barely cold in his grave. Have you no sense of the respect due the father of your child?"

She pulled herself free, striving to control the tremors quivering through her as she stepped back to Quin's side. "I have waited the required year and a day. My son's father received his due."

"Go on ahead, Siannon." Quin nodded toward the hackney. "I'll just have a word with your father, then I'll join you."

"My business is not with you, Reilly." Papa fairly bristled with indignation at not being able to satisfy his spleen. His fingers twitched and he leaned forward as though ready to lunge for her again. Quin stepped forward to shield her from the possibility.

With a dark frown her father continued. "I am here to reason with my daughter. And to protect Timothy's interests. Quite obviously I did not have enough safeguards in place to protect my grandson from the foolish notions my daughter might take into her head."

"Anything you have to say to my wife you will have to say through me, Rhodes." The hard edge in Quin's voice conveyed his years of shipboard command.

Hoping to hasten an end to the confrontation, Siannon climbed into the carriage. She squeezed herself tight into the corner and from its confines observed the exchange of glares between the two men while cold dread knotted her stomach.

"If there is nothing further, I'll bid you a good day, Mr. Rhodes." Quin touched the brim of his hat.

"Listen, you upstart pup." Although he had not stopped her retreat, Papa did not appear ready to back down from Quin either. "You'll get no more benefit from this interference than your father with his own ill-conceived attempt to meddle in my business."

Quin drew himself up and leaned closer. She strained to hear his words. "What precisely do you mean by that?"

Her father offered a mirthless chuckle. "All James Reilly accomplished when he and that old goat McManus attempted to release my wife from her righteous confinement was to set in motion the ruination of all James held dear."

Chapter Two

Anger roared through Quin, driving all speech from his tongue. He stood with his fists clenched at his sides, struggling against his overwhelming desire to pound his father-in-law's smugly superior visage into the pavement.

A perfect conclusion to the ceremony that had just been performed.

"How amusing. You didn't know, did you?" Rhodes chuckled again, either unconcerned or oblivious to the violent thoughts he evoked. "That is delicious. Make certain you share this revelation with your father and that imbecile McManus, will you?"

"Good day, Rhodes." Quin turned his back on his new father-in-law, refusing to give the man any further satisfaction. If what he claimed was true, he was a far more dangerous foe than any of them had realized. The sooner Siannon and the boy could be removed from her father's sphere of influence, the better. And the sooner he could begin to investigate the basis of the man's boast.

"You'll gain only fleeting satisfaction from this match, Reilly." Rhodes's goading followed Quin toward the waiting hackney and Siannon's anxious face. He refused to give Rhodes the satisfaction of rising to his bait.

"Mary McManus never gave me the son I required and spoiled me for other women to boot." The man's tone carried clearly through the crisp air.

"Siannon has the look of her mother, with that fey red hair and pale white skin." Rhodes raised his voice to keep up the taunts as Quin refused to face him again. "You may gain temporary solace bedding her, but in the end you'll find you'd have been **much** better off if you'd never crossed her path."

How could any man speak so of his own child? Quin's stomach clenched. His glance roved Siannon's face as he entered the hackney. Ghostly white within the carriage's shadowed interior, she pressed deep in the corner at the far side of the cramped interior. Her eyes were wide, her gaze fixed just over Quin's shoulder.

The urge to pound Rhodes swelled stronger in Quin, offering a relief from the conflicts and questions raging within. To hell with decorum. A street brawl might not solve the puzzle and insults being flung at them, but a few solid swings connecting with flesh and blood would certainly ease the tension of the moment.

"Never fear, Reilly," the man ranted on, with no regard for Siannon's pallor or the rage churning through Quin. "You'll not have to deal with my daughter very long. My plans for regaining my grandson are already in place."

Panic showed clear in Siannon's eyes and the rigid lines of her body at the mention of her son. Quin pulled the door shut behind him, effectively cutting off his new father-in-law in midsneer. He thumped the roof of the hackney, gaining a small measure of satisfaction from watching Eustace Rhodes recoil as the carriage wheels rolled back toward him before they pulled away from the courthouse.

"Oh, Quin." Siannon's words rasped across the padded interior of the carriage. She kept her eyes focused on her tightly clasped gloved fingers laced together in her lap. "I am so sorry."

Sorry? For what? For saddling him with her problems? For playing some unknown role in this intrigue her father claimed? He cleared his throat, not trusting himself to speak until he had leashed the better portion of the anger ripping through him.

Did she know the depths of her father's perfidy?

Quin strangled the urge to shake the truth from her. His new wife looked the picture of genteel womanhood in her gray widow's garments, a meek, bland wallflower innocent of the vile course of revenge her father claimed. But as he'd learned from navigating the sea's unfathomable depths, situations are not often what they seem on the surface.

Seeking the words to ask her what she knew without outright accusations, he cleared his throat.

"I do not believe the sins and omissions of our fathers are visited on us, Siannon."

Only our own. Relentless guilt had been his companion for too long. He quashed the grip of old pain as it reached for him. He needed to concentrate on the present and the future, not the past. Still, if it was possible her father had manipulated the ruination of Reilly Ship Works, how could she not have known at least a portion of his machinations?

Siannon dared a glance up at him as the clop of horse's hooves droned a steady pace on the cobblestones. Pain hovered there in the gray depths of her eyes. Though he did not want to, in that fleeting moment when their gazes first locked, he recognized her pain to the depths of his soul.

"But we are condemned by our own actions or neglects." Her words so nearly echoed his own thoughts, he wondered if he'd muttered them aloud.

She has the look of her mother with that fey red hair and pale white skin. Eustace Rhodes's pronouncement echoed, and Quin could quash neither his agreement nor his fascination with the very features Rhodes had attacked. He could not allow them—her—to divert him from this new twist. Too much, too many people, rested on his shoulders.

"What action or neglect condemns you, Siannon?"

"When he locked my mother away, he offered to let me visit her." She spoke of her father's crime in a flat tone, devoid of emotion.

"He took me to see the building where he'd sent her. Barred windows and iron gates. I could hear the fearful shrieks of the souls confined in that asylum echoing in the street. I could not make myself go inside. I was too afraid."

She closed her eyes and swallowed, then turned her attention to the hackney window and the buildings they were passing. "I never saw my mother again."

"You were still a child." Quin offered what little

comfort he could, choking back the questions he wanted her to answer about her father and his actions. Better to formulate his questions when the white heat of anger had passed. The calculated years of revenge her father claimed would not be uncovered in a few moments' conversation.

"With Gran gone, I was the only one who understood what Mama was going through." Filled with guilt that made his gut twist, her gaze shifted to him again. "I could have told her that, given her that comfort. He said she was mad. But she wasn't."

Mary McManus Rhodes had been a lovely woman, haunted and desperately unhappy despite the joy of her summer homecomings to the island she'd left behind upon her impulsive marriage to Rhodes. Mary and his own mother had been girlhood friends, one of the many ties that bound their two families.

"What did you understand, Siannon?"

"Though Gran called it The Sight, my mother was cursed to hear voices no one else could. That was the reason Papa used to lock her away, claiming it was for safety. Her safety." Bitter condemnation seared her last statement.

Quin might not believe every Irish legend and tale, but he knew better than to discount them outright. To a man like Eustace Rhodes, such behavior must have seemed lunatic enough to justify his actions.

"I knew your mother," he said in a low tone. "She was no danger to herself or to others, no matter what she heard."

Siannon granted him a fleeting smile of gratitude for his support, but regret lingered in the depths of her eyes and tears sparkled on the edge of her lashes.

He remembered too well the look on Mary's

brother, Michael McManus's, face when the news had come of her death, the furious whispers and tortured expressions shared with Da. Mary's family and friends had been unable to stop Eustace Rhodes when he'd declared her insane. Not by any legal means. And she had died before the illegal steps they plotted could be carried out.

And now the bounder who had committed her had the nerve to use the same threat regarding his own daughter. His threats, repeated in Siannon's letter and confirmed by Gill O'Brien, had prompted Quin to take these drastic steps, to wed Mary's daughter immediately and take her back to Beannacht as quickly as possible rather than chance the same fate for her. The law provided a husband with rights and controls a father no longer held.

The enormity of what they had just done, what he had just taken on along with all his other responsibilities, pressed heavily. Silence swelled in the carriage's darkened confines as they clattered through Limerick's crowded streets.

He knew very little about the woman he had just married. That fact was even more unsettling in the face of her father's revelation and The Blessing that had rocked through Quin in the courthouse. He'd thought himself finished with the family legend years before. Cursed for eternity. What choice this Blessing directed him to, he could not fathom. His choosing was done.

A sharp bend in the lane they traveled teetered the hackney on its wheels and almost threw Siannon into his lap. Her lilac and lavender scent filled his nostrils. He caught her arms to steady her. The distant crash of the sea echoed through him. He released her.

"Siannon, you are a Reilly now." He wasn't sure whom he sought to reassure, her or himself. "No one will control your fate and that of your son but the two of us. I'll see to it despite your father's threats."

His promise echoed down to his soul. This time it would be so. Surely that was the covenant behind The Blessing still reverberating in his bones. Another fleeting smile from his bride as a spark of hope softened her eyes. She offered him a nod and returned to her perusal of the buildings they passed. Did she believe him? Could he believe his own promise?

In the end you'll find you'd have been much better off if you'd never crossed her path. If only Rhodes's curse did not linger in his thoughts as well.

"Is the curried lamb not to your liking?" Irritation edged Quin's question as he took a sip from his glass and watched Siannon rearrange the food on her plate for the fourth time.

Awkward hours had passed since their arrival at the inn where they would spend their wedding night. She'd spent some time with her son while Quin made certain several of his own loyal seamen would stand watch outside during the dark hours. If negotiating the river at night were not so unwise, he might have taken ship immediately after the confrontation with Rhodes and quit Limerick without further ado.

"It's fine." He strained to catch her answer, then strangled an impatient sigh as she pushed her meal around the plate yet again without taking a bite.

Her father's threats lingered in Quin's thoughts. Damn the caution billowing inside him that demanded he proceed slowly with her because of the strain she must surely be under. He looked across the small dining table in the inn's private salon, watching candlelight gleam in the red-gold depths of Siannon's hair. She continued to stare down at her dinner as she had for the past quarter hour without reprieve. Appealingly arranged in a braided chignon or not, he'd had more than enough of this view as he considered his own meal in the silent, tension-choked atmosphere.

He frowned down at the remnants of his own lamb and potatoes congealing quietly on his plate—an apt expression of the passion that had cooled so quickly between them. The kiss in the courthouse had been born of an excess of tension and relief, nothing more.

Diabhal. He'd just as soon shove the echoes of that obligatory marital salute into the darkest depths of his mind. He'd married her solely to provide protection, out of obligation. He'd done the right and noble thing. Hadn't he?

No. Not truly. For he profited from this. Perhaps more than she did.

Another hot poker of guilt speared him. He took a swallow of wine and wished for something stronger. Rum or whiskey, to burn away all his memories and hold his guilt at bay. He let out a deep breath.

Siannon glanced up at him quickly, her gray eyes wide and turbulent as the candlelight reflected in their depths. "I find I am not terribly hungry after all, Quin."

She swallowed. The slender gold chain at the base of her neck glittered with each beat of her heart. "I suppose it is all the excitement."

Excitement indeed. So much had transpired in the

few hours since his arrival in Limerick the previous
day.

She'd greeted him with a brisk handshake worthy
of any man of business. She'd explained her needs
succinctly and described her ability to assist him with
his own requirements with the kind of efficiency he'd
learned to prize at sea. Her summary of the benefits
and pitfalls they faced would no doubt have been a
pleasure to Bryan's legal ears.

Now that all was said and done, she'd somehow
shrunk behind a protective bulkhead he seemed
unable to breach. This did not bode well for what
still lay ahead of them.

The skirmish with her father on the courthouse
steps proved many things, not the least of which was
that they must be incontrovertibly united if they were
going to win this war for her son. They would have
to consummate their marriage to render it invulner-
able to threats of fraud or annulment. Connubial
rights had not been a part of their discussions yesterday or today. Perhaps it would be best to broach the
subject now. But how?

"Does Timothy understand what occurred today?"

"He understands as much as any five-year-old." A
frown marred the pale smoothness of her brow.

"At least, I think so." She smiled and a warm glow
replaced the hesitation in her gaze. "He views today's
events as a grand adventure. He has never slept in
an inn or been more than a few miles outside the
city limits. He was most impressed at meeting a ship's
captain. I know he is looking forward to our trip down
the Shannon."

A ship's captain.

The title splashed between them like salty spume,

startling a pang of loss deep inside him and displacing his intentions. He was no longer a ship's captain. Would he ever be again? Would he taste the combined fear and exhilaration of rounding a distant cape to survive yet another day? Live the loyalty earned only through honest blood and sweat?

He blew out a long breath and forced his empty answers away. "I hope he continues to view life as an adventure. The changes being wrought for us all will be easier for him to adjust to if he maintains that notion. Would that it could be as easy for us."

The warmth left Siannon's gaze as if his caution blew a chill wind over her. He forced a smile, trying to ease the new tension yawning between them.

"Siannon." He placed his hand on hers, where it rested against the table edge. Her fingers were cold and stiff beneath his. "We must both make the best of this."

Poorly said, but true.

Wariness flickered in her eyes when her gaze touched his.

"What I mean is, our families have always been close." He tried again, wishing her distress were not quite so palpable. "We were friends as children. This marriage is bound to suit us both if we try."

She slipped her fingers out from under his. Tears glistened at the fringes of her eyes. "Yes, I'm sure you're right, Quin."

But somehow her words couldn't have sounded further from the agreement they were supposed to voice. His mind invoked a vivid revival of the feelings that surged between them when they sealed their bargain with a kiss. He refused to acknowledge the darker memories swirling just out of sight in his thoughts. He quirked an eyebrow at Siannon when she glanced at him and watched as color washed over her cheeks.

"I had thought . . . that is . . . I had never planned to . . . well, to marry again." The words tumbled out of her, deepening the color in her cheeks.

Two minds with a single thought. Quin's lips twisted at the irony.

"And now?" he prodded, wondering where she was going with this confession.

"I came to you because I had to, Quin."

He lifted his brow at her again.

She brushed invisible wisps of hair back from her forehead and toyed briefly with the gold chain, whose glittering beat had quickened. "What I meant to say is, we didn't discuss . . . any of this."

"Any of what, Siannon?"

She met his gaze. "What we expected from our marriage." The words seemed to choke her. She grabbed her wineglass and took a quick swallow.

"I thought you spelled that out rather well yesterday. Protection from your father; his threats and intentions were all too visible today."

Her gaze flew from his. She toyed with the heavy gold signet ring adorning her slender finger. His ring. She bit her lip and leveled her dark gray gaze at him once more.

"Yesterday I felt far braver than I have felt today."

"Braver?"

"Aye. Yesterday I was intent on marrying for Timothy's safety. I did not think beyond the legal ramifications of the act."

And now that she was, it was too late.

"What is it you object to, Siannon?"

Fresh color crept over her neck. "I . . . it's just that . . . with Percy." She stumbled to a halt.

The image of Percival Crofton, a man old enough to be her grandfather, touching her soft skin with his wrinkled, bespotted hands made Quin's stomach burn. He could only imagine how she had felt accepting Crofton's husbandly attentions night after night. But she was *his* wife now. Her future rested with him. He might not be able to guarantee her happiness, but he could try not to add to her distress.

He reached across the table and cupped her cheek. "We cannot fix what has already occurred, Siannon. All we can do is look to the future."

Her skin was cool to his touch, cool and soft as sand-washed satin. He ran his thumb over her silken flesh. She didn't shrink from him at least. A hint of lavender and lilac wafted toward him.

"We need to steer through the present and plot our course toward the future," he said.

She smiled then, a soft expression that threatened to steal his breath despite the hesitation with which it was offered. "You were always sprinkling nautical terms into the conversation when we were children. I thought it made you sound ever so wise and mature."

Her memory caught him off guard, and he smiled back at her.

"I was showing off, most likely. I loved to eavesdrop on the conversations in my da's office and dream of the day when I'd have a deck of my own to command."

"Do you miss your ship, Quin?" Her question sank tenterhooks. His brother Bryan was the only other person who had recognized and acknowledged all that Quin had lost in coming ashore. And even he did not know the half of it.

"I love Beannacht and the Works," he answered honestly. "But I confess after years of having my word be law, I grow impatient when I must wait upon the whims of others. Or inquire politely into progress. I am much too blunt when I grow impatient with matters outside the shipyard that claim my attention."

Siannon nodded, her interested expression prompting him to continue.

He leaned forward. "We need to present a united front to your father and to the world at large. In that respect I'm hoping you will help me.

"I'll do my best to support you, Quin." She smiled again, the expression adding a sparkle to her eyes.

"I expect no less, wife. If you can understand the strain our current project is putting on my men. Help smooth things in the village. The wives sometimes do not understand all the ramifications of the deadlines we need to meet, the pace we must maintain or risk failure."

She nodded her understanding, and he could have sworn some of the tension eased from her rigid posture. Good, she'd have her role to play, and a nice diversion from her own troubles too.

He squeezed her fingers, satisfied that he had made his point. "Now, if you've finished with your supper, perhaps you'd like to go up and check on the boy and ready yourself for bed. We leave on the morning tide. I'll join you shortly."

The eager sparks dimmed in her eyes. "I'll be ready," she said, then rose from the table to whisk out of the room on a whisper of gray silk and petticoats. The rumble and chink of merrier company in the taproom was silenced as the door shut behind her.

Quin pushed from the table, unable to sit there with the remnants of their failed wedding supper. He could only hope that this rescue truly would gift her with the kind of protection Da had been unable to provide her mother and bring an end to the haunting regrets that had hung over Beannacht for the last decade.

Siannon closed the door to Timothy's small bedchamber, leaving his nurse in charge of him. Now that it was fully night, she could not seem to still the fears battering her mind like hungry moths, gnawing huge holes in the thin remnants of her courage.

The Reilly signet spun on her finger, knocking hollowly against the solid wood of the door as she fought the urge to turn the knob and retreat to the comforting safety of her motherly duties. Just one more song, one more story—the refrain Timmy sang all too often dangled as a tempting delay to the inevitable.

She looked across the hall at the door to her own chamber. Her bridal bower. Candlelight gleamed from polished sconces set high on the hallway's plain whitewashed walls. Thick carpeting lined the corridor, most likely to muffle the comings and goings of the inn's guests.

Quin would join her soon. Would he expect his full rights as her husband? A shiver raced down her spine, chased by the wave of warmth still echoing from the embrace they had shared that afternoon. Despite the remembered thrill, the nightmare of her first wedding night twisted in her thoughts and chilled the hollows of her heart. Her girlhood fantasies of romance and grand gestures had died a tortured death beneath the cold hands and cruel finality of Percival Crofton's touch.

She and Quin had not discussed the inevitable. Yet the kiss Quin gave her in the courthouse seemed to indicate he was not averse to the idea. Indeed, it served as tacit acknowledgment of the need to unite them in a true marriage—a consummated marriage not even her father's many contacts could rend asunder.

A second wave of shivers shot over and through her and then another. Gooseflesh pebbled her arms.

She had so loved Quin when she was a child. But the memories of Percy touching her—his hands, his lips, his sweaty, aging body pummeling hers as he grunted in guttural satisfaction and spoke such vile things as to make her stomach swirl with nausea— would not leave her. She tried to imagine Quin doing any of those things, but the image of Percy was all her mind would conjure.

Cold sweat beaded her lip.

A burst of noise from the tavern below echoed up the steps as the door at their base opened. Was someone coming? Quin? It would not do to have her new husband come upstairs and find her cowering in the hall.

She hurried into the bedchamber that had been set aside for them. The massive four-poster in the center loomed out of proportion with the rest of the room. The downy coverlet and pillows should have beckoned with soft comfort; instead, they menaced with the threat of what would transpire within those

cloying depths. Her hands felt like ice despite the
fire crackling cheerily in the hearth.

She had refused the maid the innkeeper's wife had
offered to attend her personal needs. She was to be
an islander now; she would learn to manage on her
own without servants to assist and report on her at
every turn. She stood still for a while, her hands cold
and damp against her stomach as the soft rhythm of
footsteps continued down the hall past the chamber
door.

Not Quin, then. Not yet.

She forced a shaky breath past the fear that gripped
her.

Her fingers shook as she fumbled at the fastening
of her gown. Suppose he came and she was not ready.

With an icy thunk, the realization she would most
likely never be ready plummeted through her. How
foolish she'd been to think she could marry and not
have to face this inevitable duty.

She pushed out of her shoes and rolled down her
stockings, stepping out of them as she drew her nightdress from a drawer. It was new, a soft butter-cream
satin she'd purchased earlier in the day to mark this
new beginning. She had longed for this marriage for
what seemed like a lifetime. Quin was the hero of a
thousand girlhood fantasies.

"And the husband of my choosing." Her reminder
sounded far more sure than she felt. She closed her
eyes and held the satin against her face, willing herself
to relax, trying to concentrate on the smooth, silky
material instead of on the night looming ahead of
her.

But she could not stand there forever.

Before shucking her petticoat layers, she lowered

the lamp glowing on the small table by the bed. Would Quin want the light on or would he prefer the absolute, unknowing darkness Percy had favored? In all her youthful daydreams of life with Quin, she had never bothered to conjure this aspect. Oh, how she wished she had. Something to arm herself with, to fight the dark memories.

As a child, she fantasized about joining Quin on his shipboard adventures—battling pirates and exploring exotic islands. After her father had confined her mother to the asylum and forbade further visits to Beannacht, she imagined Quin sailing into Limerick and carrying her back to the island to stay with him and his brothers.

When she first married Percy, she had been too frightened to dream, but Timmy's birth had brought back all the old longings. She'd imagined Quin and herself walking with the baby in the park or chasing him across Beannacht's sandy beaches, reading him stories and playing by the fireside. Quin, a young, vital father, would be so different from the miserable invalid Percy had become after his son and heir's birth. At least the conjugal part of her first marriage had been brief. Once Percy knew she was breeding, he stopped his nocturnal gropings to allow her to rest. His stroke had ended any resumption of connubial relations.

Until now.

The satin sighed over her skin like a caress. She smoothed her hands over her hips as everything inside her shuddered. Would Quin be pleased with her choice? Would he be pleased with his? Oddly, she was no longer cold. She felt suffocated in this room, this city. She needed air and a glimpse at the night sky. That's what Gran had told her to do whenever she cried at the end of a visit to Beannacht.

"Look to the heavens, dearling—the moon and stars shine on us all and make us one where e'r we dwell. Look to the heavens and ye'll find yer way home."

She moved behind the curtain to open the chamber's window, but the latch was stuck. Trapped.

She swallowed hard, ignoring the useless latch, and rested her fingertips on a cool pane. She looked out through the wavering glass to the moonlight breaking through the clouds over the harbor.

"I'm trying to find my way home, Gran," she whispered, knowing this time she sought to recapture the home of her heart more than the actual place. Tears she hadn't realized she could still shed traced paths down her cheeks.

"Diabhal!" Quin's curse startled her from her reverie. How long had she been wandering the paths of her childhood? She hadn't even heard him enter the chamber.

"Siannon? If you're here, you must come out." His tone held equal parts caution and irritated demand. Unreasoned panic frosted her limbs, immobilizing her.

"I've given you no cause to hide from me, have I, wife?"

She wished the curtained window seat did not provide such a perfect haven. His assumptions did nothing to ease the tension building inside her. As much as she longed to avoid what was to come, she could not. Timmy's future—all their futures were—riding on this bargain's success.

She took a deep breath and pulled back the curtain. "I'm here, Quin."

Her groom stood in the center of the chamber with his brows drawn together and his hands resting on his hips, making her wish for just a moment that she had indeed hidden, as he suspected.

He'd cast his jacket on the end of the bed. How long had he stood there, looking for her? The dim light glittered in the dark depths of his gaze as he glared at her. His breath hissed through his teeth, but he said nothing as he looked at her in her fragile night rail.

Her own breath locked in her chest. All she could do was drink in the sight of him while she shook her head. His shoulders had broadened since she had last seen him in shirtsleeves a decade before. The linen stretched tight across the muscles his years aboard ship had chiseled. His brocaded waistcoat hugged his chest and tapered to his flat stomach and trim hips. He looked so much more alive than ever Percy had.

She swallowed. Percival Crofton was her husband no longer. This was Quin Reilly, her friend.

"I'm ready. Let's just get through this as quickly as possible," she managed to say, wishing back the bald statement almost as soon as the words left her lips.

A murky shadow chased over Quin's features. He crossed to her in a couple of long strides. She hadn't meant to vocalize her fears so succinctly, but for the life of her could think of no way to explain them away. Despite telling herself to trust him, she retreated a step as he halted in front of her.

Quin reached out to cup her chin in his palm's broad warmth. He grazed the moisture from her cheeks with the rough pad of his thumb. His gaze, dark and glittering in the moonlight, locked with hers as he bent down to her.

"Marriages are not meant to be *quickly gotten through,* Siannon."

Impossibly, she could hear the crash of waves against solid timber in the distance. The fresh salt smell of white water and stiff ocean breezes, like an irresistible siren's call, pulled her toward him.

He brushed his lips across hers. A sudden blinding wave of heat rolled through her, carrying the pitch and toss of an unseen sea, demanding everything she had to give and more. She clutched his shoulders for support.

She strove to hold herself back, but a tide of desire swept through her with a relentless force, surprising not only in its intensity but in her immediate response. She had felt this power only once before—in the depths of Limerick's courthouse.

With a rumble low in his throat, Quin pulled her closer and swallowed the gasp she couldn't hold back. Astonishment rippled through her as she welcomed his tongue into the depths of her mouth to seek and caress her own. His intimate touch evoked no shuddering dread, no revulsion. He pulled her tighter, as though he would mold her body against his. Her fears drained away against the solid feel of his muscled chest and thighs.

This was Quin in the flesh. No fantasy. Her friend. Her husband.

A stranger.

"*Mo ceile.*" He groaned the ancient Gaelic word for "wife" on a whisper she felt throughout her body while his lips swept her fears away before her last thought could take root.

She clutched his shoulders tighter as his fingers slid into the depths of her hair, loosening the prim knot where she'd gathered it at her nape. Like a waterfall, her hair sluiced over her bared shoulders and arms.

Another groan escaped him and tore through her as he tilted her head to more openly accommodate him. The smell of wild ocean waves and warm winter fires filled her. The masterful touch of his lips threatened to tear her soul from her and forever shred the fears she'd harbored for so long. She welcomed the release.

Her tongue slid against his, tasting him. Moonlight and sea spray splashing over rocks. Whiskey and spice. Sighing against his lips, she felt for the first time this day that she had made the right choice in seeking Quin's aid.

He pulled back. Surprised and bereft, she clutched the embroidered silk of his waistcoat for support. The cool fabric slipped under her fingers as she looked up at him. The tide surging between them still glittered raw and open in his gaze. But there was something more there, hidden and unreachable in the depths.

He brushed back a lock of hair that clung to her damp cheek. "It's been a long day, Siannon, with another to follow. You take the bed. I'll manage in the chair. We can get through this once we're home, with no one the wiser."

He released her then and strode over to the chair by the fireplace. Cool air chilled over her skin in the sudden absence of his warm muscles. Had he been as shocked as she by her unladylike response to his embrace? Was he annoyed or merely showing her special consideration? From the stoic lines of his expression, she couldn't tell.

"Good night, Quin." Her voice came out as a strangled whisper.

"Get some sleep, Siannon." He slouched back in the chair's depths, his booted feet resting on the grate.

She might have thought she knew Quintin Reilly the boy, but Quintin the man was a stranger indeed.

She lay in bed for a long time, tracing the Celtic knot and *R* on her ring, trying to decide if she felt grateful for his lack of demands or deprived.

Chapter Three

Quin placed a fortifying hand on Timothy's shoulder as the wind whipped over the railing, carrying a hint of granite and mystery from the Ring of Kerry far behind them across the water. The calls of the seamen as they worked the masts and spars echoed through him. The bow of the *Achanaich* rose and dipped across the swells created by the sudden mingling of the Shannon River's soft freshwater currents and the sea's hard, salty tang.

Heaven above, this felt good. Too good to dwell on the regrets that plagued him during a near-sleepless night and most of this day as they slid down the river. All he wanted to do was release his cares into the wind and enjoy the freedom of slicing through the seas, rigging taut at full sail. How had Bryan stood all those years cooped up in the city, studying the law? Especially without resenting Quin's role in his confinement.

"In a few minutes we'll catch our first glimpse of home," he told the boy. Anticipation bounded through Quin as it always did when headed into home port. "Beannacht Island is just over the horizon."

Standing astride, his back braced against Quin's thigh, the lad clutched his cap and glanced up. A smile lit the deep gray of his eyes, making them twinkle just as his mother's had when she was his age. Little Siannon Rhodes had observed and enjoyed everything during her summer visits to Beannacht. She'd fascinated Quin with her insatiable thirst for the joy in the simplest things.

Siannon's girlish zest seemed lost to the woman she had been forced to grow into. She'd learned to school her features into a calm mask, hiding her emotions behind innocuous complacency. Missing the girl he'd once known surprised and unsettled him. Another regret to add to his tally. But that was for later. Now he forced his attention forward.

"Timmy, what are you doing up on deck again?" Siannon's voice tossed by them on the wind. "You mustn't pester Captain Reilly when he's running his ship."

They both turned to watch her emerge from the hatchway. Not all her enthusiasm was dimmed despite the rebuke in her tone. Her love for her son showed clearly in the softening planes of her face, the sparkle of her eyes as they centered on him. A pang of a different sort raced through Quin so quickly, he refused to even name it.

The heels of her dainty half-boots rang on the deck as she came to join them. He couldn't stop the appreciative tightening in his groin as he watched his wife glide toward them, even if her attention was focused on another.

With her trim waist and generous curves, little Siannon Rhodes had most definitely grown into a woman made for a man's loving. The gentle rose color on her cheeks accented the refined softness of her skin. Her pink lips, parted slightly, seemed almost to beg for a kiss, a kiss that was his right to claim. He'd spent the better part of the previous night picturing her naked beneath his claims, begging for them. What quirk of chivalry had prompted his offer to release her from a duty she wanted to *get through,* then refused to give him peace for his sacrifice?

"We're keeping the watch for the island, Mama. Please don't make me go below again." Timothy steadied himself by clutching Quin's trouser leg.

"Thank you for keeping an eye on him. I thought he was still drawing in the salon. I'm sorry if he's been a bother." She traced a gloved finger along her son's cheek, softening her scold with the gesture. She looked at Quin, concern furrowing her brow as she clutched her shawl close about her and appeared to await his censure either for the boy's presence on deck or her neglect in allowing him to make his way there without her knowledge.

Dressed in the mist-gray silk she'd worn the previous day, she was every inch the city-bred lady, from her lace-trimmed bonnet to her gray kid gloves, a stranger as remote from the girl he remembered as he was from the lad she'd once known. And as different from the woman who nearly blinded him with the heat she'd generated with just one kiss. Furious passion and fierce protectiveness shrouded in a fog of uncertainty, Siannon Reilly drew more conflicting emotions from him than he'd thought possible even a day earlier.

Air currents ruffled the hem of her gown, playfully revealing hints of her petticoats. The brim of her bonnet concealed most of her fiery tresses, but the wind tugged a few strands free to dance to the tune it piped, providing him with a hint of the lively girl from his past. He took in a deep breath of salt and sensibility, letting the air push his lustful thoughts aside once more.

"All boys love ships and things that go fast. Leave the lad for now. A seaman's favorite part of any voyage is his first sight of home."

The light of relief that leapt in Siannon's eyes made him wish again that he had allowed himself the satisfaction of pounding her father to the pavement yesterday. No one deserved a life spent fearing the slightest mistake or misstep. Eustace Rhodes would never survive life aboard a ship, where command was built on ability and mutual respect.

He needed to change the direction of his thoughts before the whole angry mass descended on him again. "How is the young lady faring?"

Timothy's nurse had struggled for hours to hide the motion illness brought on by their voyage, finally succumbing to the wretchedness of seasickness as they'd left the smoother currents of the Shannon an hour earlier. His mother tending his nursemaid must have created enough distraction for young Timothy to creep up the stairs to stare with wide-eyed wonder at the workings of the vessel. Or so Quin had surmised when he had called the lad over to stand beside him and make certain he stayed out of harm's way.

"The tea settled Caitlin, just as you said. She's drifted to sleep despite the turbulence. Your granny's recipe works wonders. As if she were still here watching over those in need." A soft smile of memory wisped over her lips and flitted across Quin's heart.

Would Granny be pleased with his choice of Siannon for a wife? Had she sent the brume-shrouded Blessing as welcome or warning?

"Aye." He nodded and looked away to the horizon. There was no turning back now even if he'd chosen the wrong path to help Siannon. "There's many a poor seaman grateful for Granny Reilly's ginger tea. No Reilly ship sails without a plentiful supply."

"Does Devin still need to swallow it by the bucket when he sails? He hated how you and Bryan used to tease him about his queasiness. He so desperately wanted to prove he could be just as brave as you two."

"Much to his chagrin, Devin's sea legs have never grown in." The image of his youngest brother, closed and angry as he swung aboard this very vessel on the first leg of his journey back to university swam up from the depths. More regret. They hadn't parted well.

"Is Devin my uncle now like Bryan? Do they have beards that scratch like Uncle Michael's? And will I ever grow sea legs?"

Timothy's last question startled a chuckle from Quin. "Aye. No. And you already appear to have a fine set."

The lad seemed satisfied with the succinct answers Quin provided. Although he dusted his hands along the seams of his knee pants as if seeking these wondrous new legs. Finding nothing different, Timothy nodded and went back to watching the seamen as they adjusted the canvas under the mate's direction to take full advantage of the wind.

Siannon had done a fine job raising him despite the odds against her with an invalid husband and an interfering tyrant of a father. He'd have to tell her that later.

"Thank you," she said softly, as if she'd read his thoughts. Or as if he'd just passed her a cup of tea. Polite and impersonal, from the comfortable distance of strangers, the way she had sounded all through that interminable dinner last night—or through this day's voyage.

But she was his wife now and he was taking her home. He fought the desire to shake her and shout that this homecoming was all wrong—wrong time, wrong woman. Where was The Blessing in all this anger and guilt scourging his every other waking moment not filled with images of making love to his new wife?

At least she had been able to satisfy him that she knew nothing of her father's perfidious claims toward being behind the ruination of Reilly Ship Works. Perhaps Eustace Rhodes had been engaging in hollow goading. How could the man have managed to erode Reilly Ship Works after decades of growth? And how had those efforts remained hidden from Da? The sooner he got back to the office and his father's files, the sooner he could begin to try to trace some of their difficulties and see if they led to Rhodes. Yet another responsibility to juggle.

She was saying something else to him.

"Pardon?" he growled, glancing down at her.

Siannon paled and swallowed, then leaned in to speak above the wind. A waft of her lavender and lilac chafed him. "Thank you for being so patient with Timmy. Not many men would be so kind to someone else's child."

The sound of her gratitude had long ago begun to grate heavily against his nerves. She was his wife, not his guest.

"Please stop thanking me, Siannon." His words came out far sharper than he intended, drawing a wide-eyed gaze from his new bride. "Timothy is my obligation now."

"I'm sorry." Her apology came so low, he almost didn't catch it.

He bit back a frustrated groan. "You needn't apologize either," he managed to say in a more civil tone.

He could almost see the *I'm sorry* hovering on her lips.

She pressed her hand over her mouth as if holding the words back, and Quin's conscience twinged uncomfortably. *Diabhal.* He could not and would not spend the rest of his life tempering his words to keep from sending clouds across her eyes.

Where was the strength she displayed only two days before at Gill's office? Why was he so out of patience with her? She was his wife. Both answer and irritant in one.

He sighed and rubbed a hand over the back of his neck, wishing he could take back the last few moments. And at the same time he wished there were no need. He wanted to erase the whole week and start over with a different plan to save her. To save himself.

"Siannon—"

"It is an adjustment for us all, Quin," she told him with a ghost of the spirit she'd shown before. "We'll manage because we must."

"There it is!" The boy's excited cry blended with the call from the rigging. Beannacht was in sight. Anticipation gusted across the deck.

Siannon clutched Quin's arm and stood on her toes, trying to catch a glimpse of the island. Even through his jacket and shirt, heat from her touch seared his jagged nerves, blinding him to all memory, all thought save the excitement shining in his wife's eyes and the certainty that he had made an incredible mistake.

We'll manage because we must. Faint hope there. This was not the homecoming with his wife he'd imagined. Not at all the vision that had harrowed him for years.

The lad broke from Quin's side just then and scrambled to the railing to catch his first glimpse of his new home.

"Timothy!" Alarm rang in Siannon's voice as her son leaned out over the water just as the mate spun the wheel to adjust their heading. A huge swell broke against the hull.

Quicker than he'd moved in many a day, Quin scooped the now-sodden boy up and deposited him back on deck by his mother's side. His heart pounded painfully against his ribs and he felt oddly out of breath although he'd moved only a half dozen paces. Is this how it felt to be a parent? He'd rather round the Horn at full sail than face this sort of misery.

Siannon's face was pale as she crouched down to the boy's eye level. She stripped off her gloves and examined him quickly.

"We'll have to get you out of these wet things before you catch cold." Panic made her voice stern while she patted her son's dripping jacket.

"But, Mama. You said we were Reillys now. If I'm to be a seaman, I must get used to a little water," Timothy protested, oblivious to the anxiety he had created. "Isn't that so, Captain?"

"The first thing a seaman needs to do," Quin answered before Siannon could chide the lad further, "is to obey the commands of his superiors. That is the first lesson all Reillys must learn."

Timothy looked at him for a moment and then back at his mother as he digested this instruction. Slowly he nodded, then flashed a bright smile and lopsided salute that twisted an answering smile from Quin. "Aye-aye, sir."

"Thank—" Siannon halted her gratitude and took Timothy's hand in hers. The Reilly signet on her finger flashed in the sunlight. Reminders of all that ring symbolized crashed in on Quin like dark storm clouds. They were Reillys now. His Reillys. More obligations and complications.

"We'll wait below until it is time to disembark."

He nodded his agreement, although he was not sure if she'd asked permission or made a statement. All he wanted was one final chance to blow the cobwebs from his mind and order his thoughts before all the problems that surely awaited his attention on the island descended. Siannon Reilly and her son provided far too much distraction. He would deal better with this once they were home.

He watched until the last hint of his new family

descended through the hatch, then signaled the helmsman that he would take over and guide them into the harbor.

The solid feel of the polished oak wheel anchored his thoughts despite the pitch and toss cutting across currents as he steered them home. Reading the waves and winds seemed as effortless as breathing, and he welcomed the familiar routines of a ship readying for landfall. This is where he belonged, what he loved. He shouldered aside all regrets for the past and doubts about the future, giving himself up to the present until they reached Beannacht Harbor.

The red streaks of sunset glittered on the ocean and haloed the island hills as they rounded the point. His gaze snagged on the shadowy outline of the ship-yard in the distance. Everything within him tightened at the sight. It never failed to affect him so.

Reilly born and Reilly bred.

As much as he missed life at sea, he could not negate the fact that he loved the shipyard. His loyalty ran past bone and sinew—soul deep and constant. If Da did not recover enough to ever retake control, Quin faced the possibility of staying on land for a long, long time.

He rubbed a hand again over the back of his neck. Too often this possibility tormented him of late. Could he truly give up the sea? The ebb and flow of anticipating new destinations and departures had coursed through him for as long as he could remember. His brothers managed. Bryan survived, even thrived, without a deck beneath his feet. And though Devin could navigate with the best of them, he would never appreciated the rise and fall of the waves. He, too, would make a life on shore once he finished his education; how could the eldest do any less?

His new cares came crashing back. That would mean building a life here with Siannon and her son. Perhaps with children of their own. Too many obligations, too many opportunities for disaster, loomed once this current project was completed. After they'd faced down all threats from her father. So much more than he'd ever thought to face again. How would they get on through the years?

We'll manage because we must. The trust in her statement and in the depths of her glittering gray gaze was almost more than he could bear.

How was she ever going to manage? Siannon gulped back the bile that rose in her throat as panic squeezed her chest. She had no need of her Gift to read the dissatisfied bent to her husband's feelings. One day wed, and already he brimmed with regret.

Timmy burrowed his head farther into her side as he snuggled drowsily against her on the bench while they waited for the docking to be completed. She looked around the small salon outside the captain's cabin to make sure all of her son's playthings were packed and ready to transfer from the ship to their new home. She wanted to be quite certain they left everything exactly as they found it that morning. She could stand no more censure, stated or implied.

Quin's mercurial moods, blazing with passion, then cool and distant toward her, at least appeared indulgent toward Timmy, but she had no desire to test those limits. The day-long voyage down the Shannon River only added to her anxiety about what lay ahead. Her husband's frowns and pointed questions filled her with unease over the choices she had made. So much for the dreams of her return to Beannacht that had comforted her through the years.

As a child, she had fairly danced with excitement each summer when she and her mother had made the trip from Limerick to the island to visit her grandparents. She had often dashed to the railings just like Timmy earlier, breathless with anticipation for that first glimpse of the place she always thought of as home.

Not to mention the anticipation she'd felt at being able to spend her days trailing after Quin and his brothers. That had been the part she'd longed for most of all, besides her gran's hugs and Grandda's indulgent chuckles.

Anticipation of a different sort coursed through her when she thought of Quin now despite his sour demeanor. All day her thoughts had returned to last night, dwelling on the mesmerizing appeal of the man she had married. From his shirt stretched tight across the broad shoulders and corded arms that had held her so fiercely last night, to the blazing fire in his green eyes and the flames his lips had fanned to life within parts of her she had never suspected existed. Could she satisfy the passion he would surely demand from her?

From the portal she could see the reddish glow of sunset reflecting up from the water. Would they be going to Mr. and Mrs. Reilly's house, or had Quin taken one of the cottages in the village? And once they were settled in, how would they get along?

Doubts about her abilities had surely helped sour Quin's outlook on this match. Was he dreading the coming night as much as she? Would this night pass much as the previous, both of them fidgeting and unsettled in their respective resting places, or would Quin assert his husbandly rights? Most foolishly of all, she remained uncertain which Quin frightened her more, the one who scowled as he spoke to her that morning about her father's threats and claims, or the one who kissed her last night until white heat blazed inside her.

She had thought herself so ready to take this step, so sure that the love she had always felt for Quin would be enough. Why had she never considered all the aspects of a remarriage? Would she and Quin ever adjust to each other and settle into a life together? Or would this marriage prove a disaster even more painful than her first?

She would never let herself be made to feel as she did while married to Percy. As if she were not capable of holding together one sound thought. If things did not work out with Quin, she would simply go back to her original plan and work to support herself and her son. She was certain that even were she not married to Quintin, the islanders would never allow her father to find her here. The thunder of footsteps overhead and a jolt signaled their arrival at the docks.

"Are we there yet, Mama?" Timmy's sleepy question barely registered as she patted his arm and he settled back against her. The pounding of her heart nearly drowned out the sounds of the ship's company readying for disembarkment. There was no sense rousing him until Quin came to fetch them.

The clamor of boots at the hatchway signaled his summons. Seamus Keane touched his hand to his cap as he ducked to enter the salon. "Cap'n's compliments, ma'am. He'd like me ta escort ye and the lad on deck."

No turning back. She gently shook Timmy as she stood. "I can see to my son, Seamus. But you could help Caitlin. She is still resting in the cabin."

"Aye, ma'am, as ye wish." He nodded and proceeded to the cabin.

The gangplank was in place when they arrived on deck. Caitlin leaned on Seamus's arm but managed a wan smile as she looked around. "It is as beautiful as you described, Mrs. Reilly. Almost as beautiful as Ennis, my own village."

That was quite a compliment coming from an O'Brien of County Clare. It was her distaste for city life and her experience with a host of younger siblings that had led Gill O'Brien to recommend Caitlin, a distant relation, for the job of helping tend Timothy once they reached Beannacht. Siannon had no desire to bring any of the servants her father or husband had employed for her into this new life. And Caitlin was right. Beannacht was beautiful indeed, especially to one who had been gone for too long.

The hills that ranged the interior of Beannacht Island rose in orchid-colored splendor against the evening sky. Shadows lengthened from the warehouse and pilings by the docks to edge the roadway leading to the harbor village. Lanterns twinkled in the windows in the staggered row of whitewashed cottages with their thatched roofs, ordered gardens, and trim hedges. The church spire from St. Bridgid's parish rose darkly at the far side of the settlement.

Siannon took a deep breath, savoring the crisp freshness of the air—granite, salt, and welcome. She squeezed her son's hand. "Oh, Timmy, we're finally home."

"Where's Captain Reilly, Mama?" Timmy turned around to see if his new hero might be at the stern of the vessel on deck to greet them. "This is his home too. Right? We're to stay with him?"

"Yes, this is where Captain Reilly lives and works. He is a very busy man, Timmy. He has many important things to look after."

"Including us, Mama. I heard him talking to one of the seamen."

It was on the tip of her tongue to ask her son if his new father was voicing complaints over his decision to take them on as his family. How pathetic. She could not place her son at the center of any further turmoil. She would have to face this marriage and her husband squarely and make things work.

We will manage because we must. Yes, indeed.

Quin chose that moment to bound up the gangplank. Arriving home looked to have radically improved his mood. He smiled broadly as he strode over to them. A smile that tugged at Siannon's heart as it reminded her of long-ago homecomings and greetings.

"Are you ready to take a look at your new home, Timothy?" Quin asked.

"Aye-aye, Captain." A wide grin split the boy's face.

"The shipyard is closed for the night. The men are mostly gathered at the tap. I sent word ahead to Maeve Kelly to open up the nursery and such. Benen McManus will fetch your baggage.'' He reached down to Timmy, then swung him up to sit on his shoulders before offering his arm to Siannon.

This was more like the Quin she'd expected, the Quin she remembered, confident and commanding. He was a fine figure of a man, a husband any woman would be thrilled to claim so openly. Still, she hesitated.

''We must begin as we mean to go on, Mrs. Reilly, and greet the world as happily married newlyweds.'' He winked then, the joviality in his voice only barely touching his eyes. The reality of the questions and curious looks they would encounter on their way through the village crashed in on her.

Quin was a consummate actor.

Her mind fled back to the myriad imaginary games they had played as children—Viking raiders, pirates, explorers in deepest Africa—and always Quin had been the leader, the most believable during their reenactments. A pang of disappointment shot through her, but she squared her shoulders. If he could view this gauntlet as a challenge to his skills, so could she. She took his arm and forced herself to breathe in and out as the odd heat that accompanied touching him surged through her.

They strolled down Beannacht's small wharf, leaving the activity of the ship's unloading behind them. Two old tars leaning back on their stools in front of Kelly's Dry Goods stopped their whittling long enough to nod to Quin. Several shipwrights lounging in the doorway to the tap raised their glasses in salute when they caught his eye, but none called out a greeting.

''Most of the men stop by Moreen McManus's for

a pint before heading home to their suppers," Quin told her as they headed toward the village. "They'll not bother us this night, figuring all will be explained on the morrow. There are few keepable secrets on an island this size."

"Some things never change." Siannon smiled and the tension between her shoulders eased a bit. "It will be good to be in a place where secrets are not necessary."

They reached the lane that branched toward the main settlement of Beannacht. The sounds of evening echoed from the doorways. Children finishing their chores or play, mothers and wives clattering in their kitchens as they readied suppers, husbands and fathers washing up in the yards—blending together in familial harmony. Siannon looked up at Timmy on his perch atop Quin's shoulders. He was drinking everything in with eager eyes. Life here would be so good for him. Peace edged her heart.

Up ahead she could see a light beckoning from the wide front windows of her grandfather's workroom. Her pace quickened until she was swinging the gate open and fairly running past the tall hedge of her grandmother's fragrant lilacs—how many times had she pictured this place, longed for it with all her heart?

"Grandda!" Did her call come from her voice or her soul?

The door sprang open. "Siannon! Siannon! *Mo reannag bheag.*"

His "little star." No one had called her that in so long. Tears came to her eyes.

Her grandfather stepped outside. He looked so much older than she remembered. Smaller. His hair and beard were pure white and his face streaked with lines. But the love lighting his eyes was exactly as she remembered, and she ran into his open arms.

"Grandda, oh, Grandda," she sobbed over and over as he patted her shoulders and soothed her as he had done when she was little and a summer storm battered the island.

He smelled of vanilla and tobacco, just as she remembered. Pulling in a shaky breath, her face pressed tight against his shoulder, all the years of loneliness and dread dropped away like stones. And her icy fears for the present and the future melted as well. She was home with the McManuses at last. She felt safe for the first time in over a decade.

The crunch of Quin's boots on the stones behind them helped her pull herself together. Timmy mustn't see her like this. Her tears would confuse him, and she had so looked forward to introducing him to his namesake.

She swiped at her face with her cuff, ineffectually trying to swab the dampness away and praying her husband would not think he'd married a ninny who cried at every turn.

A chuckle rumbled deep inside Grandda's chest. "All grown up into a fine lady and still ye haven't learned to carry a handkerchief with ye, eh? Take mine, *reannag bheag*. I still keep a clean one in my pocket just like when ye were a little one."

He slipped one arm around her waist as he reached into his vest pocket and pulled out a square of snowy linen. He handed it to her with an indulgent smile and a little chuck under her chin.

Quin shifted Timmy from his shoulders and set him on the ground. Her son raced to her side and clutched her skirts, hiding his head shyly against her side. She rubbed his back with her hand and wondered where this sudden timidness was coming from.

"Good evening to you, Quintin." Grandda held out his hand to Quin. "So this is the urgent matter that took ye off so suddenlike ta Limerick. It appears my family is in yer debt."

"Good evening, sir. There's no need for talk of debts between our families, as well you know, Tiomoid. The ledger books on both sides would overflow." The men exchanged knowing looks as they shook hands.

"And is this sturdy-looking seaman who I think he is?" Grandda reached out a gnarled hand to stroke Timmy's head.

Using her hand to guide her oddly reluctant son to turn and face his great-grandfather, Siannon nodded. "Grandda, I'd like to introduce Master Timothy Michael Crofton. Timothy, this is Tiomoid McManus, your great-grandfather. The McManus head of our family. I named you in honor of him. Won't you shake his hand?"

Timmy turned his head to look up at Quin, who nodded his agreement, before tentatively holding out his hand. "How do you do, sir?" he whispered.

"I am much better for the sight of yer dear mother, boy-o, that much I can tell ye. And I am mighty pleased to make yer acquaintance as well." The honest joy in her grandfather's voice sang through Siannon. If only Gran were here too. She would have liked her grandmother to meet her son.

"Ye may call me Grandda if ye've a mind to."

"Yes, sir," Timmy whispered, then buried his face back into his mother's skirts.

"He must be done in from the trip down the river today. And so must ye, dearling. Why don't we step inside? We can get ye both settled in, in a thrice with a cup of tea." Grandda opened the door and prepared to usher them inside. "I was hoping the items ye had delivered here signaled yer arrival. Ye can tell me all about how ye gave that blackguard Rhodes the slip."

She was staying here? The notion offered refuge from her doubts. She wouldn't have to worry about the kind of wife she would make Quin, the kind of husband he would be. They would live separate lives. Hungering sorrow flowed from that thought.

"I'm afraid we don't have time tonight, sir," Quin answered. "We need to get this young man into his berth before too much longer."

"Surely ye do not mean ta ship them out so soon! They've only just arrived," Grandda protested. "Beannacht is the safest place ta harbor them. Yer father—"

"You misunderstood me, Tiomoid," Quin interrupted. "Siannon and Timmy are staying on the island. For good. With me."

"We were wed yesterday, Grandda," Siannon added.

"By the hounds of Chuchulain." Grandda's bushy eyebrows shot up with that news. "Married, ye say?"

His gaze roamed Siannon's face, studying her with fierce intensity. Quin stepped closer and slipped his arm around her waist. The gesture added strength and assurance to the confidence she wanted her grandfather to see in her, in them. She didn't want him worrying.

"We're Reillys now. And I'm to be a sailor." Timmy

dared a glance out from behind his mother to impart the news as he'd absorbed it.

"Seaman," Quin corrected Timothy gently.

"Ye don't say." Grandda nodded. He turned his regard to Quin. "Ye think this is the best way?"

"Aye." Siannon looked up at her husband's profile as he answered with quiet surety.

"And ye'll keep her well."

"Aye." The assurance lacing his tone added to her hopes.

Another examining look at both of them, and Grandda's face cleared. "Well then, this calls fer a dram."

"Another time, sir. I really do want to get them home and settled. I've an early day at the Works tomorrow."

"As ye think best. It is good ta see ye have such a care fer her." Grandda gave Siannon's shoulders a squeeze and kissed her forehead. "Ye come by fer that tea as soon as ye're settled, *reannag bheag.*"

"I will, Grandda." Tears misted her eyes again. She took Timmy's hand as Grandda patted her cheek. "I'll see you very soon."

Walking down the path, the rich scent of the lilacs her grandmother loved seemed to wrap her in a warm hug.

"Mama, doesn't Grandda know your name?" Timmy asked.

"What makes you ask that?" Quin asked in return.

"He keeps calling her rayneg by-og."

Their laughter blended into the night after they explained the Gaelic phrase, and Siannon's hopes for their future rose with the echoes bouncing back

to them from the shadowed depths of Beannacht's
hills under the early stars twinkling overhead.

"*Look to the heavens, dearling,*" Gran had said.
"*Look to the heavens and ye'll find yer way home.*"

Chapter Four

"Diabhal."

Quin closed the front door behind him and breathed a heavy sigh, wishing he could shut out the doubts plaguing him along with the world outside the breadth and width of this one stalwart portal. Marrying Siannon, bringing her back to Beannacht, created more change and confusion in the span of a few short days than he could have imagined, not to mention the questions.

He sighed again, closing his eyes and resting his head against the polished serenity of the door. Until this he'd always prized the kinship felt among the islanders. He'd definitely reached the end of his tolerance for the probing and inquiries he'd faced from all quarters after a full day at the shipyard.

After a second night spent apart from his reluctant bride, if just one more person asked him how he enjoyed newly married life or wondered at the haste behind the marriage while favoring him with a knowing look, he'd likely strangle the poor soul instead of attempting the increasingly awkward and uncomfortable answers he'd repeated throughout the day.

Every bit of him felt rubbed raw by the well-meaning but never-ending curiosity and good wishes greeting his every move as he worked to bring order to the chaos his abrupt absence had created.

To be fair, it was not Siannon's fault they had spent the night separately. Pale and wan, Timothy's young nurse had needed to be put into her bed even before the lad. Pluck as he was, Siannon's son then had a hard time settling into his new surroundings. Sometime after midnight, Quin had entered the nursery to find Siannon asleep atop the coverlet, cradling the boy. He'd not had the heart to wake her—she'd looked nearly as young and innocent as Timothy with her auburn curls fanning the pillows and her slender fingers clutching the counterpane. He'd fetched a blanket to cover her and doused the lamp, then spent the restless hours until dawn regretting his inability to discharge the final binding act to seal their marriage and to satisfy his growing fascination with his wife's charms.

A hint of her lilac and lavender scent teased him, although he knew she was nowhere near. The house stood too quiet and dark. She must have gone to bed long ago. Irrational exasperation chased that certainty. He'd spent too much of this day thinking of the sparkle in Siannon's gray eyes as they landed the previous night, or remembering the splay of her hair across the pillows in the lamplight, then chastising himself for his foolishness.

He could not fault the islanders for their curiosity and concern either. What they asked arose from the very kinship he had always prized. But the pain and guilt he had thought successfully excised from his soul years before throbbed anew with each mention of his newlywed status, twisting the knife already wedged firmly in his stomach.

Images of Marie had also haunted him all day, as they hadn't in years. Pretty, dark-haired, fragile Marie. She had begged him not to leave her, to take her with him when he'd sailed away from Nova Scotia. Yet he had not listened—he had left her to attend to his business, certain she would be happier in familiar surroundings. Her blood stained his conscience. Another person he had failed.

He fought to hold back the last memory, but it did him no good. He returned to Halifax after too many months away and found empty rooms occupied only by dark looks of disapproval bordering on accusation from her friends. Guilt slammed into him anew.

He rubbed a hand across the back of his neck, trying to undo the tense knots corded there. He'd never guessed marrying Siannon would unearth his memories of the past so strongly.

No, that wasn't quite true. He'd known the situations were too similar for him to escape totally unscathed. But he told himself he had long ago dealt with Marie's loss.

"Diabhal." He pushed away from the door. So much for gaining a measure of peace from the silence reigning within his home. In fact, the quiet only made him wonder where Siannon was and what she and Timothy had done with themselves this day. He'd left long before they had been up and had not returned all

day, sending for his meals, as usual, from Moreen McManus.

For months he had spent all his waking hours at the shipyard—either in his office or involved in the actual labor of shipbuilding. He didn't intend to change that routine despite the raised eyebrows he'd encountered when he stayed tonight.

He frowned and glanced at the hall clock. At ten o'clock, it was late enough for Siannon's son to be long abed. And probably her as well. The image of her in her satin nightdress, her hair tumbling like fire across her pillows, further unsettled him.

He pushed away from the door and headed for the kitchen at the back of the house. Sure enough Maeve had left his supper warming in the oven. He swallowed a few mouthfuls of soup and biscuits without bothering to sit at the table. The food warmed his belly but did nothing to soothe his mood.

This house no longer provided the refuge of the past months, the place where he could drop his guise of command and control. Nor was it the warm haven of family it had been as he'd grown up with his parents and brothers filling the rooms with light and laughter. *Diabhal.*

Where was Siannon?

He dropped his empty plate into the sink, wishing he were as unconcerned as he'd striven to portray throughout the day. But The Blessing echoed on in his thoughts, offering him no relief. As did the images of her on their wedding night when he'd taken her in his arms and been ready to make love to her right there on the floor despite her shivers. All day his thoughts had done naught but circle back to her again and again. Now that he was under the same roof as his new bride, the problem had compounded threefold.

He ascended the stairs in a few quick strides. Light glimmered beneath the door to Siannon's room across the hall from his own. Not asleep, then. Anticipation tightened inside him, and he frowned. Should he burst in and demand they bring to conclusion the duty they'd both avoided for the last two days? The duty she'd wanted them to *get through* with such an air of expectant fear and stoic acquiescence on their wedding night he'd found it impossible to reconcile with his own disturbing mixture of desire and reluctance.

He loathed the sense of coercion that necessitated the urgency of their total commitment to each other. Her father's threats to tear their union asunder set this course. Siannon was no trembling virgin. She was an experienced woman with a child. Whatever she had suffered in her first husband's bed would need to be excised with gentle care and a resolute will.

He clenched his fists at his sides as he tried to picture Siannon's response. Would she welcome him? Or would her pale skin turn whiter still, faced with actual consummation of their bargain?

It jarred him to realize that he wanted her to welcome him into her bed. Despite any other intentions he might harbor, he wanted Siannon as a lover. He couldn't seem to get the memory of the way she felt in his arms out of his mind. The sweet, open passion of her kisses. The sizzling promise of The Blessing. There was fire smoldering within the cool depths of Siannon Reilly, even if she was unaware of it, fire to match the silken red-gold flame of her hair.

Desire flared as his thoughts taunted him. He

should have put paid to the marriage two nights before instead of standing there outside her bedroom, debating the matter now.

He tightened his lips and rapped his knuckles against the door.

Silence greeted him.

Anger collided with guilt. Enough waiting. Enough mollycoddling her fears and his regrets. They'd *get through* this together.

He turned the knob.

"Siannon, we have to—"

Her room was a shambles.

Little feminine bits of clothing overflowed from her dresser drawers and swelled from the confines of her open wardrobe—fluffy pieces of linen, slippery wells of silk, and occasional tufts of starched crinoline, as though Siannon had rummaged through every garment she owned in search of something important.

Despite the plethora of lace-edged clothing and the lingering floral scent of her perfume, Siannon was nowhere in sight. Fear knifed into him, accompanied by a cruel twist of guilt. Should he have set a guard on her and the boy? Eustace Rhodes could not have snatched them back so stealthily.

Condemning memories held him frozen in place as he remembered that other empty bedroom, the woman he would never see again, and all because he had left her for too long, spent too much time in his own pursuits and not paid enough attention to the wife he had sworn to protect.

"*Diabhal.*" More groan than curse as his throat tightened.

He turned on his heel. A quick perusal of the other

bedrooms yielded no sign of her. Only the sight of her son, Timothy, peacefully asleep in his bed, with his nurse Caitlin just beyond, kept Quin from shouting the house down.

Had he missed Siannon downstairs? Best check upstairs first. He took the stairs to the third floor far quicker than he had the first set. A slender thread of light beckoned from beneath one closed door. Granny's room. Certainty that he had found his errant bride washed relief through him, followed rapidly by a fresh flood tide of anger. Why would she hide from him here?

He crossed the hallway in two short strides and threw open the door with no preamble.

Siannon's startled gasp greeted him.

She was curled in the depths of Granny's old rocker in front of the windows, her feet tucked beneath the folds of cream satin that draped her from the neck down, the same gown that had sighed against him on their wedding night and teased his memory with its revealing promises ever since. He swallowed hard as his mouth went dry and sight and memory collided.

In the light of the one candle she had lit on the fireplace mantel, her hair rippled over her shoulders, dark and thick. The irrational longing to plunge his hands into the fire gleaming deep in its silken depths nearly singed all thought from him.

"Quin." She smiled, her lips soft and parted—not the least contrite for the alarm she'd caused him. "I missed you today."

Her greeting sawed against his nerve endings. Did she think to censure him for his absence? Upbraid him for his neglect of her?

He frowned and crossed to stand before her. The

scent of skin-warmed lavender and lilac drifted up to him. His gut tightened with desire and the guilt-encrusted knife twisted still further. He fisted his hands at his sides.

"What are you doing in my grandmother's room?"

Her smile drained away at his tone. "I—"

"A man shouldn't have to search the corners of his house to find his wife, Siannon." His words came low and raw. Emotions he didn't want to name churned behind each syllable as he cut off her answer.

Her mouth snapped shut and her cheeks paled. He thought he'd frightened her into silence, until he saw the anger blazing in the smoky gray of her eyes. At that instant she was suddenly Siannon Rhodes again, the determined little girl who wouldn't accept no for an answer when she wanted to tag along with the boys.

One soft red eyebrow arched above a gaze that had grown as hard and dark as storm-washed granite. "I beg your pardon?"

"What are you doing up here?" He spoke slowly to make certain she understood. "Your room is on the second floor, across from mine. I expected to find you there."

She folded her hands together and held his gaze for several silent heartbeats. "I always liked this place. You can see both the hills and the harbor from here. If you remember, your mother let me come and sit up here to wait when you boys were not at home. Unless you plan to forbid me entrance and confine me to my room *on the second floor,* you may expect to find me here again. It holds many memories for me."

Still torn between relief and irritation, he appreciated the grit behind her answer—spoken with conviction and enunciated every bit as slowly as his own statement had been. "Memory is a thing best held at bay this night. We have a future to cement."

True to expectation, the color on her cheeks paled, but to her credit, his bride did not shrink from the idea, meeting his gaze with a steady look.

He sucked in a slow breath and admired her. Awash in the cool moonlight spilling in from the windows, the satin gown clung to her curves with an intimate caress, hiding and revealing the enticing promise of her body. No longer little Siannon Rhodes at all. A now familiar ache flamed to life in his groin.

His heartbeat pounded in his ears accompanied by long-ago echoes of Granny's tales of unseen wonders and unexpected magic. Who would ever have suspected he would find himself wed to little Siannon, let alone fired beyond all reason with the desire to make love to her until neither of them could move.

Raw with relief that should not have mattered, seeking surcease from hounding regrets and guilt for things he could not change, exhausted from the normal turmoil of working the day through, he stepped forward and reached for her.

Grasping her shoulders through the thin stuff of her gown, he pulled her from the chair. She did not resist. Her hair slid over the backs of his hands, silky and warm. She was all too soft, all too alluring in the creamy satin that clung to her. She was his.

"You don't belong here, Siannon," he growled, wishing she didn't feel as if she belonged exactly where she was—in his arms, in his home, in his soul—filling the empty places he did not want to recognize. He'd married her for her needs, not his.

"No?" Her tone held softness, but nothing disguised the light of battle glowing in her eyes. "Where do I belong, Quin?"

"Not here. Not now." He had more than his share of concerns for the foreseeable future. More than his share of obligations and guilt. He had no need of a wife—no matter the bonds between their families, no matter the mutual benefits of their arrangements—especially a reluctant wife.

"You leave before the sun is up and return long after dark without so much as a word. Will you tell me where I can and cannot go?" She lifted her chin. "I am not one of your crew. I am your wife."

"Are you?" His fingers tightened over her warm satin-covered shoulders. The scent of her filled him. He looked into the sea gray of her eyes and felt as if he were drowning. Raw desire blazed low in his middle. Did she have any idea what she provoked in him?

He didn't want to feel this way about her, about anyone, couldn't afford the distraction she was becoming. How could she expect him to fight the things she drew from him. And why should he?

"Diabhal, you *are* my wife." The wife he had yet to claim.

"Aye." She nodded, though wariness chilled some of the fire in her eyes.

Anger lashed him again. She stood before him with her expression part mutiny, part fear, as though she weren't sure whether to fight him or run. As if he had done something to her, forced her somehow.

This whole situation was her idea, and as far as he was concerned, she would not be running.

"So be it. Come with me." He linked his fingers through hers and turned. Striding from the room, he drew her along behind him, intent on leaving all regrets and uncertainty behind in the wash of moonlight. If she meant to be his wife, then so she would be. Tonight. Now. The waiting would end.

"Where are we going? Quin?"

She sounded breathless behind him, her bare feet noiseless in the wake of each deliberate echo from his boots. Down the steps and the hallway he drew her, and directly into his bedroom, avoiding the feminine frippery strewn across her own chamber.

He closed the door behind them with a deliberate click and turned to face her in the pale light from the lamp on his bedside.

"We've something to take care of, wife." He pulled open the buttons on his shirt.

She didn't pretend to mistake his meaning. He admired the way she raised her chin as she met his stare. "Have I no say in this, then?"

"Not tonight." He shrugged out of his shirt and reached for the fastenings to his trousers. "Neither one of us has a say in the course of this night."

Her gaze followed his movements. She licked her lips.

"Quin, I don't think—" She remained frozen and stiff.

"Then don't." He ceased disrobing and reached for her, his fingers closing on the softness of her skin as he pulled her toward him. "Don't think. You are my wife. I am your husband. We both made this bargain. We both must see it through."

He pulled her closer still. Warm satin touched his chest. The full roundness of her breasts teased.

"There is always a price for what we want, Siannon." He threaded his fingers through the silky warmth of her hair. "Our payment is overdue."

For the span of several heartbeats her turbulent gaze met his.

"Then make me truly your wife, Quintin Reilly."

Her request tore into him with a thousand tiny blades, stripping him of his angry determination and leaving only the desire she drew from him.

"Aye, *mo ceile.*" Ancient promise and present need collided.

He covered her mouth with his, satisfying needs he hadn't wanted to recognize. Lightning streaks raced through him from the taste of her lips and the feel of her soft body against his.

At first she stood stiff in his arms. He traced his tongue along her lips until they parted for him. Then he thrust inside, tasting the fear she could not hide laced with the barest hint of the passion and warmth he suspected her capable of.

She shuddered in his arms, though from revulsion or desire he couldn't say. It didn't matter. They could not coddle her fears forever. He pulled her closer still and slid his hands slowly downward over her body to rest on her waist. Her breasts burned against his chest. He leaned back against the door, pressed her hips to his, and sucked in a harsh breath as her softness cradled his painful length with a promise of more pleasures to come.

Ever so slowly her fingers trailed up his arms until they rested on his shoulders as her lips softened and parted further beneath his.

"I will make love to you, Siannon Reilly," he whispered against her delicate cheek. "And you will be mine."

He pulled back slightly, his gaze catching against the dazed look sparkling in her eyes.

"Aye." A breathless acquiescence. Her hands clung to his shoulders, not pushing him away but drawing him closer.

He slid his hands lower, watching her face as he cupped the rounded curves of her buttocks and squeezed gently.

Her eyes closed and her head tilted back, revealing the slender column of her throat as her breath caught. He lowered his mouth to taste the hollow of her throat, pressing her more boldly against him and kneading the soft, resilient flesh he cupped.

Her fingers slid in his hair as her breath quickened. "Quin," she whispered.

Just his name, but it was enough to make his blood race hotly through his veins. No one, not even Marie, had fired his passions to this height. He groaned again and shuttered his thoughts. It was Siannon in his arms now. Marie belonged to a past best forgotten. He didn't want to think of her, to think at all. All he wanted was to lose himself in the moment.

He trailed his tongue up Siannon's neck and nibbled at her jawline before claiming her lips again in a soul-shattering kiss that blotted out all thought save the wonder of the moment and the incredible feel of her welcome when her tongue met his in tentative parry. Siannon melded against him, soft, satin-covered woman. The stroke of her tongue against his blazed through him in wave after wave of hot desire.

"Siannon." He groaned her name against her lips, then kissed a trail over her cheek and back into the warm hollow of her neck. "I want you."

"Aye." Her answer sighed from her as he kissed and licked and nibbled the warm skin of her neck.

He sucked gently, needing to taste every inch of her. "Oh, Quin."

The breathless sound of his name on her lips blazed across his mind, tormenting him with vivid images of what she would sound and feel like in the throes of passion.

"Aye, *mo chroi.*" He traced his hands over her body. Outlining her soft, feminine shape through the confines of her gown as she pressed herself against him. She was his heart at that moment. The raging pulse of the sea.

She was a madness—a fire in his blood that could be quenched only by burying himself deep within her. His lips burned against hers as he kissed her again and yet again. She trailed her fingers down from his shoulders to stroke his chest and cling to his waist as he pulled her close against him lest her caresses provoke him into moving too quickly.

His fingers traced down her arms and over the bodice of her gown. Her heartbeat drummed beneath his hands as he undid the little buttons one by one, baring her flesh to his gaze.

"Quin—"

"Shhh." He stilled the fear in her voice and nibbled at the edge of her jaw while he dipped his fingers into the open V of her gown, tracing the slender gold chain that dangled there and then brushing the upper swells of her breasts.

She breathed a tiny sigh as he stroked her slowly, touching her only with the tips of his fingers. Back and forth over the full, high curves, the soft, warm flesh he longed to taste with his lips and tongue, waiting until her breathing evened out and she began to relax. Then he slid his questing fingers lower as his lips tasted her earlobe. More boldly his hands moved over the tempting resilience. Testing. Stroking. Squeezing.

He pulled back, his gaze focused on hers, reading the anticipation, the fear, the desire growing beneath his touch. Her gaze met and held his.

"Quin." A slight sigh of protest as his fingers encountered the tight peaks of her nipples. Then she shuddered and a groan of pure pleasure escaped her.

"Aye, beautiful Siannon." He nudged the gown from her shoulders, watching it slide like a slow caress over her breasts and downward, revealing her trim waist, the curve of her hips, and her long legs. The locket on the end of her gold chain dangled invitingly between the fullness of her breasts.

"You are lovely, my wife." The words came harshly with the tight desires raging through him. She bit her lip as she leaned toward him, questions warring with the trust in her gaze.

He dipped his head and applied his lips to the puckered tightness of her nipple. He growled his satisfaction, tasting her with his tongue and then sucking her into his mouth as he captured the other tight nubbin with his fingers.

She gasped and gripped his shoulders as he laved and teased her. "Oh, oh, Quin."

He transferred his attentions to her other breast, reveling in the sweet taste and satiny feel of her against his tongue. With one arm around her waist to anchor her, he traced his fingers over her side, her belly, and downward to the dark red thatch of curls at the juncture of her thighs.

She quivered beneath his touch, clutching him for support as he dipped his fingers into her curls and found her silken folds. Damp and slippery with desire. Triumph surged within him.

"You want me, Siannon."

"Aye, Quin, aye." She pressed a fevered kiss against his temple. There was more than a hint of wonder in her admission.

He locked his gaze with hers and teased her slick wet heat, watching as her eyes slitted at his touch. He stroked her, pressing the palm of his hand hard against the swollen nub just before the folds. She shuddered again in his arms.

"Quin." Confusion molded his name into a plea as she surged even closer.

"Aye." He continued his motions, swirling around against her wet softness.

She shuddered again. And then again. And then she clutched his shoulders and her eyes went wide.

"Quin!" Her knees collapsed, and he held her tight as her release quivered through her and shivered up his arms. Aye, indeed—there was fire and passion within the cool depths of Siannon Reilly.

And she was his.

Tenderness, triumph, and desire warred in his chest as she melted against him, sated. He picked her up in his arms.

"What did you do to me?" She panted against his neck.

"Only the beginning, *mo ceile*," he promised his wife, he promised them both.

Holding her close, he carried her to his bed and laid her gently against the coverlet. "Only the beginning."

She lifted her head, catching his gaze with her own as she sat up on her elbows. That she had never before experienced passion's release was evident from the wondering glow on her face. That he was the first to bring such profound pleasure to her pierced his heart in ways he had vowed never to experience again.

Her gaze followed his hands as he released the fastenings on his trousers and pushed out of them.

"Oh." Very soft.

He stood still for a moment, allowing her gaze to wander his length, allowing her to adjust her thoughts about what was yet to happen between them.

"Quin." She bit her lip before continuing. "You're so . . . big."

"Aye." Everything in him strained for release, but he held back.

"Are you sure—" She looked up at him, fear still in her eyes, but there was also anticipation.

"Aye," he answered. She would unman him with her questions. He joined her on the bed and leaned toward her. She stiffened. Despite his care with her, her fears raged back full force, darkening her eyes with panic rather than passion.

The ghost of Percival Crofton loomed in the bed between them. Anger flared deep within Quin's very core—anger that she could not come to his bed without her dead husband's memory, that she could go limp in his arms from his lovemaking one moment and not trust him the next. And anger that his own specters from the past sought entry into the sanctuary of this moment as well.

Nothing would help her, nothing would hold the memories and ghosts at bay for either of them save the ecstasy that passion could give.

And he was more than capable of delivering that.

He pushed past her fears and took her lips in a

long kiss. After a moment of cool stiffness, she unbent in his arms and then she was kissing him back, flowing against him, warm flesh to warm flesh. The feel of her naked breasts against his skin, her hips pressed to his, drove all remaining deliberation from his actions.

"Make love to me, Quin." Her whispered plea slid over his cheek as he nibbled her throat.

His hands caressed the curves and hollows of her sides as he drank from her lips once more. Her tongue edged along the rim of his mouth, tasting and inviting his invasion into her own with a moan that rumbled through him. Whether it was his or hers, he could not tell. All he knew was the sweetness of her awakening desire and the haze of yearning lust that enfolded him as she twined her arms around his shoulders and drew him closer to her.

His hand skimmed the roundness of her breast, his thumb circling and pressing the tip that teased his chest. Then he reached behind her and cupped her smooth buttocks, adjusting her to better fit under him. All the while his lips continued to lock with hers, tasting her hesitation and sucking away her fears.

He pulled away and parted her legs before she could protest. Unerringly he found her heat, sheathing himself deep within her velvety depths in one swift stroke that forever shattered the separate pasts they had known, melding their futures.

She gasped. Her eyes grew wide and sparkling in the mixture of moon and lamplight that spilled over them both. She was so tight, he allowed her a moment to adjust to the feel of him, although her moistness betrayed her own readiness.

"You are mine now, Siannon," he told her as he moved inside her body, beginning the ancient rhythms, the sweet friction that would bring release to them both.

"Aye." She breathed her reply as he withdrew and thrust. Her fingers dug into his shoulders and her hair splayed across the pillows in a gleaming halo of fire as she began to meet and match his motions. She was so hot, so soft, so perfect a balm to the wounds struggling deep within his soul.

She spoke something to him, urging him on, begging for release. Caught in the tidal cadence, he could not tell what she said. He focused only on his movements—on hers—as he guided her legs up high around his waist, allowing him to plunge deeper into her body. She accepted his full length, rising to meet his thrusts, gasping her pleasure.

Faster and harder and deeper he drove himself—drove them both—toward mindless, numbing bliss. She tossed her head from side to side as he continued to thrust. Finally he was lost to the sensations pouring through him, carrying them both as the tide of passion and desire welled forth. He pushed faster still, gritting his teeth as control of his actions moved from his mind to the deepest instincts he possessed.

And it was only afterward, after she had cried out and shuddered beneath him, after he had shouted his triumph and joined her over the brink, that the rest of her words registered in his mind.

And you are mine, Quin.

in nothing save her mother's locket and his own signet ring.

She shifted against the linens. Her skin smelled of Quin, manly musk and sea air, passion and sweat. Loss panged through her again. In the midst of the desire they had shared, she had expected to breach the invisible wall between them, to cross the hidden barriers. But that was not to be the case.

You are mine now, Siannon.

His words still reverberated deep inside her, humming along her nerve endings to echo each kiss, every touch, and to swirl warmth through her middle. Had he merely issued a claim of ownership with his declaration?

Heat flooded her cheeks. Everything that had passed between them in the previous hours chased through her mind in vivid detail. The taste of his skin, the feel of him inside her, the wondrous sensations she hadn't dreamed could be part of the hated duty she had endured at Percy's hands.

With Quin, marital relations proved a whole new experience, a revelation. The part of herself she had submitted to Percival Crofton had been but the smallest measure of her innocence. Her true induction into lovemaking between a husband and wife had come at the hands of the man she had loved for longer than she could remember.

The same man who had shuffled her out of his room and deposited her into her bed without a word, even going so far as to leave her nightgown folded neatly at the end of the bed. She reached for the gown, remembering the feel of his hands through the fabric, the tight look on his face as he divested her of the garment. And how utterly feminine and beautiful she had felt in his arms. Cherished. She held the satin to her cheek and inhaled. His lingering scent—wild ocean waves and warm winter fires—mingled with the soft underlying florals of her own perfume.

Just as their bodies had joined together.

A thrill pulsed through her, followed by an even stronger throb of loneliness. In the midst of the incredible intimacy they shared, she had opened her mind, her heart, and her body to him. But she still had not been able to sense Quin's thoughts or feelings. Her efforts slammed into an invisible fortress, shielding his core from her as completely as thick stone walls. As though she made love to a stranger and the Quin Reilly she had known so well was truly a part of the past.

If this intimacy they'd shared could not breach these barriers, surely the connection she had once taken for granted as much as her own breathing would remain only a childhood memory.

That bleak conclusion twisted a different kind of pain through her. Tears stung, tempting her to spill them for all the pain she'd been through in the last ten years—for her mother and the choices that could never be taken back, for her marriage to Percy, for her father's underlying perfidity and the cold black emptiness that filled him where his soul should have existed. And for the friendship she had valued above all and its loss.

She blinked hard as her throat tightened. None of the past could be changed or remedied by giving in to the tears welling inside her. None of her mistakes could be taken back. Her father's decisions could not be rectified. Did she really want to commemorate her hours with Quin by sobbing into her pillow?

She swallowed hard and swiped at the wayward teardrops staining her cheeks as she struggled to pull herself under control. "Enough," she whispered, the sound swallowed by the darkened bedchamber. "There has been enough sorrow, enough fear and loneliness in my life."

She took a deep breath and sat up on her elbows, feeling bolder. Quin's signet ring weighed heavy on her finger, a solid reminder of their unity. "How many women can claim to have married the man of their dreams? I am Mrs. Quintin Reilly, in fact now as well as name."

Satisfaction rolled through her with this declaration. So she said it again, louder. "I am Mrs. Quintin James Reilly."

Let him hear her across the hall. Let him hear her through the doors he'd put between them. Let him hear her behind the barriers he placed around his heart. She had longed for this title during the happier days of her childhood and during the lonely days of her first marriage. She had achieved it, mayhap not the way she had intended in the beautiful mist of her fantasies, but she had achieved it. That and Timmy's safety were something to cling to.

She settled back against the pillows. She had Timothy and now she had Quin. She had managed to place her son beyond her father's nefarious reach for good. These were accomplishments to be thankful for and to celebrate each day for the rest of her life. On that thought she drifted to sleep in her lonely bed.

When she awoke, bright daylight streamed through the lace draping the windows. The sight brought her upright in the bed. The quick motion jostled the mattress, making her bite her lip and suck in a hiss of breath. She was sore in places she had not been sore in for a very long time. Yet it was a far different type of ache than she had experienced before. A tight, almost pleasant kind of pain.

Almost, she winced.

"Best to go slowly."

As she moved in a more gingerly fashion toward the edge of the bed, the state of her room hit her with a second shock. She had left her wardrobe doors open and the bureau drawers a shambles, knowing she faced the chore of cleaning up after herself in the morning. Now all were closed with not a scrap of clothing in sight. Even the items she had dropped in a heap against the dark blue swirls in the rug last evening were gone. Neat as a pin. Both puzzling and unsettling.

Who had tidied the room while she slept?

Quin had no servants beyond Maeve Kelly, whose job was light housekeeping and meals during his mother's absence. Maeve had her own household and children to tend with her husband, Dan, gone to sea at the helm of Quin's own schooner.

She and Siannon had shared a pot of tea the previous morning and discussed the running of the Reilly house at great depth. Maeve would continue tidying the kitchen and downstairs, and to shop and cook breakfast and supper, leaving them light luncheons, since Quin regularly had his dinner brought over from the tap. Caitlin would attend to Timmy's and her own needs.

Siannon had insisted that she was fully capable of seeing to her own wardrobe. Although after discovering she'd never so much as rinsed a pair of hose, Maeve had insisted they enlist some extra help with the laundry.

Maeve's relaying the information that Quin cared for his chamber had prompted Siannon to take on responsibility for her own. Never having done so before, she had spent the better part of the day trying to decide where and how to unpack her belongings. Siannon was sure that if someone had entered her room, she would have heard. The mystery drew Siannon from the bed to check the drawers and the contents of the wardrobe. Not only had the drawers been closed, the contents were neatly folded and organized for her. Even her brushes and combs had been tucked into a corner of the top drawer.

The wardrobe showed signs of organization as well, from the straightened dresses to the arrangement of her shoes. How disconcerting to think she had slept through such a considerate intrusion. Not once in all the years she had suffered her father's servants, or the elderly retainers Percy favored, had she slept through someone entering her room.

Her curiosity more than piqued, she poured water into the basin and hurriedly washed and dressed, choosing a soft day dress of pewter-blue Canton crepe with Swiss muslin sleeves and chemisette, mostly because it buttoned down the front instead of possessing unwieldy back closures. It was slightly looser than her other gowns as well, allowing for her lack of corseting. She'd need more dresses like this one for life here on the island with no personal maid to assist her. Freedom followed that thought. With no personal maid to spy on her and report her every action.

After fixing her hair into a simple chignon, she tried to fold her nightgown as efficiently as the items that now graced her drawers. It ended up looking suspiciously like a ball. She tugged at the bedcovers and tried to pull them into a semblance of order, but she could not even out the counterpane no matter how she tried. Now that she had left her father's servants behind, she would have to learn to do such things much better. She would practice later. But first she wanted to find her family, to find Timmy. Judging from yesterday, Quin had surely left the house by this hour.

Yesterday and Quin . . .

The events of the previous night raced through her thoughts again, halting her as she reached for the doorknob. The mesmerizing power of Quin's kisses in the moonlight surged through her, pulling her along with him in a haze of need and desire as he stroked her skin and claimed her. Her body tingled anew. She blew out a long sigh. She did not have the luxury of reliving her hours in Quin's arms, tempting as the memories might be. She was a wife now, and it was time she set about discovering her wifely duties, whatever they might be.

"I am Mrs. Quintin James Reilly." She renewed her claim to the title.

She pushed out into the hallway. Quin's room was empty, just as she'd thought, with his door wide open now that he had no need of barriers between them. The idea that their lovemaking of the night before had unsettled him warmed her unexpectedly. Perhaps he had not been rejecting her but merely trying to restore some order after the wild tumble of passion they had shared. She could only hope as much. His room stood so tidy with its stiffly made bed, no one would ever guess what had occurred within those walls just a few hours before. Only the scent of him, wild ocean waves and warm winter fires, lingered in the air—laced with a musky whisper from their love-making.

She turned and headed down the carpeted hall. The nursery proved equally empty.

Where was her son?

A twinge of fear clutched her, and she hurried toward the stairs, telling herself he was fine, here in the house with Caitlin somewhere. She had taken the first few steps, when a burble of laughter drifted up the staircase.

"Timothy?"

"Tchh, young Timmy, ye're a devil of a charmer, aren't ye?" Maeve's voice teased, followed by another burst of giggling. "Would ye like to come fer a walk with me down to the village? Mr. Quin said to leave your mama sleep in. Yer Caitlin's hanging the wash and I've chores that need doin' at my own house. I've also a fine couple of lads who'd be happy to have yer company."

Quin had said to let her sleep? Warmth flowed through her middle and stung her cheeks at his consideration. Or had he just wanted to be sure to avoid her? The quick conversion of her hope and confidence into doubt stunned her.

Siannon glanced over the banister to see Maeve kneeling, eye-to-eye with Timmy, her gaze sparkling with invitation. Her son had never played with other children before. Percy had not believed playmates would be of any benefit to his son, and after his death, Siannon had been too afraid of her father's intentions to allow her son far from her side. The idea of him gaining a more normal childhood warmed her heart.

Maeve glanced up and caught Siannon's gaze. "Oh, Missus." She straightened. "We've woken ye."

"No, Maeve. You didn't. I should have been up long ago," Siannon assured her. "I almost never sleep this late."

"Mama!" Timmy's smile shot straight through Siannon, as it always did. He ran up the stairs toward her, and she met him at the landing, engulfing him in a hug that offered her the warm, sweet scents of clean skin and soft child. "Can I go with Maeve? She has lads for me to meet, and she's offered to let me see the shipyard, if only from the hill."

"If it's all right with you, ma'am." Maeve sought her approval. "Young Caitlin's offered ta help with the household chores here, as we thought yer lad might like a playmate or two some of the days. Boys like ta be out and about."

Thinking of the Reilly boys and how she'd loved to follow them around the hills and hollows of the island as they played, Siannon kissed her son's cheek, forcing back her ingrained need to keep him close. She was on Beannacht now, and Timothy was safe.

"Yes." She could not wrap him in cotton batting for the rest of his life.

She was instantly rewarded with a tighter squeeze from her son's arms. "Thank you, Mama."

"I'll bring him back when I come mid-afternoon," Maeve assured her. "Or you can send that Caitlin O'Brien ta fetch him before then."

She'd forgotten the island tradition of referring to one another by both first and last names. It had been a matter of deep pride to her when she was here for the summer to be named Siannon McManus, marking her as one of them. Now she would be Siannon Reilly. That realization brought a sweet burn of satisfaction.

"Thank you, Maeve." Siannon released Timmy, who skipped down the steps and linked his fingers with Maeve's.

Maeve nodded, her somber gaze holding equal parts approval and appraisal. Siannon was not surprised. Quin was the eldest Reilly son. The islanders, despite her links to Beannacht or her new name, would want to be certain she measured up as his wife. She was not yet one of them. She would have to pass muster first.

She knew several of the bolder neighbors had called yesterday with welcome gifts, but Maeve had turned them away, insisting they give the lass a little time to adjust.

Obviously Maeve believed one day was enough. Pray God she was right. "Please call me Siannon, Maeve. It will help me feel more at home."

"Aye, Missus." A smile creased Maeve's eyes as she caught herself. "Siannon. I've left ye a pot of tea and some biscuits on the stove fer yer breakfast. Come along, boy-o. It is a fine day, and time is wastin'."

Timmy waved, his face glowing with his smile as he and Maeve disappeared toward the doorway. Siannon watched them leave, realizing only as the door shut behind them that she hadn't asked Maeve about her bedroom. Perhaps Caitlin would know. She made a mental note to ask later and turned her gaze out the landing window.

Beannacht Harbor sparkled before her with the tall masts in the shipyard and dark blue of the sea stretching back toward County Kerry. Opposite that, the deep green edge of Beannacht's hills drew her. Her throat tightened. She was here, really here, as she had thought never to be again, the whole day spread in front of her before she would see her husband again. And her son gone to play. Another pang of loneliness threatened.

If only Quin were here—taut muscles gleaming in the moonlight over her, his eyes glistening with passion as he thrust into her and she urged him closer, tangling her fingers in his dark hair as he kissed her and made thorough, sweet love to her. Siannon held those images at bay with an effort and turned away from the window.

"Enough of that, my girl. You're his wife, a Reilly now. He's got more important matters to occupy his day than helping you spend your time." She lifted her chin and marched down the remaining steps, wishing she had matters requiring her attention.

Yesterday had been devoted to settling their belongings into their new home. She had spent the hours alternating between her own chamber and the nursery with Timmy. Today they would begin to settle themselves into their new lives, Timmy making new friends, herself kindling old friendships.

First things first. She would refamiliarize herself with the Reilly household. Then she would go to see her grandfather.

She drifted through the rooms, feeling almost a ghost as memories scaled her heart. Echoes of the times she had spent here and the people she had known in her childhood whispered through her. Their feelings still draped the rooms like old colors, faded by time but still recognizable.

She could hear Quin's father, James Reilly, commanding his sons to spin the globe in the parlor. She trailed her hand over the ridged continents and gave the globe a turn. Wherever someone's finger landed when it stopped was where he would begin his tales of adventure and ancient mystery that held them spellbound in the evenings.

Many of Devin's penciled sketches hung with honor in James Reilly's den. She lingered over the familiar faces of people she remembered from her summers—Dan Kelly Sr. rolling a barrel of flour into his dry goods store; Bryan reading a book by the fire; Jimmy Doyle whittling on the stoop outside his cottage with several of his children playing in the dirt beside him; Quin standing proud on the deck of what must have been his first ship; and the one that made her sigh the hardest, their two grandmothers, Granny Reilly and Gran McManus, laughing and sharing a cup of tea as they had so many afternoons.

Other memories of cricket bats and spirited games on the lawns, of laughter and people crowded into the dining room and spilling into the kitchen, made her smile as she moved on at last. Mrs. Reilly was known for her pies and sweets—Siannon and Devin had spent many summer afternoons sneaking to the pantry for samples. His mother had always known, choosing to allow them the triumph of their stolen booty, then telling them to wash up and helping brush away any crumbs of evidence.

The specters of old pain entered her thoughts too. The corner of the table where baby Meaghan had fallen and knocked out her tooth. Devin standing by the front window, watching his brothers race their sculls in the harbor, knowing he could not join them without losing his dignity along with his lunch. Bryan's tight-lipped acceptance of his father's mandates regarding his future legal studies after he'd lost Quin's ship and Bryan and his little brother nearly drowned. Standing in the foyer, Bryan had vowed to eschew all impulsive behavior and the havoc it could wreak. What would he think of his older brother's actions this week?

As she walked the rooms and passageways of her memories, Siannon noted the number of items that were no longer there. Mrs. Reilly's collection of delicate porcelain figurines. The exotic vases and artwork brought home by various seafaring Reillys over the years. The china service and crystal missing from the butler's pantry along with the full silver service that had sparkled on the table when the Reillys had entertained clients. She and Devin had received quite a scolding for absconding with the ladle one night and using it to feed Bryan's new puppy.

Perhaps these items of value had been packed away in storage during James Reilly's convalescence in the Mediterranean? She would have to remember to ask Quin.

She took the last steps to the third floor, drawn to Granny Reilly's room as she had been the night before just as surely as she had been the long-ago day of her funeral.

The melted remnants of the candle she had placed on the mantel stood mute testimony to her visit and abrupt exit with her fingers irrevocably twined through Quin's, just as the scent and feel of him was now irreversibly twined through her mind and heart.

The ghost of Granny Reilly's lavender perfume seemed to linger in the air, drawing Siannon's thoughts into the past. . . .

"Ye must be ready fer The Blessing at any time. And ye must heed it, fer a blessing missed is a curse indeed."

The Reilly Blessing. The tale they'd all loved the best and had never willingly shared. She could still hear Quintin as he set about recounting the oft-told tale, using all of his granny's inflections, missing not a word or glimmer of magic, missing nothing.

" 'Tis a sound once heard that lingers on. A sight once seen and never forgotten. A feeling once felt, always remembered. 'Tis in the blood of all Reillys."

Sound, sight, and feeling—so like her own family's Gift. A discovery that had both comforted her and filled her with wonder and envy as she listened to him invoke the ancient favor. The Blessing added a luster to the future for each Reilly.

"Reillys take heed and Reillys beware, for unto ye is delivered a great gift. A token of esteem, a promise, a fearsome gratitude." Quin had said after warning his brothers, *"It will be up to you to make of it what you will. Capture The Blessing or suffer The Curse."*

"The joy of their hearts, the wish of their souls," she repeated from time-shrouded memory. "The direction of their life. The path of their choosing."

Siannon covered her mouth with her hand as those remembered feelings roiled through her as powerful and poignant now as they had been so long ago. She'd listened from the wardrobe but not dared to reveal herself to them. Their grief had been too raw, too personal at that moment.

How those boys had loved and revered their grandmother. Quin had seemed so strong and heroic in the face of his own tremendous loss and the pain his young shoulders struggled to support. Her heart had cried out to him then, longed to give him the love he mourned, but she hadn't dared to go him, hadn't dared to breathe a word of her feelings to anyone.

Her own gran had surely known. More often than not, she had caught her grandmother's gaze dwelling on her with the kind of sad knowledge Siannon recognized now as a silent message things would not go as she wished.

In her childish fervor to believe she could change the darkness she sensed looming ahead, she had never asked Gran to tell her what she saw in store for her own future. Perhaps it was just as well she hadn't. Knowing Percival Crofton would dominate her life, even for only a few years, would not have helped at all.

Siannon slid into Granny Reilly's rocking chair and curled her feet beneath her as she had the night before. All those years ago she had promised herself she would care for Quin. She would take up where Granny had left off. She would love him and support him and be there for him when he needed her. So far all she had done was turn to him and lay yet more burdens on his already loaded shoulders.

What could she do to lighten those burdens? She would have to see that she did not further vex him.

"A man shouldn't have to search the corners of his house to find his wife." She repeated his words to her last night, recalling the worry in his glittering green gaze. And the anger that had flared so swiftly into passion. The least she could do was wait up for him and greet him on his homecoming, no matter how late.

And what was it he had asked her to help him with during the strain of their wedding supper? The other wives on the island struggling to adjust to their husbands' long hours and preoccupation with the ship-yard's demands. That was it. She sighed, feeling more than a little lost. How could she help them when she had so little idea how to adjust to her own husband? She would have to find a way.

She had thought herself so prepared for this mar-riage, so ready for the fulfillment of her dreams. Even during the worst of her fears when the physical reali-ties of marital relations had menaced her, she'd thought she had the emotional aspects neatly cov-ered. But like the mess she'd made of her bedding and folding of her nightgown, showed there was far more work and practice she needed to get it right.

She rested her head against the back of the rocker and gazed out the window toward the deep green hills of Beannacht. Granny Reilly had favored this view because it looked toward the inner valley, where her cottage yet stood. The sight both unsettled and soothed her.

"*That's where her soul lies,*" Siannon's grandmother had answered when Siannon asked why Granny Reilly looked so wistful when she gazed out her window. Yet she started each day with quiet contemplation of that view.

"*She willna' go back there, for it holds the memories of her husband and her pain at losing him, but she longs for it every day.*"

How could pain and longing become so entwined in loving and missing someone? Siannon hadn't understood, but she had accepted the explanation because she respected her grandmother's wisdom and Sight far more than her own meager understand-ing. And because there had been something in Gran's eyes, in the misty tone of her voice that bespoke truth.

A man shouldn't have to search the corners of his house to find his wife, Siannon.

Then make me truly your wife, Quintin Reilly.

Quin's words and her own. Entwined.

You are mine, Siannon Reilly, he'd shouted in his passion.

And you are mine, Quin, she'd answered.

She was beginning to understand. A depth of emotions and needs should well between a woman and her husband, a man and his wife. Timeless. Wordless. Shared.

Against the reference frame of Percival Crofton and his grand town house, she had never truly been a wife. She had been the trophy of his dying years, the means to the continuation of his line, but not a wife. Not the wife she intended to be for Quin.

She'd spent the better part of a year planning to escape her father's household and raise her son away from his influence. Independence and a source of income had been a big part of that plan until matters had come so urgently to a head. Perhaps she could interest the women of Beannacht in her project and accomplish two things—gaining them all some worthwhile occupation and pleasing her husband by helping as he'd asked.

"Oh, Gran." She sighed, wishing she still had her grandmother's wisdom to guide her. "I hope I can bring Quin the kind of happiness he deserves."

"Well, ye'll not do it sittin' in a deserted bedroom, dreaming the day away, Siannon Reilly."

The crisp retort brought a smile to Siannon's lips. Whether real or imagined she couldn't say, but the tone had been Gran's through and through.

"All right, Gran." Siannon pushed to her feet and

left the rocking chair swinging gently in her wake. This house felt more like home already.

She descended the stairs with her spirits lifted. There were many problems yet for Quin and her to sift through and adjust to in their marriage, but that was normal and expected. All newly married people had some adjusting to do, didn't they?

She paused at the second-floor landing for just a moment.

The shipyard.

Maybe she needed to make a visit to her husband and share her newfound realizations and plans before she went to see Grandda. Her heart raced at the thought. Surely a chance to talk things through would help them build their future. The heat of a green-eyed gaze and the chance to taste desire on his lips threaded through her decision as well. And why not? They were truly married now.

Yes. She would visit her husband in his office and remind him of the help she could offer him during the day and the newly discovered passion that awaited him when he returned home tonight.

She nodded to herself and hurried down the remainder of the steps, humming softly. Reillys were not known for being faint of heart. Neither were the McManuses, for that matter. And she represented both families now.

Eustace Rhodes and his empty heart could just stick that in his pipe and smoke it.

She stopped in the foyer to settle her bonnet atop her head and tie a jaunty bow beneath her chin. Life sparkled back at her from the gray eyes of her reflection in the mirror, surprising her with a flash of recognition for someone she had not seen in a very long time—herself as she had been before she married Percy and before her mother's death.

How odd to think she had missed herself along with the rest of Beannacht. And that coming to Quin's home had given her back a part of herself that had been missing, something else she had gained from their bargain while giving so little herself.

Well, that was about to change.

Chapter Six

Quin sighed and raked a hand through his hair as his thoughts continued to stray from the task at hand, snagged again by a pair of gleaming gray eyes glazed with passion in the night. He'd just incorrectly added the same column of figures he'd battled for the last half hour and laid the blame for this impediment to completing his task squarely on the distraction he'd struggled through all morning.

Instead of providing the clear-cut relief he'd envisioned, making love to Siannon had served only to complicate matters between them still further. His conscience taunted him for his lack of control, his lack of vision, in a tone more than a little reminiscent of his brother Bryan but failed to offer him any solutions. Having tasted her sweetness in the hopes of satiating his desire, he found himself craving more.

The Blessing he'd thought he'd detected in their

earlier kisses mercifully had not swelled between them the night before. Obviously the rippling waves of fervent passion Siannon set off in him had nothing to do with Granny's tales. An edge of loss struck him. Whyever had he thought himself worthy of The Blessing? He'd failed everyone in his life—Bryan, Marie, Devin, Da. With all the pressures and obligations dependent on his success here in the Ship Works, he was allowing himself to be distracted by lust for a wife he'd never wanted—surely this was to be his curse. To recognize what was needed from him and know he could not deliver.

A swift, salty breeze ruffled the edges of his erasure-darkened ledger book, drawing his gaze out the window toward the ship slowly coming to life. Clean lines of yellow-leaf pine stretched the length of her great skeleton and bowed beneath her stalwart keel. The work in the yard thrummed with a rhythm all its own, a life and heart developed over generations of experienced shipwrights plying their trade. This was the female who should command his every thought, his full concentration.

Despite the appreciative pride curling through Quin's chest as he observed the ship slowly being born, his traitorous mind supplied ready images of the tempting white curves of Siannon's body—her supple breasts, the taut arch of her back, the velvet-soft smoothness of her stomach. Her passionate cries echoed on in his thoughts. Desire tightened within him, driving him mad with urges that had no place in his office, no place in his life.

He knocked the ledger to the floor with a satisfying clatter. He should be sailing the Atlantic, seeking new contacts to supply the lumber the Works so desperately needed. Or trading cargoes for profits that could purchase the hemp whose price had mysteriously doubled over the past year. That was his true calling, his trade. Not shuffling these papers. And certainly not striding up the path to enter his house and make slow, sweet love to Siannon over and over again, as he longed to do.

He'd sworn never to damn himself through his attachment to a woman again, yet he'd clearly wasted his entire morning doing little else but musing over one. The image of moonlight shimmering over Siannon's alabaster-pale skin as he drove himself into her last night sent him to his feet. His chair crashed to the floor.

"Diabhal." Nothing good could come of this overwhelming lust. If only he could have married little Siannon Rhodes as he remembered her. The pesky young girl had turned into a woman he was finding harder and harder to turn away from.

Hell, he hadn't even tried to resist her. Truth be told, after a day spent today much like yesterday, thinking of her tantalizing curves, he had stridden toward the house at night with every intention of claiming his rights as a husband and bringing to an end his growing obsession with Siannon Reilly.

He rubbed the knots of tension at the base of his skull as he strode over to the window. Well, having achieved the first part of his objectives, he had certainly fallen short of the mark on the second. The reality of making love to his wife was beyond anything he'd imagined possible before last night.

"Problems, Captain?"

The question jolted him. Quin turned toward the doorway, torn between throttling whatever hapless

soul intruded and thanking him for stopping the
untenable direction of his thoughts. Part of the tension wound between his shoulder blades lessened as
his gaze met the twinkling spark in the eyes of the
wiry seaman standing there.

"Run into a bit of a squall, I see." Declan Rogers
looked down at the ledger and papers on the floor
in front of the desk and then at the overturned chair
before he entered the office and closed the door
behind him.

Declan had been a fine seaman, captain of his own
Reilly ship until a freak accident sank the vessel and
left him with only one good arm. By all accounts,
despite his own grievous injury from the mysterious
explosion that sent the *Earrach* to the bottom, Declan
had worked feverishly to make sure all hands were
safe before he'd abandoned his post.

Without answering his friend, Quin retrieved the
ledger and correspondence that had fallen in its wake.

"Give us a tell, then." Declan crossed to the desk.
He set the chair to rights and perched on the edge
of the desk, his empty left sleeve swinging gently in
the breeze.

"Just figures." Quin tapped the ledger and took
his seat with a heavy sigh.

"Hmmmm." Declan squinted his dark eyes and
lifted one skeptical brow. "It's more than that, I think,
Captain Reilly. There's a foul wind scuttering your
sails."

He peered at the papers in front of Quin and
offered a good-humored chuckle and wink. "That,
or your thoughts are far from the ledger in front of
you. I thought the currents were changing in our
favor for once."

Declan knew enough details of the shipyard's financial straits to recognize how close they were to foundering, a realization it had taken Quin the better part of his first month home to reach. And during that month he had more than regretted sending Devin away so abruptly.

The best way you can help, stripling, is to get back to Dublin and finish your term, he'd growled, and practically tossed the lad onto the *Achanaich* for the first leg of his journey after a parting shot about seeking a pot of gold if he truly wanted to be of use. It was Declan who told Quin, in no uncertain terms, how hard Devin had worked to keep things together here on the island once their father's illness became apparent.

He could use his brother's help now, but it was clear Dev was not speaking to him, for it had been nearly two months with not a word from him in Dublin. And who could blame him after being taken to task by his brother for being green-gilled and naive. The same brother who was now putting the island's very livelihood in danger acting like a lovesick seal.

Quin shot Declan a scowl he really meant for himself. "There is nothing scuttering my sails save the endless delays we've faced with this barque. Any word on the hemp for the seams and rigging?"

"Aye." Declan accepted the change of subject smoothly. "If it's not on the packet that's just rounding the point, it should be here by week's end when the *Achanaich* returns. We've scrounged enough decent logs for the planking and I've set the crew to work on it. We'll be on schedule soon, don't worry."

"Good." Quin sat back and rubbed a hand over

the back of his neck. "I'll feel a hell of a lot better once this one's done and gone."

"Aye, Captain. As will we all." Declan nodded and let silence build between them for a moment. "The lads were hoping your marriage was a sign fortunes were looking up for yourself as well as for the shipyard. A blessing that arrived just in time."

Fortunes. A blessing mayhap, but not for him.

The aftertaste of accepting Siannon's money stung the back of Quin's throat. The capital she'd accumulated had allowed him to pay enough creditors to ensure the delivery of the hemp despite a sudden increase in price. But it galled him that his word was not enough to obtain what they needed to complete the project. The Reillys had always stood good for their debts.

"Have you been sent to ascertain matters?" Agitation rasped his tone.

Declan offered a shrug. "It's a strange sight to see a new groom, with a bride as fair as Siannon McManus, brooding over a scarred ledger book. Are you sure you'd not like to tell me what's bothering you, Quin?"

The image of Siannon in his bed, sprawled beneath him, flashed through his mind—brooding over her, was he? For all to see and wonder about, no less. He shook his head, trying to banish his wife from his thoughts. "Nothing I can't solve with a little concentration, a new lumber supply, and a mallet."

Declan's snort of laughter sparked Quin's own. It felt good, freeing, despite the skepticism still lingering in the other man's eyes.

"You mentioned what you sought in your father's files yesterday. Is that what troubles you? Can I lend a hand? I've one to spare." A wry joke.

"Thanks, boy-o, but I think I'll have to pilot this one on my own." Quin shook his head. "A decade and more of orders and correspondence will take me some time to get through. The best thing you can do is keep things moving in the yard and leave me to the sorting. I'll sing out as soon as I get a sounding and we have some idea which vessels are burdened and which privileged."

Declan accepted the answer and moved to his feet. "Then come and look at the trimming crew with me. I've an idea for the final plank and I want your opinion before I try it."

It was on the tip of Quin's tongue to turn down the invitation and return to the damned ledger. But his efforts so far had been fruitless. Despite the upswing in their fortunes, courtesy of his bride, they would be damned lucky to squeak through even if they delivered the barque on time. And they'd fold if any delays forced them into a contract penalty. A turn in the yard might be just the thing to clear his mind of Siannon and allow him to focus back on the tasks at hand, the truly important matters facing him.

"An idea for the final plank, eh?" He pushed to his feet and stretched out the kinks knotting his back. "Now, that I'd like to see."

Work continued in the yard as he passed with Declan. Hatchets chopped at long strips of lumber, slowly hacking the ship's design from the wood, a vision solely in the minds of the men working diligently to produce it. Generations of skill and commitment and an uncompromising knowledge of what worked at sea abounded here in the Reilly yard. He admired and valued each and every one of these men for their contribution and their unflagging enthusiasm. Untold numbers of seamen's lives depended on each swing of the hatchet, each nail pounded through, each bend in the wood. Such was the life of the shipwright.

After an hour of sun and fresh salt-tinged air, some of the cobwebs seemed to have cleared from his mind. He could thank Declan for that. The ex-captain hadn't really needed to show him anything. It had been an excuse to pry Quin from the office's musty confines and the ledger's less than promising scribble. He felt better for it.

Crossing back toward the office, he wondered if his elevated mood would last. A flash of red hair disappeared through the door at the top of the stairs, sinking his hopes.

Apparently not.

Siannon. That color could belong to only one person here on Beannacht. Even her McManus relatives sported a darker hue. Hers were the only tresses with those rich spun-gold highlights. The only ones to curl so seductively against pale white skin and haunt a man's thoughts. And now she was there in person, just as he'd banished her specter from his thoughts.

Everything that had passed between them in the dark, sweet hours of the night echoed through him with far more power than he should allow. Far more than he wanted or had the time to entertain.

They would obviously have to come to an understanding about acceptable intrusions into his life. He had let her into his house and into his bed and been plagued by thoughts of her all day as a result. He had no intention of allowing her invasion here as well. The policy he had set for all the shipwrights' wives must apply to her too. Hadn't he told her as much at their wedding supper?

Will you tell me where I can and cannot go? Her question from the night before stung him anew, adding impetus to his pace as he took the stairs.

With her bonnet slung down her back and her bottom pointed saucily in his direction, his wife leaned over his desk, peering at the grim ledger book, when he reached the open doorway. Anger sliced into him. He tamped it back with an effort, waiting to voice in private his dismay not only at her audacity but at the wanton display she was making.

"Siannon." She jumped guiltily and stepped away from the book as he closed the door behind him. "Most of the wives on this island have too many things to occupy themselves with to waste their husband's time during the working day."

"Surely you can best advise me on what things your wife could do that might please you, Quintin." Color washed over her cheeks and down into the bodice of her gown as she met his gaze with a slight rise to her chin.

She wasn't dressed much like any of the women on the island. During flush times they might order a special dress from a catalogue, but most used fabric purchased from Kelly's Dry Goods and made do with their own skills with a needle. Siannon's outfit had obviously been made by one of Limerick's finest seamstresses. The pewter-blue gown emphasized her trim waist; the white fabric of the bodice accented the full lushness of her breasts. His trousers tightened across the front as desire splashed through him despite himself.

She took a deep breath and exhaled slowly, dimming some of the stubborn light in her eyes.

"I didn't come here to provoke you, Quin." She offered him a soft smile that sank beneath his guard. Petticoats rustled beneath her skirts as she moved toward him.

"Why are you here, Siannon?" The words came out with a harsher sting than he intended, stopping her before she reached him. The smile died on her lips.

"I . . . you had gone already. . . ." Her voice trailed away as fresh color washed her soft skin.

"Aye. I've much to get done and far too little time to do it." And little patience to spare. He certainly shouldn't be standing there, longing to pull her into his arms and ravish the hesitation from her lips.

He raked a hand through his hair and struggled to control the impulse. So much to be done and so many obstacles to face before he finished. He turned from her and strode over to the window to stare out into the yard.

"Siannon, I've many matters to attend. Ledgers do not balance themselves. Is there something urgent? Else—"

"Urgent?" She moved closer. The scent of lilac and lavender, so seductively Siannon, teased him. He caught back a groan.

"What is it you want?" He knew what he wanted. The fullness in his groin demanded release. The rustling approach of her petticoats halted again. He was handling this very poorly. He turned to face her.

"I wanted—" Her gaze moved over his face, halting at his lips. He could almost feel her mouth beneath his. Hot blood boiled through his veins, making it difficult to concentrate on anything beyond the need rising inside him.

"What?" He prompted, needing her to finish her sentence—to state her demands and be gone before he lost what little restraint remained at his command.

"I—" She licked her lips.

The sight of her pink tongue tracing a delicate circuit along the path he himself craved mesmerized him, snapping his control like dry twigs beneath a booted heel.

He reached for her without conscious thought, closing his hands over her shoulders and pulling her against him.

"Was it this you sought, lass?"

He covered her mouth with his, tasting her uncertainty and the untried passion he had sampled the night before.

She made a tiny sound in the back of her throat. Protest? Welcome? It didn't matter as he pulled her closer, anchoring one arm at her waist to settle her fully against him. He traced the soft line of her mouth with his tongue, gaining entry as she parted, accepting him.

Desire pounded through him, wave after inescapable salty-sweet wave, crushing his intention to put her from his mind and to keep her from his heart. To keep his distance altogether. She was a cursed distraction he could not afford, and he did not care. He wanted her. Their tongues slid together, mating in seductive parody of the act he truly wished to engage in.

Her fingers threaded his hair as he spanned her waist to pull her closer and closer still. It was not enough, not nearly enough. Her scent enveloped him. Sweet lavender, lilac, and Siannon.

Her breasts pressed into his chest, so soft and full. He longed to strip her out of the gown and take her. Damn the location. He would lock the door and introduce her to the pleasures of lovemaking in the broad light of day.

He released her mouth and arched her chin upward with his fingers, teasing and licking and nipping the small pulse beating beneath her skin at the side of her neck.

"Oh, Quin." She moaned and clutched his jacket as he nibbled her, tracing his hands over her back and sides to cup the full swells of her breasts through her gown.

"I want you, Siannon."

"Aye." Their gazes locked as the mingled sound of their quickened breaths filled the office. More than acceptance glowed in the luminescent gray sparkling before him. She wanted him. And he wanted her, perhaps more now than he had last night. Cursed indeed. Damnation.

He could drown in the depth of her gaze.

Footsteps pounded up the stairs outside the office. A thump sounded at the door as though something heavy slammed against it. She released a shuddering sigh and turned her head at the noise.

"Ye canna' go in there."

"Stand aside." Officious English tones answered the challenge.

Siannon's gaze darted toward the door and then back to Quin's. Passion had been replaced with dread.

"Ye've not the captain's leave. State yer business or be on yer way." Young Benen McManus seemed to have appointed himself gatekeeper against this unknown invader who must have sailed in on the packet he'd spotted earlier.

"I will not be questioned by some lackey. I've business with your master. I doubt he'd want it spread about as fodder for the gossip mill."

Siannon's grip on his jacket tightened. Annoyance flared deep in Quin, accompanied by a quick flash of unease. *Rhodes*. Siannon's father had to be behind those weasely tones demanding entrance. He had lost very little time in causing trouble. Benen was handling matters just fine for the moment. Let the blackguard cool his heels. Quin wanted to give Siannon a moment to collect herself.

"Reilly." The lass called through the door in the same officious tones, but louder and clearly frustrated. "Reilly, are you in there?"

"Here now, it's Captain Reilly to ye. If he's interested in yer business, he'll let ye know." The lad held his ground. There was obviously quite a bit more starch to young Benen than Quin had surmised.

"How ridiculous. *Captain* Reilly, it would be in your best interests and those of your wife to open this door immediately."

Quin sighed and reluctantly released his wife.

"Quin?" Fear laced his name as she whispered.

He reached back and squeezed her fingers. "Don't worry."

Then he crossed the short distance to the door and pulled the portal open. Benen nearly fell through the doorway, so determinedly had he been blocking the smaller man's way.

"Sorry to bother ye, Captain. Captain Rogers set

me ta stand outside the door and said ye was not ta be disturbed by anything save—"

"Are you Quintin Reilly?" The nasal fellow cut off Benen with complete disregard. He straightened his blue worsted jacket by tugging at it with one hand while clutching a bulging leather satchel in the other. He adjusted his bowler and fixed Quin with a look of intense study.

"Aye." Quin bristled beneath the man's beady-eyed perusal.

"At last." He gave Benen a dismissive look and brushed at the front of his jacket as though merely talking with the stalwart young seaman had been beneath him. "May we carry our discussion inside, Reilly? Or would you like to discuss our business here on the open steps, as this burly youngster seems want to do?"

"Captain?" Benen continued to block the older man's way. Quin respected the loyalty, though he doubted even a barricade of ten capable shipwrights could put a stop to the sort of trouble their visitor portended.

As much as Quin longed to toss the intrusive fellow down the office steps and off his island, no good would come from satisfying the moment when it would only multiply problems for the future. That much he had learned from experience, if only last night's. "Let him pass."

"Aye, Captain." The lad nodded and moved out of the smaller man's way.

"About time." The man sniffed as he stepped forward.

Quin waved a hand toward the office interior. "Stay

nearby Benen, but see that word gets to Dan Kelly Sr. He'll know what to do."

Benen nodded and closed the door. The man stalked into the room, stopping short when he noticed Siannon standing by the window. He drew himself up to the peak of his bandy height and puffed out his chest.

"Excellent," he exclaimed as he gave her a long look. "Your presence will expedite matters."

Quin brushed by and went to stand between this threat and his wife. Her skin was pale with her apprehensions, but with her cheeks still flushed from his kisses she looked serene and unconcerned by the intrusion. Recognition showed in her gaze as she watched their visitor.

The man nodded to her, retrieving a pair of spectacles from his pocket. "Mrs. Crofton."

"Mrs. Reilly," she corrected him.

"Yes." He placed the spectacles on his face and gave her a more thorough perusal. "Very well, Mrs. Reilly, then."

"I have come on behalf of . . . Timothy Michael Crofton's grandfather, Eustace Rhodes. My name is Nigel Franklin. I have been Mr. Rhodes's solicitor for many years."

Quin lifted a brow at Siannon and received a quick nod in return. She'd had more than enough experience with Mr. Franklin if the tense expression on her face was any indication.

"And your purpose here, Mr. Franklin?"

"I'm certain you are aware of my client's objections to his daughter's hasty marriage to you only a few short days ago. He very carefully selected her first husband, and he intended to manage the second just as painstakingly. There was even some question as to whether he would have her marry a second time at all. Due to the . . . er . . . delicate condition she is prone to.''

"Delicate condition?'' Was she pregnant? But how and with whom? The absurdity of the notion rippled through Quin, chased by a prickle of rage so primal and dark, he felt as if the walls were closing in on him.

No! He wanted to shout. Such could not be the case. She would have told him. Surely he would have sensed such a secret last night, buried so deep within her that he couldn't tell where he ended and she began.

Yet, was that the true reason for her hasty proposal? Gut-wrenching sickness churned through him. Dark betrayal slithered through him. He forced himself to ignore it. Little Siannon Rhodes could not have changed so much. She would have told him all before they said their vows; he had to believe that.

"Yes.'' The man rummaged in his broad leather satchel to pull out a ream of papers. "Her father has been pursuing various ways to deal with the problem for some time now.''

"No.'' Siannon barely whispered the word. Her face had gone pale.

Quin reached out and linked his fingers with hers. They were icy cold and stiff beneath his own. This man's intentions terrified her. Quin drew her to his side and squeezed her hands, trying to tell her without words that she was safe, that he would not believe anything, no matter how damning the evidence, until she had spoken first.

Her gaze stayed fixed on her father's solicitor.

"What condition would that be, Franklin?"

"Why, her mental state, of course." The man darted a superior look at Siannon.

Her fingers gripped Quin's.

"Her mental state? Speak plainly, man. So far you have done naught but take up valuable time."

"Oh, I see." The man lowered his papers and returned his gaze to Quin's. "I'd assumed you knew. Well, that changes everything, doesn't it? An annulment will be much more easily obtained when the magistrate realizes she married you under false pretenses."

Cold solidified in Siannon's stomach, as thick as winter's ice, completely obliterating any lingering warmth from Quin's kiss. Numbness pervaded her limbs. She wanted to scream at Nigel Franklin to go away, to Quin not to believe anything the man said. But in doing so she would prove the case.

Oh, why hadn't she reminded Quin of her abilities? Her Gift had never seemed so much a liability as it did at that moment. Though he had scoffed when they were younger and teased her many times, that didn't negate the fact that she'd had the opportunity to explain things to him. Many times, even in the short span of their reacquaintance. Franklin would take advantage of anything Quin said now, and she could stop nothing. She couldn't even gain command over her own tongue as she stood frozen by her husband's side.

Silence hung in the office, a doomed cloud predestined to deliver her and Timothy back into her father's control. She should have known her father would brook no escape.

"There were no false pretenses about our marriage." Quin's warm fingers squeezed hers.

"Indeed? But you were not aware of her mental problems." Franklin did not even bother to phrase his statement as a question, so neatly did the admission fit into his schemes.

"My wife has no mental problems."

Bless Quin. He sounded quite certain.

"Ah, but I assure you, Mr. Reilly, she does." He proffered a folder to Quin. "If you like, you can peruse not only the statements made about your wife by those who tended her but those about her mother as well.

"Living outside the civilized world as you do, without benefit of formal education, you may not realize it, but these things are often inherited." Franklin dropped his voice and nodded conspiratorially to Quin.

The evidence dangled between them. Siannon longed to snatch the papers and rend them to shreds. Her own mother's condemnation hovered there, ink against paper. She swallowed over the tightness gripping her throat. The screams from within the dark gray walls of the asylum echoed afresh in her mind.

"I need to see no papers. No doubt Mr. Rhodes paid quite handsomely for them, but I have known my wife for a very long time, Franklin. Be on your way back to civilization. You have nothing with which to threaten either one of us."

"Mr. Reilly, it is paramount for you to know—"

"That my wife has The Sight?" Quin laughed as though he had known the full extent of it all along.

Incredulity rippled through Siannon.

"Then you do know." Nigel drew the words out.

Quin had surprised him as well. He replaced the folders in his satchel. Siannon's knees felt weak. She continued to cling to Quin's hand for fear she would go straight to the floor if she did not.

"That does not change the reason for my visit."

"Which is?"

"As his nearest male relative, Mr. Rhodes merely wishes to regain guardianship of his grandson now that the boy has seen his mother settled into her new life. Being that Siannon Crofton is not mentally sound, she did not have the right to take the boy from his grandfather's home"

"No." Siannon blurted out the word. "You cannot take my son."

"Please do not distress yourself, Mrs. Crofton . . . er . . . Mrs. Reilly. I am aware how fragile you are at times. Your father is not seeking to block all access to the boy. You will be granted frequent visitations. On the condition that you turn the boy over to me immediately."

The horror of what he was proposing tore into Siannon. "Never—"

"Let's hear Mr. Franklin out, Siannon, before we deliver our answer." Quin squeezed her hands as he spoke.

How could he even consider listening to this? Why would he? She took a deep, racking breath, trying to fathom Quin's strategy. By listening, at least they might gain some insight into her father's plans. Insanity for sure—what else? She nodded.

Franklin smirked. "I did so hope you were a man of reason, Reilly."

"No matter my lack of education?" Wry humor laced Quin's barb.

Franklin ignored this last. "There is no reason this transfer cannot be handled in an amicable manner. Since your husband is aware of your . . . indisposition, Mrs. Reilly, and has accepted you anyway, that is his affair. But Mr. Rhodes's grandson is of primary concern. As the heir to both Eustace Rhodes and Percival Crofton, the boy will have a certain standing and responsibilities in society. This can more beneficially be fostered by his grandfather in Limerick than here on this remote and somewhat provincial island. Provided this custody matter is settled today, in his role as trustee Mr. Rhodes will expedite the release of your widow's portion from Mr. Crofton's estate."

Silence reigned for the space of a single heartbeat before Quin answered.

"As I suspected, Franklin, you have nothing of interest to either one of us. I have given you more than enough time to spout your nonsense. Good day."

"I assure you, Mr. Reilly, this is not nonsense. If you force Mr. Rhodes to fight for his grandson, the proceedings will not be a pretty affair. Mr. Rhodes will tie up your rich little widow's nest egg for quite some time. You may very well lose your wife and your business in the bargain."

"Get off my island." Angry control underscored Quin's command. "Benen."

"Aye, Captain." The young shipwright answered Quin's call immediately.

"Escort Mr. Franklin back to his ship. His business here is finished."

Franklin's lips grew pinched, a look that signaled further trouble for whoever had placed it there. "Very well, sir. I will leave for the moment. But remember, when the time comes, you were offered an amicable settlement. It is you who have chosen to make this a protracted battle."

Nigel replaced his spectacles in the pocket of his jacket and closed his leather satchel with a cool click of the brass latch.

"Good day to you both. You will receive my missives within the week."

Quin released Siannon's fingers long enough to close the door behind Nigel with somewhat more force than was necessary. Everything in her shuddered with relief to have her father's solicitor on his way off Beannacht. But for how long?

"That went better than I expected."

He seemed so calm in the face of her father's threats, so unsurprised by everything that had just been revealed. Her head spun and she tried to focus on all that had just occurred. "But you never believed when we were children. How did you know?"

"I guessed his intentions from his tone, *mo ceile.*" Quin cut through her confusion and sighed. "Remember, wife, I knew your grandmother. Our families have shared a heritage here on Beannacht for generations. And I remember your intervention the night of Bryan and Devin's accident." A sad smile chased across his lips.

The danger they faced rolled through her again. "Even if my father were only goading you with empty boasts in Limerick, he will be quite angry by our continued refusal to allow him sway. I've put everything, everyone here, at risk. I'm sorry, Quin."

"You are my wife, Siannon. Reillys hold what is theirs. It's one of the tenets of living in an uncivilized portion of the world."

The fierce possession in his tone brought back the

memory of what had almost happened before the solicitor had intruded. She met the blaze in his green eyes and saw the truth and the promise reflecting in them. "Timothy is now my responsibility. I knew your father would try something. He was just a bit quicker than I anticipated."

"What do we do now?" Weariness ached through Siannon.

Quin laced his fingers through hers again and pulled her toward him, where he rested his hip against the desk. "We solidify our position, sweet Siannon."

He kissed her, a feather-light brush of his lips against her brow. Warmth raced along her already raw nerve endings. She sighed. With his arms around her and his lips teasing her skin, somehow Nigel Franklin's threats held less power.

"How do we do that?" she whispered as his hands stroked over her back, soothing her fears.

"We contact Gill O'Brien," he answered, his breath stirring the hair at her temple. "And we fight for what is ours. For Timothy."

Chapter Seven

And we fight for what is ours.

Resting her head against Quin's broad chest, Siannon caught back a sigh and wrestled the paralyzing demons of fear and dread that had plagued her whole life where her father was concerned. Faced with Nigel Franklin's horrifying accusations and proposals, and the threats they yet posed, she needed the strength of her husband's embrace to seep into her and become her own.

We fight for what is ours. For Timothy.

She tried to lose herself in the mesmerizing beat of Quin's heart. Heeding the strong rhythm helped her to order her thoughts.

Safe. Secure. Safe. Secure.

The message thrummed against her ear, promising all that she could wish for and more. All she had ever wished for herself, for her child.

Wistful prayers curled through her as she gave herself over to the haven Quin offered. She truly had found protection for her son with Quintin Reilly. Perhaps she had found more. His promises seemed genuine enough in light of his defense just now and the shattering revelations he had accepted without question.

And given the tantalizing covenant their new intimacy from the prior night harkened. The kiss they'd shared had promised a furthering of those intimacies in the future. A happy ending.

At the moment, despite Nigel's intrusion, all things seemed possible. Such moments were seldom destined to last. She clung to this one, willing to hold her doubts and fears at bay for this small moment out of time.

"In the meantime"—a chill pebbled her arms as Quin set her from him, his face ordered into an unreadable mask—"I will achieve very little of benefit to anyone if I do naught but entertain uninvited guests."

The glow in the depths of his green eyes flared to life as he held her with his gaze, belying the crisp business edge to his words. The sounds of a working shipyard outside replaced the cadence of his heart. The security of the entire island pulsed with each rhythmic swing of ax and mallet.

Heat bathed her cheeks once more as Quin's stare traced her lips. The tender ardor of their kiss in the moments just before Franklin had appeared shimmered again in her thoughts like seamist wisping in from the harbor. Would Quin make love to her here in his office, extending the magic of this moment?

"We've a few matters to clear up between us before you leave me to my business, wife."

"Aye?" Her cheeks warmed still further beneath his brilliant green gaze. She'd always loved his eyes, had dreamed of them for years.

A shout from the yard drew his attention to the window for a fleeting second, enough to break whatever had been brewing between them.

"Aye." He nodded, his lips tightening as his gaze shuttered, hiding the emotions that had brimmed in those dark green orbs. "What manner of Gift do you possess, Siannon?"

"My Gift?" She had been willing—eager—to set aside their worries for a few minutes and lose herself in the magic of his embrace. And he had been concentrating on their strategy. She should feel grateful. Frustration at her inability to read him had never pounded harder through her.

"Yes—the McManus Gift. Your gran was both a healer and one who saw things before they happened. Your mother heard these things. But we need to prepare a rational explanations for your father's attacks. How does it manifest in you?"

He spoke so matter-of-factly about the deep secret of her childhood. Her own mind, her thoughts, could not drop the desire that had sizzled through them just a moment before despite the situation they faced. Obviously her appeal did not have such a devastating effect on him.

"I . . . I can read emotions, sense what is to come from the underlying feelings people do not recognize." That was the best way she could think to explain.

His dark eyebrows shot up. "Then why were you surprised by your father accosting us outside the courthouse. And—" His voice hardened as he stood up straight. A glint she did not like came into his eyes, as if he'd caught her stealing something precious. "What do you know about—"

"I cannot sense things with people I know best. The ties I share with family seem to muddle things to the point where I cannot tell what my father or Timmy or . . . you feel. Only in random pieces when I least expect it. And only the strongest of the most basic emotions."

He nodded and stared off into the distance for a moment. When he glanced back at her, it was like looking at a stranger.

"It is against our practice here to allow wives to visit the shipyard save for the direst of needs."

He scooped up her bonnet from the floor and handed it to her, his eyes impersonal and implacable as he took her arm and guided her toward the door. "There have been enough delays for this day, especially with the impending threats from your father's solicitor. I have much to do. The ledgers will not audit themselves. Nor will I ever uncover any connections between your father and the Works if I do not get to the files. This ship must be delivered on time, and I've the next one to contract for as well."

Disappointment and alarm clashed. So much rested on Quin's shoulders. His family and the islanders counted on him to get them all through this crisis. She and Timmy added enough to his burdens. But so much of his demeanor had changed when she'd explained the manner of her Gift to him just now. Why?

She longed to stay, to make him explain the coldness of his reaction. But perhaps it would be best to wait and discuss this when he got home that night.

To give him time to digest the information as he dealt with the immediate matters clamoring for his attention.

They stopped before the door. Another shout rang from the yard, calling his attention to the window again.

"Did you see Franklin's ship arrive, or did you come here for some other purpose?" he asked politely enough, though his gaze remained fixed at the window.

Purpose? All the things she'd intended to say rang through her mind—her burgeoning hopes for their marriage and how his lovemaking still sang through her blood, her need to know what he intended for their future and her own plan to help the island. In light of her father's looming threats, Quin's varying acceptance of her Sight, and all the other demands on Quin's time and energies, her visit now seemed frivolous—childish.

"No purpose other than a visit." She reached toward the latch, embarrassment scorching her cheeks where just a few moments earlier desire had warmed them. How could she feel so safe and secure in his arms one minute and so terribly alone the next?

"Siannon." He halted her before she opened the door.

"Aye?" She couldn't turn back to him—couldn't bear the thought of him seeing just how thoroughly confused she felt. She had vowed never again to place herself at the whim and mercy of another husband, of any man for that matter.

"Do not fret yourself over your father." His words vibrated through the air toward her, tightening the invisible band squeezing her chest. "I promised you protection. By my word, you shall have it."

I want more than protection. She bit back the words.

"I believe you, Quin." She gripped the brass handle and gave it a twist. "I have trusted you with all I hold dear. It is my father and Mr. Franklin I do not trust."

She could feel his dark gaze measuring her as she passed through the doorway without another word and resolutely shut the door behind her.

Her skirts rustled overloud as she hurried down the steps away from Quin's office. She could only hope that this marriage would be enough to ensure Timothy's continued safety. A quick rush of fear shot through her, stilling her footsteps.

Thank heaven Maeve had taken the child with her that morning. If he had been at the house and Nigel Franklin had made his way there instead of to the shipyard, would her son still remain on the island? A shudder ripped up her spine in a fresh mingling of fear and relief. She would not lose Timothy to her father's designs no matter what she had to do to achieve that end.

She looked across the busy shipyard as she reached the bottom of the steps. As far as she could see, men worked—at planks of lumber with hooks and chains and hatchets—in a familiar rhythm, almost a music all its own. Slowly, as though a spring wound down on an invisible music box, the work around her ground to a halt. Fresh embarrassment stung her cheeks.

They all knew the policy that women should provide no distractions. Yet there she was, creating just the interruption her husband forbade. Waves of speculation surrounded her in the near silence. If only Quin were so easy to read. She closed herself off and blew out a slow breath. She would not come here again. The least she could afford her husband in return for all he provided her was respect for his boundaries. And if that guarded her heart and pride into the bargain, so much the better.

She steeled herself to walk slowly through the shipyard on her exit, holding the ponderous cloud of their disapproval at bay. Rounding the small hillside that finally put her out of sight, she renewed her vow to stay away from the shipyard and breathed a sigh of relief.

Her relief was short-lived as fingers snagged her arm in a painful grip, halting her before she could take another step toward the docks or the village.

"Your husband is vastly overconfident, Mistress." Franklin released her as she turned toward him.

She fought not to rub her arm and to keep her fears from showing on her face under his all too astute gaze.

"With reason," she offered, wishing she were still in sight of the yard and didn't feel quite so vulnerably alone with her father's man of business. "I thought you had left, Mr. Franklin."

"My ship makes ready as we speak." He glanced over his shoulder at the harbor to the sloop anchored there. "I managed to elude that insufferable lout foisted on me long enough to afford you one last opportunity to see reason. Your father will forgive you this irrational behavior and allow you to make amends if you hand over the boy to me at once."

"Never." How had he gotten away from Benen McManus? And if he could outwit Benen, what chance did Timmy stand? "Besides, what makes you think you can appeal reasonably to someone in my mental condition?''

"So, you agree with your husband's recalcitrance. Pity, but not unexpected. Given your father's extensive history with the Reilly and McManus families, we had anticipated this stance.''

He took a step closer. A gleam sparked in the icy blue crystals of his eyes. Siannon stopped herself from retreating from his suffocating presence.

"Your father has unlimited resources at his disposal, both monetarily and with the influence he can bring to bear. More, I've no doubt, than your husband currently has at his command. Mr. Rhodes is fully confident in the rightness of his position regarding Master Timothy.''

"My father has always been fully confident of everything, Mr. Franklin. That does not mean he is right and it does not mean he will achieve his ends." Her voice sounded far more sure than she felt. "I am afraid that in this instance you are both mistaken.''

She sighted Benen McManus coming around the corner of his mother's dockside tap just then. He was scanning the landscape, and when his eyes fixed on Siannon and Mr. Franklin, he set off toward them at a lope. Relief rippled through her.

Franklin offered a derisive shrug. "Have no fears, Mrs. *Reilly*. Above all else, Mr. Rhodes loves his grandson. He wishes only to ensure that Timothy grows up properly prepared for his position in the world. There is no mistake in the matter; the boy will be returned to Limerick. It is only a matter of time.''

He stiffened and turned at the sound of Benen's boots scraping on the graveled path below them. "I'll leave you to your illusions, my dear. I see that my ship is ready. I must return to Limerick immediately. There is much to be done." His words eerily echoed Quin's sentiments.

Franklin tipped his hat in a bare minimum of courtesy and strode away from her as though he hadn't just stabbed steel-pointed knives of worry through her over and over again.

"Sorry he bothered ye, Missus. I thought he'd gone aboard his vessel, but he turned his skip around on me when my mum called me in. Cap'n'll pin my ears fer losin' sight of the man."

"Don't fret, Benen, just make sure he really leaves this time. No one else came ashore, did they?" Immediate concern for Timmy still beat through her.

"Dan Kelly Sr.'s kept an eye out and swears he's the only one." He looked down the path to Franklin's hasty retreat, then nodded to Siannon. "Maeve Kelly's got yer boy with hers while she does a spot of tidying up fer Father Dunnavan at St. Bridgid's. Now, I'd best catch that one up and wave a tearful farewell till he's well and truly out of sight."

He touched his cap and trooped after Franklin's retreating back.

Siannon let them both get far enough ahead of her so she could be alone with her thoughts. What she really wanted to do was run straight back to Quin's office and pour it all out on his shoulders.

Thinking of his coldness as he sent her away, she resisted. Franklin had told her nothing new, nothing she did not already know. Her father did love Timothy. His feelings for her son had been the only thing that made life bearable under his roof. When it came to his grandson, Eustace Rhodes seemed to have finally grown a heart almost as strong as his ambitions.

But that did not excuse his previous vile actions or his lack of remorse for what he had done to his wife. And it did not offer Siannon any solace in connection with his plans to raise Timothy himself.

You'll marry again, my dear. Whom and when I decide or you'll follow your mother. Your very defiance shows how closely your behavior mimics hers. His final edict after she had tried to argue against remarriage had been the catalyst that sent her running for sanctuary.

She shuddered, unable to keep her thoughts from turning to Percy's hands squeezing her flesh and remembering the cold calculation oozing behind her father's words when she'd practically begged him not to marry her off to another of his cronies. She had never meant anything to Eustace Rhodes beyond a means to an end. After Percival Crofton, heaven only knew who her father would have deemed his next suitable alliance.

Fresh winds whipped in from the hillside, lifting tendrils of hair from her nape and carrying the mixed scents of the sea, fresh sunshine, and new grass. Home. Beannacht had always felt like home, yet being here was somehow not the all-encompassing haven she had expected. Now her troubles followed her here in the form Nigel Franklin.

She blew out a quick sigh as the sun drifted through clouds overhead, teasing her with warmth and then letting her cool in the shadows.

Just like her husband. She pushed that realization away along with the painful twinge it engendered, determined to concentrate on making some positive headway in her new life.

With that in mind, she took the path toward Beannacht Harbor with an odd mixture of anticipation and reluctance. What she really wanted to do was turn toward the Reilly house and take a long nap. So much had happened in the space of a few hours, she couldn't face the awkwardness of meeting everyone. But she couldn't avoid it either. She was no longer an islander. She was an outsider. Related through her grandparents and now her marriage to Quin but an off-lander just the same. The only way to renew old acquaintances was to begin. Holding herself aloof would only make matters more uncomfortable.

Besides, Timmy was on the far side of the harbor village if he was with Maeve at St. Bridgid's. Quiet echoes of alarm still rang in her heart. She needed to see him for herself; then she would stop and spend some time with Grandda at last.

She nodded to the few women she passed as she walked down the lane that wound past the neat stone cottages with their thatched roofs and trimmed yards edged with stone fencing. No one actually spoke to her, but everyone smiled pleasantly or waved as they went about their business.

A baby wailed inside one cottage she passed, but the mother came to the door anyway. Her faded blue dress was mostly hidden by her white apron. "Will ye not come in fer a visit, Cousin?"

Siannon tried to place the young woman. She was small and pretty and had curly, deep red hair that marked her as a McManus.

"Mary?" Happy recognition flooded Siannon. "Mary McManus?"

A broad smile spread across the freckled cheeks of the young woman as she beckoned from the doorway. "I'm Mary Rogers now. Married to my Declan these past two years. I just put Davey down fer his nap. I'll put the kettle on.''

Siannon gave her cousin a quick hug. "Another time. I need to check on my own son. And I've yet to spend more than a minute with Grandda.''

"Make it soon. We've so much to catch up on. We're all so glad ye're back safe with us. We missed ye.'' Tears sparkled in the blue-gray depths of her cousin's eyes.

Siannon blinked away her own tears. "I can't wait to hear everything. I have missed you too.''

Just at the bend by her grandda's, she spied Timmy and two slightly larger towheaded boys playing with a ball while a small puppy nipped at their heels. Two-fold relief bounded through her when she also observed the vessel that had brought Franklin to Beannacht weighing anchor and unfurling its sails to head out of port.

"Mama, Mama, look! I've got friends! Seamus and Kevan. And they're letting me play with their dog!'' Timmy was fairly jumping with all his news. Then he stopped and looked crestfallen. "Is it time to go back?''

"Not yet.'' She resisted the urge to snatch him up and run for the safety of a door she could lock and bar. His shirttail was untucked, his cap askew, and dirt streaked his cheeks. He looked happier than she'd ever seen him, save for that once on deck with Quin.

"As long as you mind Maeve, you may play a little longer. I am going to visit Grandda, if you'd like to join me there. Or I will see you at home.''

"Home?'' Genuine alarm leapt in Timmy's eyes. "I saw that ship. We can't go back to Limerick yet.

I'm going to be a sea captain just like Seamus and Kevan's dad. Like Captain Reilly. Grandfather will never allow that."

Sometimes the level of his awareness surprised her. Perhaps he, too, had inherited a portion of the McManus Gift?

She crouched down to his eye level. "Timmy. This is our home now. Here, with Captain Reilly. I just meant I'd see you back at his house. We're not going to live in Limerick anymore."

His face cleared a little. "So that ship wasn't here for me? Maeve said we had to have a care as long as it was in sight."

"She was right to be wary. But you must know that Captain Reilly will never let anyone take you away." She gripped his hands, willing herself to believe her own assurances. "I will never let anyone take you away."

"Good." He nodded, then bent to pick up the wiggly puppy that licked his chin while he giggled. "Do you think Captain Reilly will let me have one of these? Ross McGee has three more to give away."

"We'll see."

Apparently satisfied that he hadn't gotten a no, Timmy raced off with his friends. "See you soon, Mama," he called back to Siannon.

Fresh lilac drifted on the salt-tanged sea air as she reached her grandfather's house. He faced the sea, just as the Reillys did. The west side bloomed with Gran's favorite lilac bushes, white and pink and delicate purple, grown far taller than they had been the last time Siannon had attempted to call Beannacht Island home.

Beyond the lilac blossoms, large windows poured

light into her grandfather's work space and gave him a view to place his miniature ships upon the ocean. As the shipyard's longtime model builder, his was an important job. Quin had told her how Grandda, even semiretired, still held high status among the shipwrights and that many sought his training in hopes of one day attaining such a position.

Her grandfather sat as she had seen him on so many other bright mornings, before the wide windows, peering intently at the ship before him on the table.

"*Dia duit, reannag bheag.*" He didn't look up, but the warmth in his tone was enough to slough some of the loneliness from Siannon's shoulders.

His Gaelic greeting made her giggle just as it had when she was little and first learned its meaning. "It's not possible to wish good day to a star, Grandda." She'd spoke aloud the old argument. "They come out only at night."

"Ye shine in my heart all the time, my Siannon," he answered. And they both laughed.

With a careful flick of his wrist he pared away the tiniest fleck of wood before lifting his gaze to hers. "Ye look a bit lost." More question than statement.

She made her way toward him as the combination of the sunlight streaming in the windows and the lingering essence of her grandmother's love still permeating the house gave a lift to her spirits.

"Nay, Grandda." She leaned in to kiss his leathery cheek and catch a nostalgic whiff of his pipe tobacco. "Not so much lost as displaced. But I'll work my way through it."

"Displaced?" He settled back and plucked the magnifying glasses from their perch at the end of his nose to peer at her more closely. "And who here would dare displace ye, my Siannon?"

The displeasure sparking in the depths of his astute blue gaze showed her a glimpse of Tiomoid McManus in his younger days. Gran always said he was a fearsome man, not one to be taken lightly. He was The McManus, after all, head of an ancient family.

"No one would dare, Grandda. Not with you on my side." She settled next to him on a stool, admiring the lines already beginning to show in the model he still held.

"Hmmrph." He nodded, somewhat mollified by her answer. "They'd best not if they know what's advantageous for them."

"Your next project?" She touched the clean edge of the keel.

"Aye. Young Quintin has big plans. As did his father." He held the model out against the view of the distant horizon. The last of Franklin's ship was disappearing around the point. "She'll be fast and efficient, I'll give him that. Quintin Reilly's not ta be trifled with, as yon scurvy no doubt discovered this day."

So, Grandda already knew of Nigel Franklin's visit. And of his threats, no doubt. Not much passed unnoted in Beannacht.

"Have ye been to see Mary McManus?" Grandda put the model back on its stand. "Yer cousin's been asking after ye."

"She's married to Declan Rogers—the captain who lost his arm a few years ago?"

She received a nod.

"Not really, but I will. I want to see the baby."

"Mmm." He studied her for a moment. "Tea and a visit, then?"

She smiled. "Aye, Grandda."

She pressed a second kiss to his cheek and preceded him into the small kitchen. Another wave—almost an echo—of her grandmother's love washed over her. How many times had she sat at this table, absorbing all Gran had to teach her and basking in the warmth of her approval? Too many to count.

She put the kettle on to boil and set Grandda's favorite tea in the pot.

"Siannon, ye've a frown settled across yer brows big enough to hold a spar."

"It's all so different than I thought." She settled cups on the table in front of him. How to explain it. "I married Quin—"

" 'Cause ye always loved him." Her grandfather chuckled when she couldn't keep from looking at him in surprise. "I may be old, but I am not blind, Siannon. Never have been. We all knew how ye felt. It was plain in the worshipful looks ye cast his way since ye were old enough to toddle after him."

Heat bathed her cheeks. "But that is not the reason." *At least not the whole of it.* "I could not agree to my father's plans—"

"So ye grew a backbone at last." Old pain and banked fury etched her grandfather's words as he nodded his approval. "I wish yer mother could have done the same before it was too late. And I hope someday yer father receives the payment in hell he's earned."

Siannon turned back toward the stove, fetching the kettle as the water boiled. Deep inside her she echoed his sentiments about her father, but her mother was another matter. She knew firsthand how difficult it was to oppose Eustace Rhodes. Her mother had not lacked strength or intelligence. What she had needed was the means to see her way safely clear of him and the ability to turn her back on the man she had loved enough to leave Beannacht in the first place.

"Here, Grandda." She handed him a cup and rejoined him at the table. Hot tea scalded the back of her throat as she sipped.

"Tastes good, lass. Ye remember just as yer gran taught ye." He complimented her with a small smile; then his face grew serious, and his gaze bore into her again. "But I've strayed from my true intent. After yer mother's unhappiness with her choices, I allowed stubborn pride to prevent me from interfering until too late. I vowed I'd not stand aside should one of my own act rashly and then feel forced to live with regrets.

"Yer first marriage was two months past afore yer uncle Michael brought the news." He reached across the table and patted her hand on her cup. "I can tell from looking at ye that ye're not happy, my Siannon. Is yer new husband not all that ye had supposed him to be? Has he been . . . unkind?"

She shook her head, caught between the warmth she felt for his concern and indignation that he could ever think so of Quintin Reilly. "Quin has done all that I have asked of him. And asked very little of me in return."

Steam curled up from her cup, and she blew it away. "He brought me home to the only place I have ever wanted to live. He added Timmy and me to all his burdens without any hesitation."

"Then it's grateful ye should be fer what ye have.

There's few who can claim to get exactly what they bargained fer." Grandda swallowed tea for emphasis. "Still, ye're finding that what ye asked was not what ye wanted after all."

Again a question phrased as a statement, leaving the way open for her to tell him what was bothering her. If only she could put her finger on it herself.

"I am just feeling my way. A new marriage, coming here after so long away . . ." She tried to cut off further questions before he could ask them. She had no way to explain that Quintin didn't love her, that holding her secret may have cost her any chance of gaining his love, let alone his trust if the shuttered coldness in the gaze he'd fixed on her was any indication. That she'd thought she could live with that, but the developing passion in their physical relationship only made her miss the emotional connections all the more. "I feel like I do not fit anywhere. That my past and future might belong here, but right now I do not."

"Ah." He nodded, accepting her reasoning. "There is much truth in what ye say. But there is also a great deal of Beannacht heart and soul lurking within ye. Yer history is here, Siannon. Yer family's anchors dig down almost as true and deep as the Reillys themselves. No time away could take that from ye. A lesson young Quintin is yet discovering fer himself. Ye'll find ways to settle in together."

"I've staked everything I have on that hope." She fingered the gold chain at her neck, tracing the outline of her locket. Her mother's locket. "In the meantime, I need to rediscover those anchors you speak of and find my place here. I promised Quintin I would help him, not create more for him to carry."

Grandda scratched his ear for a moment, then tilted his head and lifted his brow. "If it is yer keel ye seek, ye'd best start in the attic."

"The attic?"

"Aye." He nodded, a twinkle sparkling in the depths of his gaze. "There are trunks up there from yer mother. And some with yer gran's things as well."

Excitement surged through her. "Thank you, Grandda." Everything that had belonged to her mother had been stricken from her father's house immediately after her death—clothing, jewelry, personal items. Siannon had nothing left save the locket around her neck and the memories her father had not been able to take away. The idea that something had survived was intoxicating.

"Don't feel ye have to sit here with me, Granddaughter. There is a spark in yer eyes now that was not there when ye entered my home a short time ago." He laughed and reached out to brush her cheek with the warm backs of his fingers. "As much as I'd like to think it was my company that put it there, I know better. Ye know the way to the attic, lass. Go and look fer yerself."

"Thank you, Grandda." She swallowed the rest of her tea in one decidedly unladylike gulp and rose to throw her arms around his neck. "I love you."

"Aye." He cleared his throat again as he patted her shoulder. "Just be careful going up those steps. Ye've a few more layers beneath yer skirts than ye did the last time." His laughing caution trailed after her.

Indeed, the steps she remembered as more than ample were quite narrow and challenged her enough to make her shed her walking slippers and climb up in her bare feet. She gained the top, exhilaration racing over her skin to raise a myriad of tiny bumps along her arms and neck.

Sunlight streamed across the rush-covered floor from the narrow windows at either side of the attic. Dust-shrouded memories filled the corners along with old whispers and echoes from the past. She remembered searching the rafters with Devin and Mary, looking for old ship models and dreaming of the lives they would lead someday.

She closed her eyes and slowly lowered the layers of protection she habitually wrapped around herself. Oh, yes, Gran's belongings, her mother's. Her throat tightened and tears burned. It was as if their spirits still dwelt here. Or at least traces of them—pain and hope and ethereal happiness from her mother—a lifetime of commitment and responsibility from her grandmother.

"Oh, how I miss you both," Siannon whispered as she padded barefoot along the straw-covered floorboards. She stopped at an old sea trunk, closed her eyes once more, and traced her fingers over the strong contours of the oak chest, ignoring the fine layer of dust coating her hand as she touched it.

Gran. Colorful feelings shimmered up from the trunk in bright waves of blue and green, so strong it was, like being wrapped layer by layer in the embrace of a rainbow. Tears slipped from beneath Siannon's closed lids. She swallowed over the tight lump in her throat.

"I love you too, Gran."

She moved from trunk to trunk, not stopping to open them to investigate their contents. That would come later, after she adjusted to the emotions flowing like an unseen current around and through each of them. She had learned to protect herself from the raw feelings forever undulating past her; this was the longest she had ever spent with her guard lowered since she had been just a small child.

Slowly, as she moved toward the far end of the attic, searching for her mother's things, she recognized a darker undercurrent lurking in the depths of the tides swirling through her. She reached the last two chests and halted. Pain and fear radiated like a barrier. Entreaty and warning wrapped together.

"Mama," she breathed. Her pulse quickened as cold foreboding mixed with the anticipation in her stomach. Nausea swirled beneath the mix. A dull ache began in her temples. She had almost reached the limits of her endurance as the emotional torrent battered her. She struggled harder with each passing second as her instincts screamed for protection.

She drew in a deep breath of dusty, straw-scented air as she concentrated. Alarms shrilled over her nerve endings. The pain throbbing in her temples blazed. What terrible secret could her mother's trunks harbor? There was only so much more she would be able to sustain, but after coming this far and being so close, could she back away?

"No." She gritted her teeth and pushed herself the last few steps. Blood drummed in her ears as her heart pounded so hard, she feared it would leave her chest.

She closed her eyes and forced herself to breathe. Once. Twice. She could hesitate no more. She placed her hands flat against the cool, time-worn lid of the first trunk.

A hot frisson sizzled under her palms and shot straight up her arms, raising the fine hair on her skin. She stiffened and shuddered beneath the onslaught.

Wildness ripped through her, grief, agonizing worry, and a despair so strong, it tore jagged holes in her heart. Pain exploded at her temples. With a cry she crumpled to the floor, cradling her hands in her lap as though she had been burned.

"Oh, Mama," she choked out, and drew in a trembling breath. "So much sorrow. So much anger." Hot tears came then, welling from the depths of her soul to pour unchecked over her cheeks.

Chapter Eight

The floor.

Siannon concentrated on the floor as she tried to push past the fountain of sadness and anger welling up from her mother's trunks.

The solid symmetry of the planks, lined one against the other. The grain in the wood. The variegated color in the straw wisps covering the boards—brown to blond to white. Order and reality. She covered her mouth with one hand and slid the other into the straw, letting the dried pieces crackle against her palm.

When she'd entered the attic she'd sensed her mother's love for her, mingled with Gran's welcome, in an embrace she'd missed for far too long, and as real to her as memory and wishes.

"What is this darkness?" Her whisper felt as arid as the straw. She swallowed hard. With so much understanding and acceptance flowing elsewhere, why this inky curtain of despair and warning here?

Mustering her strength, she blocked the emotions pouring from her mother's hidden possessions. But she could not block the knowledge of them eddying deep within her own heart. Her mother's misery— righteous sorrow and guilt-tinged indignation as she packed this trunk—reached out across the years. Beckoning and warning at the same time.

A merciless cadence at her temples and the nausea that accompanied this extended use of her Gift swirled through her, making it difficult to think clearly. Opening herself always exacted a price—but she needed her wits about her, especially when such jagged shards of emotion snagged her, threatening to shatter her with their intensity.

"What should I do?" Her question barely penetrated the roiling panic and dread swelling in her. She swallowed them back. Surely, here of all places, she was safe. These were lingering emotions, not a real threat. The trunk itself could do her no harm. And the contents surely contained the answers she had long sought to explain her mother's aborted attempt to flee her marriage.

Natural curiosity warred with reflexive caution. The unshakable love Mary McManus felt for her daughter laced through the utter despair hidden in the depths of the trunk all these years. Bittersweet comfort. Her mother's palpable affection provided a balm to Siannon's soul, to the guilt she had carried for the past ten years at not being able even to say good-bye when her father had prevented their departure by having her mother confined.

Pushing past her raging headache and weakness,

she reached out her hand toward the trunk. Opening it would surely bring her the answers to so many of the questions she had bottled inside her for years. What had forced her mother to finally leave her father after all their years of patent unhappiness? If she were as ill as he claimed, why had her father felt it necessary to confine his wife rather than let her return to her family to heal?

The answers lay in that trunk. That much Siannon knew for certain. But was she ready to deal with those answers? A fresh surge of pain and nausea swept through her. Not now, not yet.

Whatever her father had done must have been truly horrendous for her mother to feel this way as she packed the trunk to be sent ahead. Worse than anything Siannon had suspected. Worse than her mother had wanted anyone to know at the time. Beyond the disintegration of naively plighted troths and marital dreams destroyed. Siannon rubbed her temples as the beat of her mother's bitter disappointment in the past compounded the pain searing her own thoughts at the moment.

Wait. Caution whispered through her again, carrying an echo of her mother's soothing tones. But why? Surely the time had come to know the truths that had shattered her childhood. Did she have the strength to accept those truths? To face them on her own? Only once before had she felt so utterly bereft— felt as if there was no one to whom she could turn. Knowing Grandda was downstairs provided no solace even as she considered calling him to join her.

No. That thought from beyond and her own conviction answered as one. Grandda carried enough guilt over his failure to protect his daughter. She couldn't expose him to whatever raw information had sealed Mama's fate until she knew for herself what was in the trunk—until she could protect him from the dark secrets that had shorn him of his daughter.

"Quin." The certainty that her husband would charge right in and make short work of whatever secrets the trunk contained scoured her. Although she trusted him to see to Timmy's safety and to her own, he so clearly set limits on their intimacy after delving into her version of The Sight, the thought of laying bare any more secrets from her past clenched her stomach anew. She couldn't bear to add more frost to the depths of his green gaze should she make another demand on his time.

Pride stiffened her spine. She must face this alone—when she was stronger, when she was better prepared. The problems in her parents' marriage, the anguished secrets of their past, could not be allowed to hinder the present. They needed to remain hidden until a safer time, when she could deal with them.

Later. A comforting wash of understanding and encouragement surrounded her. Her shaky marriage, her father's threats to take Timmy, the pressing needs of the present must take precedence over curiosity about the past.

The ache in her temples lessened as her decision was made.

Just knowing her mother's trunks were here—that they existed at all—would have to suffice for now. The contents and the heartache her mother had packed away so long ago had waited all these years. She would come back and sort through them when she felt more rooted in her own marriage. She pushed to her knees and then to her feet.

"I'll be back." She promised, her voice sounding as cracked as the straw she still clasped in one hand. She dropped the pieces back to the floor and dusted her hands over her skirt. Her barefooted retreat was accomplished much more quickly than her entrance.

Only when she had once again closed the door and slid her feet back into her walking slippers did she breathe a sigh of relief. She headed to the kitchen to splash cool water over her face from the pitcher and basin there.

"Grandda?" She couldn't face him; she knew she couldn't hide the shattering effects of her visit to the attic from his penetrating stare. He was a McManus, The McManus, after all. The Gifts spread through his family might be varied, but the prices they exacted remained unmistakable. His own wife had been a second cousin endowed with a healer's touch that left her wrung out too many times for him not to recognize the depth of the experience she had just undergone.

"In here, darlin'." His answering call came from his workroom. Good. She could leave from the back hall and he'd be none the wiser.

"I'm going on to Mary's now," she called in what she prayed was a cheery enough voice to mask her turmoil. "I'll come another day to look through the trunks."

At least that much was true. Another wave of nausea had her gripping the edge of the basin for support. The cool edge of the enameled bowl cut into her palms with a bite of reality she welcomed.

"Are ye all right?" Sharp concern underscored Grandda's question. "Ye weren't up there long. I thought finding yer mother's things would bring ye some joy."

She fought to keep the emotional turmoil she faced in the attic to herself and out of her answer.

"Aye. I'm glad to know those things are here, but I promised Mary I'd stop back, and I'm sure opening the trunks will take the rest of the day. It's a bit stuffy up there's all."

"Go on, then, but come back soon," he called. "Ye brighten my sky as always, little star. Mayhap I'll get the lads to bring the trunks downstairs fer ye so ye can go through them where the air's not so musty. Ye sound a bit peaked."

"I'm fine." She took a deep breath to bolster this claim. "I'll see you tomorrow, Grandda."

She edged out the back hall past the larder and the keeping room, still feeling shaky. The keeping room's door stood slightly ajar and the heady mix of old herbs and ancient spices filled her with the consoling aromas of the past. Her headache faded as she paused to inhale a deep whiff and remember sitting on the doorsill, watching Gran measure and mix the healing potions her neighbors depended on her to provide. Gran rarely consulted the recipe cards she stored in the room, relying instead on instinct and inner assurance.

"Each plant has its purpose, just as we do," Gran had told her one day when she'd asked why she could not have been given the healer's touch instead of a Gift she could fathom no real use for. "It's not up to us to question what the good Lord provides us, Siannon. Ye might as well question why ye have yer mother's red hair. Ye must learn to control The Gift ye have so that ye may direct it when needed."

She'd learned the control part very early, given her father's adamant rejection of what he'd termed *that ancient rubbish*. She'd certainly never brought the subject up with Percy. Quin at least had seemed to accept and support her ability despite the nasty twist Franklin had tried to give it. That is, he accepted the possibility, although her revelation of her particular form of The Sight had turned him so cold.

Picturing Quin in his office—the fire that had seemed to smolder in him when he'd kissed her and then the ice block that had chilled her when he'd sent her away—she sighed. She'd buried her ability to read emotions so deeply, it either eluded her when she tried to summon it or threatened to overwhelm her when it spilled forth. Perhaps one of her grandmother's curatives could help her sort through the tangle that left her unable to read her own husband.

She edged the keeping-room door open farther and found it filled with barrels. Her barrels. She'd almost forgotten her original plan to escape her father and support herself. What would she do with all this pottery? She had invested a pretty penny in the plates and mugs and paints stowed in these barrels. Money she'd carefully hoarded and handed over to her uncle Michael to set her original plan in motion. The plan to save herself until the immediacy of her father's scheme to marry her off again had prompted her to contact Quin.

More to sort out. Her head pounded anew. She shut the door and left her grandda's house. Father. Franklin. Quin. Secrets. Threats. Uncertainty. Faces and questions spun through her mind. Whyever had she thought that having made her escape to Beannacht, all her troubles would be over?

As she made her way to her cousin's cottage, she turned her face up into the sunshine, letting it bathe away a portion of her worries and warm the lingering effects of her discovery in the attic. She had no wish to alarm her cousin with any traces of strain on her face.

"Siannon, I am so glad ye came back today." Mary waved her in when Siannon knocked at the open door. "Davey's having a wee bite before he goes back down to his cradle."

Siannon step into the small, neat cottage and let her eyes adjust to the interior as she breathed in the pungent aromas of the herbs and plants drying in the kitchen rafters. Happiness and an abiding contentment dominated this dwelling. The room was small but comfortably welcoming with its rough-hewn furnishings and the homey touches of lace and pottery that adorned the shelves along with a number of small boxes and tins. A larger oak box, oddly familiar, held a place of honor on the sideboard.

Mary sat in a rocking chair near the hearth with the bodice of her gown loosened. Her babe nestled against her, suckling contentedly as she fed him. Reddish-brown wisps dusted his head, and a small, chubby fist reached up to play with his mother's chin while he ate.

"Mary, he's lovely." She sat on the bench Mary pointed to nearby. "It seems only a short time ago that my Timmy was that small."

She felt a pang of envy as the baby drank greedily and gazed in rapture at his mother. Her father had not approved of her feeding her son herself. So many things he had controlled. The more distance she put between them, the more amazing it became that she had tolerated his bullying. Or managed to escape him.

"I think he's a handsome lad, the spit of my Declan save for the hair. Our red marks him as a McManus for sure." Mary kissed the top of her son's head as the babe drifted to sleep. "I'll just go and put him down again and then we can have a real visit."

The pulse of Mary's joy and satisfaction with her life hovered in the room even after she left, feelings Siannon had no wish to block. *My Declan* echoed on in her thoughts. She would never have considered Percy that familiarly, nor at this point could she imagine using the phrase with Quin. They were still too separate despite the intimacy they shared the night before. Quin's greeting at the outset of her impromptu visit to the shipyard seemed to promise a new bridge between them, that she herself had felt blooming in the warmth of his gaze and the passion promised in his delicious kiss.

But following Nigel Franklin's visit, her father's threats, and her own revelation, Quin's haste to be rid of her and concentrate on his work demonstrated how tentative any growing bonds between them remained. Perhaps if their lovemaking resulted in a child they could share—the image of downy black waves and deep green eyes gazing at her as Davey just had his own mother filled her.

"There now." Mary came back and gave Siannon a quick hug that chased away the last vestiges of her headache. A true healer's touch. "I've a mite of good tea set by for a special day and some fresh oatcakes ta go with if ye'll join me." She barely paused to note

Siannon's nod of acceptance as she turned to fetch a steaming kettle simmering on her stove. "I'm so glad ye're here. I saw yer Timmy with Maeve this morning. He seems a fine lad."

"Thank you. He's a bit bedraggled but absolutely ecstatic to have friends to play with." Siannon waited as Mary reached into a cupboard to retrieve mugs and tins with a calm efficiency she'd possessed even as a child. Curls of bright red hair escaped the knot at Mary's nape. Always small for her age, she did not appear to have grown much in height since Siannon had last seen her, but mature assurance and cheer radiated from her cousin as she worked in her kitchen. An edge of envy sliced through Siannon.

"I've only some wild honey Ross McGee gathered in the hills ta sweeten it by. Sugar is too dear these days," Mary apologized as she handed Siannon a steaming mug.

"Honey will do fine," Siannon took a quick sip. "Reminds me of the time we sneaked into Gran's larder—"

"—trying to concoct a cure for Devin's weak stomach." Mary giggled, her red curls bobbing and her eyes twinkling as they'd done that day.

Siannon laughed too. "Gran swore the only thing that saved him from our brew doing him in was the honey."

"Aye." Mary nodded. "And she made us scrub the counter and floor of the whole keeping room since we'd made everything—"

"—and each other—"

"—and each other—so sticky, the herbs we ground clung in great clumps to everything we touched." A merry twinkle lit Mary's eyes as the memory transported them both back to their childhood.

"I've gotten a good deal better at concocting tonics since yer grandda passed yer gran's recipe box to me," she declared with a chuckle.

Siannon's gaze followed her cousin's to the large oak keeping box with a worn knot carved in its lid. No wonder it had looked familiar when she'd entered the cottage. No wonder she had felt so welcome here. A part of Gran lived on in Mary's work.

"Uncle Michael told me you'd become quite the healer—respected by all on the island. You are fortunate that is the portion of the McManus Gift you received. He told me how you saved Declan's life with your skills."

A blush of embarrassment spread across Mary's freckled cheeks at the compliment. "I try to do right by folks for simple things. Kiernan—ye might remember, he's Declan's younger brother—brings the doctor from Tralee over once a month on the *Achanaich*, or ferries those in dire straits there when the need arises."

Mary took a sip of tea. "But I am fortunate indeed, for it was my healing skills that first brought me to my Declan's notice. He was so despairing after that terrible explosion took his ship."

Siannon nodded. "The sinking of the *Earrach* made the Limerick papers for days. Even my father devoured the news of the tragedy and the descriptions of the bravery displayed by Captain Declan Rogers in saving every man of his crew." The heat of the tea Siannon swallowed warred with the cold shadow that crossed her heart with the memory.

"Aye, but his bravery cost him dear." Mary's eyes held a faraway look and she pressed her lips together.

"Uncle Michael said the doctors in Tralee gave up on saving his life once he lost his arm. They sent him home to die."

"He was in a sorrowful way when he arrived here," Mary agreed. "Being scuttled, as he called it, was the hardest part for him. Losing his arm meant he'd never be able ta run the rigging or steer a vessel as he knew it should be done. He didn't think he could bear a life without the sea."

Like Quin. And she'd just anchored him more thoroughly to the shore by marrying him. No wonder he blew so cold at times.

"How did you convince your husband otherwise?"

"Being married to a strappin' lad like Quintin Reilly, and as quick as a wink, I might add, I'd say ye could teach me a thing or two." Mary grinned over the rim of her mug.

If only that were so. Regret pulled at Siannon as Mary continued. "But I loved Declan and couldn't let him fade away through his own stubborn pride. There are too many wonders in life to fret over what ye cannot have."

She put the mug down on her planked table with a thud. "So I told him that if he was going ta waste my time by dying on me, to be quick about it so's I could stop trying ta tend him and look after someone who wanted my company and my caring."

"What did he say to that?" Siannon almost shuddered to think of Quin's reaction to such a challenge.

"He smiled." Mary's lips curved at the memory. "For the first time. He called me an insolent wench, then he took my hand . . . and asked me not ta jump ship just yet.''

"And he improved from there?"

Mary shrugged and smiled. "Oh, ye know how men are. They love a challenge. When ye're all sweet and putty in their hands, they can't wait ta let you slide away. But should ye get a might slippery, then they must hold ye fast."

That was food for thought. She'd never made any secret of her feelings for Quin. Perhaps he viewed her as too eager? Definitely something to add to the tumble eddying through her.

"Mr. Reilly and the shipyard did the rest. Declan's thrown his heart into making sure the ships others sail are as true as can be. As Mr. Reilly's health failed, Declan was the one who finally sent for Quin and alerted Bryan and Devin to the state of things here on the island. I tried everything I could to help yer father-in-law, to no avail."

Siannon nodded. "I'm sure you did your best. Even the doctors in Tralee and Limerick were stymied. The strain of keeping everything running certainly didn't help. When Bryan told me of his father's illness, he also told me he was trying to do all he can to help raise new capital while Quin was handling things here."

"The lads all pitching in must surely comfort Mr. Reilly," Mary agreed. "When his parents left for Italy, Devin took a leave from his schooling and came here until Quin returned. He did a fine job, too, by all accounts. Declan said it was a pity he'd never command his own quarterdeck."

"Devin's never outgrown his seasickness?" During the few letters they'd exchanged or the couple of quick visits they'd arranged as he passed through

Limerick on his way to the university in Dublin, Siannon had never found the right way to ask if her friend had gained the one passionate wish of his boyhood.

"No, he still fights the nausea, much to his chagrin. He'll never be able ta handle a long ship voyage." Mary shrugged. "His talents lie elsewhere for sure. He'll find his own way and surprise the lot of us one day soon, I do suppose."

Siannon smiled her agreement. Devin's disappointment in his weaknesses compared to his older brothers had always hidden his other talents more from himself than from others. "He always includes a sketch or two for me when he writes, and he did have a way with horses even when we were little. Grandda always said he was his best stable boy."

"True, and Declan said he had a knack for handling the shipyard's figures. We were in even direr circumstances until he came home and straightened things out as best he could. Then Quin made landfall."

Mary shook her head, and the sparkle in her eyes dimmed as her thoughts obviously turned to something that disturbed her. She started to open her mouth but stopped herself and clamped her lips shut. She reached for a bundle in the basket next to her rocker.

"What?" Siannon prompted.

"Quin was rather abrupt when he hustled Devin back to school's all." Mary sighed and began making neat little stitches in the shirt she held. "There's always something that needs mending these days. Everyone's a mite distressed."

An undercurrent of worry swelled and threatened to overwhelm the peace Siannon had felt from the moment she'd entered her cousin's house. Devin would discover his strengths when he needed, and being at odds with Quin was nothing new for him either. Mary's distress ran deeper than concern for an old friend's hurt pride or even the threadbare state of the shirt she stitched.

Siannon slid over on the bench until she was right across from Mary and could look her straight in the eye. She touched her hand. "You're not just talking about Quin and his brothers anymore, are you, Mary?"

Mary looked up from her sewing. Her gaze held Siannon's for a moment. "There never was much use trying ta hide how I felt from ye, Cousin. Ye often knew before I'd sorted things out for myself. But it is not just me. With things as strained as they have been at the shipyard, we all must make everything last longer and stretch further than it's possible. Tempers fray as easily as linen, especially yer husband's."

She bit her lip. "I didn't mean to speak out of turn. Quin is doing everything he can, Siannon. He gave up his ship and all. From Declan I know how hard that is on a man. His parents sold most of their fine things to keep up with the demands at the Ship Works. We're not going hungry, at least, but with all the men working at half wages for so long, things are ever so tight, and it's hard for the little ones to do without. Nora Doyle can't keep her clan in shoes, and Bridget McGee and Kiernan have put their wedding off twice because they can't afford to set up housekeeping. The coins are jest too dear."

"I wondered at the changes up at the house, and hoped things had simply been put in storage before the Reillys left. But I'd had no idea how dire things were all around." Siannon clasped her cousin's fingers. "You must tell me everything. Perhaps there may be something we could do to ease things a bit. If you are interested."

Mary settled the shirt against her knees. "If it provides the money we need to keep things afloat, I won't be the only one interested."

Siannon's spirits rose with the anticipation sparkling in Mary's eyes. Mary would add just the eunthusiasm needed to bring the project to fruition, especially if they were to entice Beannacht's other women.

Siannon leaned closer. "I have these barrels . . ."

"There, that makes our third barrel for this week alone." Bridget McGee wrapped the last of the plates they'd worked on the day before and put the lid on the barrel with a satisfying thud that warmed Siannon's heart.

The women of Beannacht, assembled in Maeve Kelly's cottage as they had each day since Siannon had first broached her plan to Mary a fortnight before, cheered as they continued cleaning up from their day's labors. Paint-smudged aprons were hung on pegs by the back door for use the next day, stencils were wiped clean, and the floors swept as the extra tables and benches they'd used were cleared out to the lean-to so Maeve's family could have a portion of their house back for the night.

"It's a good thing yer Dan is out to sea, Maeve. My Dermot would never stand for such disarray." Grania Keane tucked a lock of her gray hair back under her cap and rested her hand on her ample hips as she put away the last of the lamps they'd used to improve the light in the cottage while they stenciled the crockery.

"Oh, I don't know, Grania, by the time our menfolk get home from the shipyard, most days it's so dark and they're so tired, I doubt they'd notice anything beyond their supper plates and pillows," one of her friends called from the front room.

"I know mine hasn't noticed me in over a month," another one said.

Everyone chuckled. Siannon leaned against the doorjamb between the rooms as the comaraderie swirled past her. It felt so good to be a part of something worthwhile, to have accomplishments of her own, shared with these women. Mary's friends and neighbors had enthusiastically joined in with the plan to earn extra money through decorating pottery. Siannon's original plan to support herself and Timmy when she escaped her father would benefit them all. Over the weeks, with Timmy busy with his newfound friends and Quin at the shipyard from dawn until well after dusk, the decorating of the china she'd purchased to paint on consignment had provided her with a sense of belonging she'd hadn't felt since her summer visits when she and Mary had played with the Reilly brothers. Since she'd first fallen in love with Quin.

She certainly wasn't getting those feelings of fulfillment from her husband. Since Nigel Franklin's visit, Quin had maintained a cool but polite detachment during the few minutes she saw him each night. She swallowed the lump of pain that swelled in her throat just thinking about the chasm that yawed between them.

Maeve patted Grania's shoulder. "We're lucky

indeed that I've no one but meself to answer to right now—save the boys, and they know better than to touch our work. They are proud of what we are doing."

"Even if our husbands are not," Grania sighed. Her sons were both sailors on the *Achanaich* under Kiernan Rogers, home only a day or two each week. "All Dermot and my lads care about is that their shirts are not pressed the way they're used to. Not that ye didn't do a fine job, Fenella Doyle, it's just not the way they are used to things."

Fenella brightened with the compliment, although her gaze slid to her mother, Nora, standing nearby with her eyebrows raised. A becoming blush covered the fourteen-year-old's fair cheeks. She'd proven a godsend, marshaling the older girls to help watch the little ones and do the odd chore as the women of Beannacht organized themselves into a small work-force, some painting china and the others pitching in to help with the mutual laundry and housekeeping.

With a smudge of green paint on her cheek and Davey nestled against her shoulder, Mary counted the pottery plates that lined all the available flat surfaces in Maeve's kitchen. "There's near enough here to fill the next barrel by half, Siannon," she said as she finished. "If we put in a few extra hours tomorrow, we may have enough dried and packed ta send four barrels back with Kiernan this time."

"I don't know about that." Grania chuckled and shook her gray head. "Dermot already protests that I spend too much time away from home."

A chorus of rueful agreements underlined her statement.

"He'll worry less about that when we're able to

help put food on the table and clothes on the backs of our children." Mary nodded for emphasis as her gaze caught Siannon's.

Siannon picked up one of the delicate dessert plates with little green and yellow flowers dancing across the cream-colored rim. "Turning things around so quickly should please Mr. Cartwright. His last note said how impressed he was with the quality of our work."

"I'm more interested in the size of the bank draft he'll enclose than his compliments." Nora Doyle looked up and winked as she washed the brushes and handed them to her daughter to set on the hearthstone to dry. "Have a care not to put them so close to the opening, Fenella. Ye singed one the day before last, putting it too close to the flame. We can't afford to have all our profit going back into supplies because of carelessness."

Fenella tossed her dark braid over her shoulder and sent her mother a withering look but wisely held her peace over the warning. "James will be disappointed we're not going to be home in time to fix his supper," she observed. "He complained that he was tired of Aunt Moreen's stew last night."

"And he'll be complaining again tomorrow night." Nora wagged a plump finger at her daughter. "The island needs us to make a success of this pottery painting. Things have slid by fer too long to let the grumblings of our menfolk stop us before we've even been given a chance."

"With Moreen tied to the tap, I think it a blessing to have her to cook for some of us." Maeve spoke up and Siannon observed many heads nodding in agreement.

"And Dan's mother baking the extra bread the way she has," Maeve continued, "frees some of us to get more done, though my father-in-law complains she's in the kitchen too long and not in the store enough with him."

"At least my Kiernan thinks we're doing a good job." Bridget wrapped her shawl around her shoulders. "He even delivered the first of our work in person to make sure Mr. Cartwright didn't try to cheat us. And he's told me how impressed he was with the whole business."

"That's cause ye're not wed ta him yet, dearie." Grania picked up her own worn wrap and shrugged it over her shoulders. "Once he's got ye well and truly tied to him, ye'll be surprised how quickly all those compliments he used while courtin' ye turn into complaints."

Almost as one, the other women nodded as they, too, made ready to go.

"There's too much starch in my collar," one woman offered in a mock remonstration.

"Or not enough," said another.

"There's enough salt in the stew to turn the oceans to freshwater," Nora chimed in with a chuckle as she and Fenella waved farewell from the doorway.

"My mother always put in more leeks." Maeve laughed and shook her head.

Trying to best one another, the wives and mothers of Beannacht walked out into the early evening, shouting exaggerated grievances. At least, Siannon hoped they were exaggerated. A pang of envy shot through her. Quin never complained of anything she did or didn't do. She doubted he even knew what the island's women were trying to accomplish to ease the financial strains—or her role in setting the scheme in motion.

She sighed and fingered the chain of her locket. Mary laced an arm around her waist, and comfort flowed from her cousin, easing a little of the strain.

"Tired?" Mary asked.

"A little," she admitted. "Though I was really thinking how little Quin cares about how I spend my days. Nor does he seem to worry that I spend too much time away from his home."

"Things are no better between the two of ye?"

"Worse." Ever since experiencing the depths of passion and pleasure the joining of a man and woman could bring, Quin's lack of interest ached through Siannon to a depth she'd never thought possible. Her admissions sounded so weak even to her own ears. What had she expected from her hasty marriage bargain? A happily-ever-after? She was housed, fed, and protected—but very unhappy. This was not the life she'd always dreamed of.

"Tchh," Maeve joined them. "Newly married men are unpredictable beasties in the best of cases. This business with his father brought Quintin Reilly home a changed man to begin with. There's been so many demands on him ever since, ye must not take his moods to heart."

"Declan's often short tempered when he first gets home. That's the tension and strain from barking commands all day. He sometimes forgets I am not one of his sailors or shipwrights." Mary grinned, then nuzzled her sleeping son, who stirred on her shoulder. "But he more than makes up for it in the bedroom once I remind him. He's far better at showing his love than talking of it." Mary gave her another squeeze and then retrieved the bundle of Davey's things in the corner.

"My Dan always grouses a bit as he tries to take over running the household during his leave," Maeve chuckled. "But we both know who's in command. If he's too miserable, neither one of us will enjoy his stay, so he keeps himself in check. Ye'll see, once Quintin knows his heading, ye'll have smoother sailing."

Siannon couldn't bring herself to confess as they made ready to leave, even to Mary and Maeve, that her husband had taken her to his bed just the once since they were married—one time to ensure the fulfillment of their contract. He had not so much as kissed her save in his office during her one visit. He must have found her woefully lacking, where his caresses had seemed to set her very skin on fire and left her near to begging for more even weeks after.

Pitiful.

The light was rapidly dimming outside. "I must get home to hear Timmy's prayers." At least with her son, Siannon felt the rightness of this move to Beannacht. He blossomed here, and so enjoyed his lessons and friends. Caitlin had taken him on ahead over an hour before for his supper and bath.

The three women ducked through the door and out into the gathering dusk. A sharp breeze tainted with salt and the promise of rough weather greeted them.

"I'm off to the rectory to fetch my lads," Maeve said. "I hope the boys have been good for Father

Dunnavan. He's training them to be acolytes. Tomorrow they're going fishing with Ross McGee after their lessons if it doesn't rain.''

They all looked up at the clouds gathering overhead, adding to the darkness, as Maeve headed to the far side of the harbor and St. Bridgid's-by-the-Sea, hugging her shawl around her.

"I'll feed Davey one last time and tuck him up. Then Declan should be coming home. If he's whistling, it means the day's work went well." Mary headed toward her own cottage with a final wave.

Siannon made her way up the hill toward the Reilly house, wondering if tonight things would be different for her and Quin. Determined to do her part and show him that she could be a good wife—without making any demands on him—she stayed up each night, hoping to bridge the distance between them when he dragged home later and later.

A man shouldn't have to search the corners of his house for his wife, he'd said. And so she'd waited for him each night, usually greeting him in the kitchen, where she'd moved Granny Reilly's rocker from the third floor.

He seemed alternately pleased and disapproving when she greeted him, telling her there was no need for her to wait up, he was well used to life on his own. After inquiring about her son, he always dismissed her, telling her to seek her bed and not to bother about him the next night.

Still, she clung to her rotating list of excuses for her late-night vigils. There was often just enough warmth radiating from her husband's gaze when she caught him looking at her out of the corner of his eye, to give her hope. So far this week, she'd been hungry, thought she heard a noise, come downstairs to get a drink, and had just helped Timmy with a bad dream. What reason would she give him tonight?

Make love to me, Quin. The words she longed to repeat from their one interlude would not do.

Chapter Nine

"Come along now, Captain." The humor in Declan Rogers's voice woke Quin with a start. He'd been sailing a lilac-and-lavender-scented sea with the sun at his back and a fair wind filling his sails.

"What time is it?" Quin muttered as he sat up and scrubbed his eyes with the backs of his hands. "How long have I been asleep?"

Declan moved into the halo of light from the desk lamp, amusement scrawled across his features plain as the day that had clearly faded away while the master of Reilly Ship Works snoozed over tattered ledgers.

"When I sent Benen McManus in to tell you I was dismissing the crew a good half hour or so ago, he said you were sleeping like a babe. Tho' the way my Davey keeps his mother up some nights, that's not saying much."

Quin frowned, still thick-headed from his im-

promptu nap, but Declan threw back his head and
laughed at his own joke. "We made good headway
in the yard today. It's time to chart a course for home.
We've got a pair of winsome lasses awaiting our attention and I for one plan to take advantage of my wife's
comfort. Although from the looks of you these past
weeks, you might want to consider taking a little less
comfort from your wife and a tad more from your
slumbers."

"Very funny." Quin pushed to his feet and doused
the lamp before his too astute foreman could read
the conflict churning through his thoughts. He left
his jacket slung across the chair and followed Declan
out into the night and down the steps.

For two weeks he'd avoided Siannon as much as
possible—given her as little attention as he could
and still be polite when he could not avoid her. And
certainly not engaged in any of the *comforting* Declan
suggested. He'd not so much as kissed her. It was too
risky. Still, not taking Siannon to his bed, and refusing
even to touch her, only added to his desire, which
now claimed far more of his attention than he could
afford.

Much to his chagrin, she seemed determined to
taunt him, lying in wait for him each night when he
finally quit the confines of his office. Every night he
sent her to bed, hoping she would finally understand
he did not want her there, tempting him, practically
inviting him to expose himself—to expose her—to
the raw lust and emotions she'd awakened in him.
But the next night she'd be there and he'd send her
away, remaining condemned to twist on his barren
sheets, knowing she was across the hall while he lay
sleepless.

Make love to me, Quin, she'd whispered the night he had claimed her and every night since in his thoughts. But he couldn't; he wouldn't. Too many rocks lined that course; he would founder them both.

"*Diabhal,*" he swore.

"Anything in particular you're wishing to the devil?" Declan paused and then fell into step when Quin caught up with him. "Have you made any progress with your investigation?"

Quin rubbed the stiffness from his neck and nodded. "Aye, I think I may be on to a thing or two. The moves were very subtle at first, but over the years a pattern seems to have built with broken contracts and doubling of costs. Difficult to pin down until the last year or so."

"During your father's illness?"

Quin nodded. "I'll know more come tomorrow. Provided I have fewer interruptions. What was Dermot Keane nattering on about when you diverted him earlier? What could I possibly do about the amount of starch in his collars? Thanks for stepping into the breach on that one."

Declan gave Quin's thanks a shrug. "It's the china painting again."

"The what?"

"China painting. My Mary and your Siannon. They've got the other women in on this scheme to make their fortunes. Something about piecework and commissions." Declan shook his head. "The men are all grumbling at the disruptions to their households with all the wives and mothers so absorbed with this business."

"And you say Siannon's involved?" Quin had given no thought as to how his wife spent her days, how any of Beannacht's women actually spent their time, for that matter.

"Involved?" Quin could feel Declan's grin, though the clouds overhead made it too dark for him to see the amusement behind his foreman's surprised tone. "It was her idea. Apparently, until you swept her up with your marriage proposal, she'd hoped to do this very thing on her own to support herself and her son."

They stopped at the fork in the path that led behind the McManus tap, where, from the sounds flinging by on the breeze, more than a few of the shipwrights still lingered over their nightly pints.

"It seems you asked her to help keep the other wives occupied and away from the shipyard while we finished this contract," Declan continued, and then nodded to the crowded building. "Now it is the men who are disgruntled by the hours their spouses spend away from home."

Disbelief stung Quin. He'd asked Siannon to help, envisioning afternoon visits over teacups, not a revolution. No wonder he'd been the recipient of so many disgruntled looks from the shipwrights of late.

"You are certain Siannon is behind this with Mary?" He felt stupid having to ask a second time. Must be the lack of sleep.

"Aye, thick as thieves they are together. But my Mary's happy because she thinks she'll be able to help with the expenses one day."

Both men stood in silence for a moment as the chill breeze from the harbor nipped around them. "Well, I'm off to my supper." Declan gave Quin's shoulder a hearty pat. "I only hope I can stomach another night of Moreen's stew. See you in the morning.''

He struck off toward the village at a brisk pace, whistling as he went while Quin headed up the hill toward the deceptive peace of his darkened home.

Across the dark gleam of polished oak floorboards in his foyer, soft light spilled toward Quin from the kitchen. Too soft and all too familiar, curling unwanted heat through his middle to couple with the burning slash of anger and regrets that smoldered there. She was waiting for him yet again.

Why could she not offer him surcease from the tensions hounding him? Wasn't it bad enough that he suffered too many thoughts of her during the day? Must he be confronted with his desires in the flesh every evening as well?

Just the direction of his thoughts drove a fist of frustration through his stomach. There was only so much a man could take.

He realized his footsteps had come to a complete stop at the entrance to the kitchen. He was hovering just beyond the reach of the welcoming glow of candlelight—just beyond Siannon's reach, as though he dared not come too close.

"*Diabhal.*" He forced himself forward as anger burned hotter in his belly. He would not show himself the coward here. He had rounded more than two dozen capes and navigated many shoals in his life at sea, seen his ship and crew through more storms than he could count, faced down situations that would make lesser men tremble. One slight woman should not disrupt him like this.

He would not allow it!

For a moment as he entered the kitchen he thought

he had been mistaken, that she had gone to bed and left him in peace with naught but the pungent smell of ginger tea lingering in the air like a reminder from Granny—a token of ancient tales and long-ago promises. His relief was short-lived and only tightened the knot of his frustrations further as his gaze registered the soft and tempting form of his wife curled asleep in the depths of his grandmother's old rocker.

Siannon's hair was piled loosely atop her head, as though she'd been too weary to care if a few perverse red-gold tendrils slipped free to tease her neck or rest against her cheek, tempting and enticing him. She had removed the outer jacket of her dress. Pale-ivory-colored lawn traced her collarbone and bared her arms. He stifled a groan that pushed from his very depths.

Bare toes stuck out from the edges of her charcoal serge skirt, as she had tucked her legs under her in the chair, almost as white as the edges of her petticoats that peeked at him as well. A yellow wool shawl was draped partially across her chest as she slept.

He wanted to shake her awake, to demand an explanation for her continued plaguing of him when he had told her each night not to bother. To go to bed and leave him be. He couldn't risk touching her. Already he was too close. The lavender and lilac scent of her enticed him to come closer still. He fought the urge to take her in his arms and satisfy all the ways he had dreamed of enjoying her soft curves and tender hollows over the past two weeks.

Her hose lay in a heap near her half-boots. He bent and retrieved them, rolling them into a smooth packet and tucking them into her boots as he struggled to suppress tantalizing images of the shapely calves and creamy thighs they had recently caressed.

How could one slender red-haired female destroy a man's very sense of himself like this? What was he to do with her?

As though he'd asked his questions aloud, she stirred beneath his gaze and opened her eyes.

"Hullo, Quin." She moved in the chair, uncurling herself and stretching with lithe movements that tightened the pale lawn across her rounded breasts as the yellow shawl pooled in her lap.

He swallowed, strained tension gripping his throat and tightening his groin.

"Why aren't you in bed?" The only greeting he could grind out invoked images of her in his bed, the burnished fire of her hair fanning his pillow.

"I'm sorry I fell asleep. You seem to get home later and later." Her teeth tugged her bottom lip, and he fisted his hands at his sides, fighting the urge to reach for her, to test for himself just how soft and warm her skin would feel as he caressed her. "I hope all is progressing well at the yard?"

"Aye." He forced the one word out of his throat. It came harsh and tight with the yearning she invoked so easily in him. He didn't want to stand there in the intimate half-darkness of the kitchen with the scent of Granny's tea lingering between the two of them like a benediction from beyond the grave. "You've yet to answer my question."

"Oh." Siannon's teeth worried her lip again as storm clouds gathered in the gaze she fixed on him.

He could almost taste the sweetness of her lips beneath his own.

"Would you like some tea? I've kept it warm in case—"

"Nay." He cut through her attempt to placate the beast stirring within him, knowing he wasn't being anywhere near fair to her and yet unable to help himself. "I seek only your answer. I've no need for tea."

Diabhal. Why had he voiced anything about needs to her? The word fell like an anchor from his lips, splashing into whatever murky waters dwelled between them, impelling ripples he had no intention of following. His needs had nothing to do with tea or food or any of the things she no doubt waited to offer him as the measure of her wifely duty and support.

"Is there something else you would like?" she asked with irrational innocence, as though she had no idea the notions she set loose inside of him with her pale white skin and fey red hair.

Pale white skin and fey red hair.

Siannon has the look of her mother. . . . You may gain temporary solace bedding her, but in the end you'll find you'd have been much better off if you'd never crossed her path.

A rush of cold surged through Quin's gut as he realized how very closely his thoughts echoed the vile words Eustace Rhodes flung at him on the day he and Siannon had wed.

"Aye, there is something else I'd like, since you can't see fit to mind me or to answer me. Rum will do just fine." He turned from her to stride from the kitchen's warm confines into the darkened depths of the house.

Rum. Whiskey. Brandy. At the moment it didn't

matter what spirits he helped himself to. He needed something to deaden the awful knowledge coursing through him that he responded to her exactly as his father-in-law predicted. That he wanted Siannon every bit as much as Rhodes's terrible claims decreed. Surely his desires did not dump him into the same slop bucket as Rhodes. Surely he was a better man than that.

The lust continuing to sear Quin belied his attempts to believe that was so.

He reached the whiskey decanter in the front parlor and splashed a healthy portion into a waiting tumbler. He tossed it back with complete lack of the normal respect due the potent elixir.

Releasing a long sigh, he rolled the cool glass over his forehead as the liquor's burn tried to loosen the twisted knot formed by his many failings and unanswerable questions.

"Quin?" Her voice sounded from the hall.

Awareness sizzled through him, raising the fine hair on the back of his neck and streaking down his arms. It was as if every inch of his body cried out a welcome to her before she even entered the room. Disgusted with himself, he put the tumbler down with a thunk.

"*Diabhal,* Siannon. Cannot a man come home in peace?" His question lashed the room's inky darkness. He wished back his harsh tone almost as soon as it left his lips. Nothing good would come of having an argument with her despite the warring factions inside him that demanded some kind of release from this cursed tension. "What is it?"

"That is my question." Her words came soft and low through the darkness of the room, but they held the undercurrent of strength he so admired in her.

Despite anything that had happened in her past, she refused to be cowed. She'd planned her escape and even schemed to support herself, far-fetched as the plan Declan had outlined seemed. Nothing life had thrown at her had intimidated her.

Not even her disagreeable husband. But then, look at the type of man her father had become or who her father had chosen as her first husband. Lord above, was he really no better in her eyes than they had been?

That he could not bear. He bit back a sigh and struggled for control.

"There's nothing I wish to discuss. Go to bed, Siannon."

"Quin—"

"Go to bed, wife." He spat out the last, hating himself for hiding behind his own churlishness but needing her to go away and leave him in peace. "Unless it is your desire to hear things you would rather not."

"What do you mean?"

"Is that not obvious?"

Her petticoats rustled as she crossed the floor toward him. He could feel her sympathy and her concern wafting almost as seductively toward him as the lilac and lavender scent of her perfume.

"Perhaps you are not as obvious as you think you are, Quintin Reilly."

Challenge laced her tone. *Challenge.* She dared him to reveal the things he kept bottled inside him. Did she really want to be confronted with the thoughts and desires that plagued him daily? Not likely. She would not understand how deeply it humiliated him that he had failed all of the people he cared about in life. Failed the very people who depended on him most—hurt the people who dared to trust him.

He poured another drink and swallowed it, relishing the fire that burned through his regrets. He had failed Bryan so long ago. Failed Marie. He would not fail Beannacht, not even for Siannon. She asked too much.

"Talk to me, Quin." She moved into the room, her voice reaching out to him like a caress.

With the whiskey loosening his tongue, he was sure to tell her much more than she would truly wish to hear.

"You need hide nothing from me, Quin. I may be your wife. But I have also, always, been your friend."

His friend? Aye, she had been his friend. And her family's ties to his went bone deep. But what he felt for her now held no resemblance to friendship. Didn't she know that?

"Let me help you as you have helped me." She moved even closer.

He could almost feel her warmth against his back. He couldn't help wondering where the breaking point would be and how much longer he would be able to retain control.

"I seriously doubt there is anything you can do to help me," he told her, splashing yet more whiskey into the now-empty tumbler. He knocked back the third drink and sighed as it burned its way into his stomach. Warmth surged through his middle, helping to displace the vile chill from Rhodes's words, from his own fears.

"But—"

"How many times must I tell you to go to bed, wife? Just give me the answer and I will happily voice the command as many times as is necessary. Can you not judge when your presence is not wanted?" The question ended on a near shout, venting some of the poison in his mind and soul.

"Oh." The one syllable wrenched out of her.

He gritted his teeth, locking his guilt and apologies behind his lips. Silence reigned for the span of several heartbeats.

"I will endeavor to work on that, my husband." Cool control iced her words despite the thickness in her tone. She spun, her petticoats rustling toward the doorway, promising him the empty sanctuary he was no longer sure he wanted.

"I am not your enemy, Quin." She paused by the door. "I never have been. Since it is your wish to be a rock alone in a stormy sea—so be it. I will cease trying to remind you you're a man."

Siannon moved away from the front parlor, her lip firmly clenched between her teeth. She would not cry within earshot of him, would not allow him to know just how much hurt he had inflicted with his words.

And not only his words. There in the darkness of the parlor, with his back rigid in front of her and whiskey fumes slicing the air, she had found the connection she'd been seeking for so long. But it failed to bring her the solace she hoped for, indeed craved. Instead, flashes of anger knifed her along with the cold certainty that Quin regretted every moment they had spent together, especially on the night he had made her his wife.

A tremor went through her and she swallowed hard, determined to hold back tears long enough to return to her lonely bedroom, where he need know nothing of her pain.

A roar from behind her brought her up short as she reached the kitchen. The sound of shattering glass splintered the air just as Quin's booted footsteps rang over the hallway floor.

She turned to face him as he approached her, and her courage failed at the sight of him striding out of the dark, anger evident in every line and angle of his tall frame. She gripped the doorframe to hold her place, willing herself not to run.

He stopped in front of her.

"You will cease to remind me I am a man?" He laughed, the sound stinging and harsh. He gripped her arms, his fingers tight against her shoulders. "*Mo ceile,* you remind me I am a man by just standing there. By breathing. By existing. If only I were the rock you proclaimed me to be. Then perhaps I would not be haunted with the constant desire to do this."

He pulled her against him and slanted his hot mouth over hers. He tasted of wild anger, whiskey, and pain. So much pain. But beneath all of that, he was Quin. And she could not hold herself from him. She tried to relax against his onslaught. He groaned low in his throat and thrust his tongue against her lips, sliding boldly inside to stroke and taste her. His pain and hers seemed to hover and collide in the air around them. She shuddered against him and spread her fingers against the front of his shirt, longing to heal him, to heal them both.

Her heartbeat drummed in her ears as he thoroughly ravished her mouth. She provided no resistance, welcoming each deep thrust of his tongue, struggling to help him fill the void she sensed in him.

He released her mouth moments later. Candlelight flickered over his features and the dark sparkle of his eyes.

"If you would have me be a man, *mo ceile*, then so be it. I am a man. With a man's desires. To hell with your father's words and my own better intentions. I'll have you right here. Right now."

"Quin—"

"Nay, darlin'." He slid his fingers into her hair and arched her head back. "Do not think to deny me now."

"I have never denied you." The words whispered out of her as his lips caressed her neck. He pressed the open heat of his mouth to the pulse beat just below her ear and laved her roughly with his tongue. Raw desire curled through her middle. Did he really mean to make love to her here in the kitchen?

"It doesn't matter." His words teased the fine hair just behind her ear as he gripped her arms tighter. He traced her lobe with his tongue and then bit gently. "Nothing matters but this. And how I will feel sheathed inside your body. I want you, Siannon."

"Aye." Again the floodgates opened between them and she could feel the darkness churning inside him, hot, wanton blackness whipped to a frenzy in his soul by the pain he couldn't bring himself to voice. He wanted her down to the deepest part of himself, needed her. And almost as deeply wanted to thrust all desire from his heart and feel nothing.

But he couldn't.

A surge of satisfaction swirled through her despite the undercurrents of doubt and despair lingering in his depths. He wanted her. He needed her. And she needed him.

"Nothing else matters." His hands moved over her arms, stroking, teasing with knowledgeable fingers, and then he spanned her waist as his lips teased her collarbone.

"Then make love to me, Quin," she urged as he swirled a hot path along the top of her gown, his breath stirring the heat deep inside her.

"Love has nothing to do with this. Nothing to do with us." Harsh words, but she could feel the denial pulsing deep inside him.

He flicked open the buttons of her gown. One, two, three. In rapid succession he bared her, parting her bodice and tugging at her chemise to gain easy access to her naked flesh. Her breath quickened as his lips followed the path of his fingers and nuzzled the curves of her breasts. He fingered her locket for a moment and continued his quest. Her nipples tightened as his moist breath swept over first one and then the other.

"Quin." She gasped as he fastened his lips to one sensitive tip and sucked her deep into his mouth. She slid her fingers into the ebony of his hair, cupping him to her breast.

He groaned, sucking her, teasing her with the rapid flick of his tongue.

Cool air touched her ankles, her knees, her upper thighs as he lifted her skirt and loosened the tie to her petticoats. They dropped to the floor with a sigh, leaving her open to his touch as his fingers unerringly found the juncture of her thighs and slid between. His arm cradled her waist when her kness would have buckled from the sensations assaulting her as he entered her.

"Aye, sweet Siannon." His words traced her breasts

as his fingers tested her willingness. "You are so hot and so fine. Everything a *man* needs." He thrust his fingers inside her, forcing a gasp from her at the sudden invasion. Deeper and deeper he pushed, stretching her to accommodate the length of his fingers. And then in and out, in and out, as his dark gaze moved over her face.

She couldn't hide her response to the forceful rhythm he invoked as she clutched his shoulders for support. She bit her lip and fought for breath as the exquisite sensations undulated through her. He triumphed in his power over her reactions to his touch.

"Quin, please," she begged, uncertain whether she needed him to stop or to demand more of him.

"No man should feel this way about any woman," he told her. He increased the rhythmic invasion of his fingers, forcing her to cling to him even as his words lashed her. "I want you far more than I should. Far more than you should want me to. I want to watch you as you are now, enthralled by what I make you feel. I want to taste your passion. I want to bury myself deep inside your body and hear you cry out for me. I want to make love to you every moment. There is no sanity in my life. No sanctuary. And that is because of you."

"No." She shuddered as he swirled his fingers deep inside her, surely stroking her very womb.

"Aye. I don't want to feel about you the way I do, *mo ceile*. And yet I cannot stop."

She shivered beneath his touch as he expertly drew from her the things she could not deny him even as his anguish clogged her throat and brought the hot sting of tears to her eyes. She could feel all the awful things churning inside him—goading him beyond endurance.

"Oh, Quin." She laced her fingers up into his hair to draw him down toward her.

Resistance stiffened his neck and swirled through the darkness inside him. He didn't want her forgiveness or her gentleness. He wanted to hurt both of them in an effort to create enough distance for him to tell himself there was nothing between them but the old friendship of their two families and his need to protect her.

But there had to be more than that. It welled with each broken beat of her heart and pulsed deep inside her. She loved him enough for both of them. Would that be enough? For now it would have to be.

"Take me, Quin," she urged. "Here. Now."

He closed his eyes and groaned from deep inside. Pain and hunger and the desires he feared twisted through the sound. Memories of an earlier time and a woman who should still be at his side rippled over Siannon, tenuous and uncertain. She tightened her lips and pushed the images away. Nothing mattered at the moment but this man, this time, and the passion and promise welling between them.

"There is more to marriage than this," he managed to say through gritted teeth even as he allowed her to draw him closer.

"It does not matter," she gasped as their breath mingled. The whiskey he'd drunk made her head spin.

"Aye, it does. This solves nothing," he whispered just before his mouth closed over hers, releasing them both from their frozen postures.

She tasted all the fear and reprisals on his lips, all

that he strove to hold back from her, to keep locked behind the walls of his heart. They ripped their way through her. For some inexplicable reason, he was nearly as open to her now as he had been so long ago.

So much so, she could almost wish he were not. To sense the things he felt for her now was almost too honest, too open, too much to accept. She ceased trying to understand the sensations battering her mind and heart, letting them roll through her and pour out into the air around them.

He scooped her up, his hands cupping her bared buttocks as he carried her farther into the kitchen. She clutched his shoulders. The sound of his boots against the floor and then the scrape of a chair. He settled himself against the wall on the chair and drew her into his lap. Her legs slid to either side of his as she faced him. The hot bulge of his desire pressed intimately against her own as her skirts settled around them. Heat spread upward over her cheeks. She squirmed atop him and watched as his eyes slitted.

"Siannon." He cupped the back of her head and freed her hair from its loose knot. Pulling her down for a hot, hungry kiss that invaded all of her senses, he tangled his hands in her hair as it spilled around them. He groaned low and deep in his throat. She could only cling to him and meet his tongue thrust for starving thrust as his needs poured through her soul.

His fingers shifted between them, releasing his hot flesh from the confines of his trousers. He sprang against her, thick and hard and velvety smooth.

Their gazes locked as the sound of their breathing echoed around them. His face was tight with desire and pain. Siannon's heart twisted within her. Whatever else lay between them, she could not deny her own feelings. She loved him. And for this one moment she could give him exactly what he needed.

"Take me now, Quin," she urged, her voice coming husky and low.

"Aye." His answer came in a harsh rasp. He gripped her hips and lifted her, sliding her down over his hard length.

Her body parted, stretching to accept him fully. A rainbow of sensations filled her. The crash of waves on timber and the sharp light of the stars in a winter sky.

"God, Siannon," he groaned as she settled atop his lap. He was deep inside her, so deep, she could almost not bear the sensation.

She squirmed again and gasped at the whirl of pure pleasure that shot through her belly and swirled straight into her heart.

He groaned again and slid his hands over her arms. Looping his fingers into the top of her bodice, he pulled it down, baring her completely to the waist so that he could fasten his lips to her breast. Her sleeves trapped her arms to her sides, confining her yet freeing her to accept all that he pounded into her without making any demands of her own.

There was no need for demands. Wild ripples of heat tore through her as he sucked her, nipping with his teeth, teasing with his tongue. She shuddered in his arms again and again, unable to hold back the sensations he built to fever pitch inside her. She cried his name, uncertain whether she begged him to cease or never to stop—until the tension inside her exploded, washing wave after sweet, rich wave of satisfaction through every inch of her body.

And still it was not enough. His hands guided her hips, and they began to move, first in an awkward rhythm and then like silk as she caught his cadence, driving his pulsing length in and out, grinding her need against him, gripping his sides with her knees.

"Oh, Quin." *I love you.* She bit back the words, knowing he didn't want to hear them, could not face them. He pulled her arms free of her sleeves.

"I can take everything you have to give me," she challenged him as she slid her hands inside his shirt, caressing his chest and moving slowly atop him, teasing them both to madness with the slow, sweet feel of their bodies sliding together. "I can be what you need me to be."

"Nay." He grunted his rejection.

She could feel the denials swirling inside him even as he held her closer. His needs, his secret fears, pulsed through her.

"Aye. Let me please you." She kissed him then, taking command as she tilted his head back, sliding her tongue boldly inside his mouth.

He groaned from deep inside as he accepted her kiss, accepted her command. She pressed her bared breasts against the heat of his chest and moved her body to accommodate his. Back and forth, her nipples stroked his muscles, and the tempo built the white-hot fires inside her again even as she concentrated on him.

She could feel his need growing and tightening, nearly bursting. He was deep inside her body and she deep into his mind, his soul, as she tormented him with her slow movements. Rhythmic, undulating, entwined—physical need and sentient barriers shattered and merged.

With a savage roar that echoed from the rafters, he gripped her hips and reasserted his control, increasing the rhythm, thrusting his body so deeply into hers that she cried out and clung to him. And still he drove faster, harder, deeper, allowing no respite as he took what she had offered him, took what he needed.

Tears stung her eyes for the pain and loneliness inside him. For the pain inside them both.

"You are mine." His words ripped the air as she shuddered atop him and then felt the fiery spurt of his seed fill her again and again.

In the aftermath, silence filled the room, broken only by the sputtering candle burning low to the wick. Siannon's legs trembled against Quin's hips. What would happen now? She rested her forehead against his shoulder as they both fought for breath, for sanity. Too much sorrow. Too much guilt. Too much. Too much.

"Go to bed, Siannon." Quin's voice was distant and controlled though his body was still locked intimately with hers.

Tears clogged her throat and she swallowed hard. There was her answer. Despite the intensity of the lovemaking they had just shared, nothing had changed. Grief tore through her, jagged and sharp. His grief, hers—it did not matter.

With awkward haste she pulled away from him, adjusting her skirts and tugging up her chemise. Questions screamed through her mind. Had it meant nothing? Merely sex and nothing else? But she could not voice them. She had offered. She had challenged him. She had laid herself bare for this rejection.

"Good night, Quin," she managed to say on a husky

rasp that hurt her throat but could not match the pain and self-condemnation that pounded through her.

He didn't answer. She bit back a sob, then turned and left the room, finally giving him the solitude he seemed to want more than he could ever want her.

Chapter Ten

Warmth stung Siannon's cold cheeks, at odds with the icy emptiness pervading her. Snared in a shaft of unyielding morning sunlight, she could no longer avoid the awful questions twisting through her mind and heart. She turned onto her back and stared up at the ceiling, cool and white—as barren of hope as the night she had spent wrestling with Quin's inner demons and her own doubts.

Pain such as she had never expected was kept locked away deep inside her husband. Pain and emptiness and guilt he had no wish to share with her. With anyone, for that matter.

She caught back a sigh. Avoiding her inner certainties had never done her any good. Never. Last night had not proved the exception to the rule.

She had made a dreadful mistake in marrying Quin. Acknowledging the truth so plainly shot anguish and loss through her middle. She bit her lip and forced herself to face it anyway. For herself, for Timothy, her decision had been sound. But for Quin—strong, stoic Quin, her childhood champion who held true to her fantasies and charged in to save her when she needed him most—their marriage forced him even further into a hell she could not fathom. A private hell filled with black and unspeakable misery that haunted him and hounded him and had increased because of the burdens he had taken on for her. For Quin, their marriage was a disaster.

The flash of his anger and the chilling certainty that he regretted every moment they had spent together still clashed in her heart, rubbed raw by desire neither of them could hide. Tears gathered at the corners of her eyes. She swiped at them with the back of her hand. Her eyes itched and burned from the weakness she had indulged in during the night when she could no longer avoid the truth of what she had contributed to the burdens already crushing someone she claimed to love, had claimed to love for as long as she could remember. Claimed to love but did not really know at all.

Crying never solves problems, Siannon. Her mother's familiar admonition, repeated many more times than usual the last year she had been home, echoed through her loneliness. Siannon had known then the words offered her mother no comfort and they did little to help her daughter now. Still, she had never suspected the true depth of the pain that could fall behind them.

What could she do at this point to resolve the situation? She and Quin were well and truly married, legally and physically joined. They'd done more than consummate their marriage, though last night had surely not been the connubial relations Father Dunnavan explained, red-faced, to Bridget McGee and Kiernan Rogers prior to their betrothal. A gentle and godly man, Father Dunnavan had surely never envisioned marital duties in any way approaching the raw, driving hunger that passed between her and Quin.

Siannon pressed her fingers over her lips as the thought sparked a hysterical urge to laugh, salty and acrid in her throat. She couldn't stay hidden away in her chamber much longer. Whatever she could do to alleviate the situation, to help Quin, she would not find it in bed. A second bubble of laughter burned. Last night had surely proven that if nothing else.

"Enough." She flung back the covers and sat up. Her heart ached, her head spun from the pummeling of Quin's emotions, her body twinged from the rigors of their kitchen tryst, but she felt oddly alive and more aware. At least she knew now how he felt—what he faced. What she faced. That gave her something to work on.

At the moment she had no desire to try to explain to Caitlin or Maeve what she was doing in bed past her normal hour, laughing like she was truly as demented as her father would have people believe. If only he could see her now, with her tear-streaked face and the frenetic hysteria bubbling inside her. It would be all he needed to confirm his claims and wrench Timmy away.

Marriage was supposed to be a joining beyond connubial relations, Bridget had whispered—asking for confirmation more than sharing information with the only bride she knew. The pooling of resources, the sharing of two lives so that each could be a comfort in sorrow and a companion in joy, that's what Father Dunnavan had said to Bridget. Siannon hadn't had the heart to deny this to the girl still anticipating her wedding with such hope. She'd shared that hope for herself right up until last night.

But now she knew there would be no such sharing, no such joining. Not for Siannon Rhodes Crofton Reilly. Not from her first marriage. Not from the marriage of her parents, and now, almost certainly, not with Quin. He'd never allow her to comfort him and she could get no sense of any joy hovering over the horizon for them to share either. Unhappy years stretched out before her, before them both.

How could she save Quin from the bargain she had foisted on him—lighten his load and save him from a lifetime of misery that piled guilt upon guilt until it raged out of control? Divorce was out of the question. She could not do that to Timothy, and it would surely bring a stain to the Reilly and McManus names as well.

That she simply would not do.

"Oh, Mama." Had this been the path her mother had followed inexorably toward her doom? Had she suffered through years of unhappiness and then finally worked up the strength to walk away from her husband, trying to save them both further misery? Was this the warning looming from the trunks Grandda kept? It certainly shone a slightly different light on her father and his actions. Siannon pressed the heels of her hands over her eyes and forced herself to take long, slow breaths until some of her internal balance returned. She would have to deal with those trunks, and soon.

She blew out a long sigh and forced herself from the clinging depths of rumpled linen and regret. Mary would be waiting. The plates would not paint themselves, and she could not stay here all day and hide like a frightened schoolgirl. Her goals all along had been sound and directed on the right course. She may have fallen afoul of a bad wind, but that did not mean she shouldn't continue to hold the wheel and—

She stopped mid-step as she heard the echo of Quin's old shipboard analogies in her own thoughts. How quickly and completely she had aligned herself to his way of thinking. She bit her lip as the torn emotions that had coursed from him last night shuddered through her again.

You will cease to remind me I am a man? You remind me I am a man by just standing there. By breathing. By existing.

"Enough." She slapped her palms down on the top of her dresser, welcoming the sting as she locked gazes with her tousled reflection. "You cannot solve anything if you do not first take charge of yourself."

Her own resolute gray gaze glared back at her from beneath puffy lids. She tightened her lips and nodded for emphasis. First things first. She would bathe the telltale redness from her eyes and cheeks and then she would address the things she had set her mind to before the events between herself and Quin had muddied her thinking. And somewhere in the midst of this she would find a solution for all of them.

She had to.

"It's worried I was after ye, Siannon Reilly." Her cousin Mary welcomed her into the warm confines of her own small kitchen an hour later. The room smelled of tea and biscuits and happiness, a mix that tugged at Siannon's heart.

"I'm sorry." Despite herself, hot color spread over her cheeks beneath Mary's scrutiny. "I overslept."

A bald lie but the best she could come up with. If anything, she had underslept, listening to Quin's footsteps as he readied for bed and again a few hours later as he left for the yard. And worrying.

"Ah, don't fret yerself. I take it Quin arrived home whistling like my Declan yestereve." Mary squeezed her hand in understanding, a sparkle lighting her eyes as she obviously mistook Siannon's hesitation for shyness. "I well remember the times when I *overslept* before Davey was born."

She smiled down at her infant son, who cooed in his basket, ready for another day at Maeve's.

Siannon kept her face averted lest Mary's all too keen gaze determine the spark of tears her well meant comment engendered. Envy over Mary's relationship with Declan hit Siannon once again. The quiet ripples of contentment that radiated along with her cousin's words pierced Siannon like swords.

"Thank you, Mary." She managed to get out the words in a normal tone. "But we've much to do and I've wasted half the morning."

"Well, seems ye've come with a renewed sense of purpose, Siannon Reilly." Mary nodded approval and handed her a cup of tea before scooping up Davey's basket. "So be it. Let's go join the others."

Women with a purpose. Yes, that was it. Siannon nodded to herself. That's what she had hoped to achieve. Praise be, in that at least it seemed she might succeed. She let the essence of the women around her wash through her, soothing and rhythmic like the ocean's tides as they greeted her with a mixture of smiles and murmured good mornings when they arrived at Maeve Kelly's. Each bent to her task, a brush stroke here, a turn of the wrist there, and the plates stacked, neatly awaiting their packing in the barrels they had come from.

Soon they might begin to reap the benefit of this labor. And then they would really start to see just what they had accomplished. Hope burgeoned inside her. Perhaps that would help ease Quin's burden just the tiniest bit and then . . . She cut her hopes off before they lingered down that well-worn path. Enough was enough.

She bent her head to the task of her own plate. In the meantime, she alone was garnering a boon none of the other women seemed to be truly aware of, and she couldn't help the warm curl of pleasure the thought gave her. They had begun to treat her as one of them. Gone were the wary glances and puzzled stares—the slight standoffish distance they had held when they first gathered at Maeve's house and wondered what Siannon was up to.

She hadn't faulted them for their misgivings. The distance they had held her at seemed natural. After all the time she had spent away from Beannacht, she had become an outsider, an offlander. Now the open welcome of their acceptance warmed her. At least here she could imagine herself at home. Even as the thought gave her a fleeting moment of peace, a niggling tweak of disquiet stole in.

Siannon tilted her head for a moment, pulling her concentration from the women surrounding her and their gentle hum of conversation. She lowered her guard and searched for a moment, even as a slight pain twinged at her temple. Nothing.

"Don't ye think, Siannon?" Grania Keane's question seeped into her thoughts.

Siannon forced her attention back to the group. After coming so far, it would not do for anyone to realize she'd not be minding what they said. With a quick flash she sensed questions and boys and scraped knees.

"Oh, aye, indeed," she tried, hoping she understood the blur of emotions she was sensing. "Although Timmy is not usually one for climbing."

"Then ye've not seen him over at Ross McGee's recently." Nora Doyle's knowing laugh rippled through the group.

"No, I haven't." Siannon laughed in return, and then that slight pang hit her again, stronger than before, but still undirected. There was nothing to cling to, nothing. It was frustrating and worrisome, but there was no way to make the sensation come sharper or clearer. And in the process she was only strengthening the pain in her temples.

She released her efforts and smiled at the women surrounding her. "I shall have to make a point of checking his knickers for tears."

Approving laughter and knowing glances greeted her pronouncement, and the talk drifted to other topics. But the chafing sting of worry stayed with her like an itch she couldn't quite relieve. Gran had often described her visions that way. Sometimes they came clear as day and she could truly be of help, but other times it was just enough to tease and torment.

Siannon well remembered the beginning of her own fears for Quin's brothers, Bryan and Devin, that day so long ago. Her feeling then had been like that as well. Undirected, sporadic, and frustrating—in the end matters had nearly come to disaster. She frowned at the comparison, her concern tightening within her. What could be wrong?

"Siannon, are ye all right?" Mary glanced at her as she saw Siannon peering at the clouds darking over the harbor.

"She's fine." Grania answered with a chuckle as she nudged Nora. "Probably mooning over her strapping husband. Aye, Siannon? Ye certainly got the pick of the litter, I'd say."

"All of the Reilly men are worth a little swooning or mooning over to my mind," Nora answered before Siannon could think of her own reply. "I do appreciate the set of their shoulders and the twinkle in those green eyes they all use to such advantage."

"Aye, but knowing them since they were little scamps takes some of the luster out of the admirin', fer me at least."

"They all scare me," Bridget confessed, her gaze sliding shyly toward Siannon.

The women laughed again, and Siannon tried to smile even as another stronger pang of warning hit her.

She lifted her gaze from the plate she'd been painting to see Caitlin approaching down the hill. Timmy was not with her, but then, that was not unusual given his preoccupation with the other boys and the time he spent attending the hedge-school with Father Dunnavan. But there was something in the set of Caitlin's sturdy young shoulders that stiffened Siannon's and made her put the plate down on the table with a clatter.

"Siannon?" Mary looked toward her.

"I don't know." Siannon answered the questions flowing gently from her cousin as she pushed to her feet. "Something is not right."

Siannon reached the doorway as Caitlin came up the walk.

"Oh, Missus." Caitlin attempted a smile, but the concern radiating from her twined around Siannon's heart and gave it an uneasy squeeze with fingers of dread.

"What's wrong, Caitlin?" Siannon strove to keep her worries from her tone.

"I . . . has young master Timmy come to show ye one of Ross McGee's puppies? The one he still hopes ta call his own?" Caitlin's eyebrows rose, and her questions, wreathed with a mix of worry and hope, clamped the vise around Siannon's heart tighter.

"No, I have yet to catch more than a glimpse of Timmy this day." *Where is my son?* Fear knifed her, but she held it back. Losing control would only confuse matters. She needed to hear the whole of the young nurse's tale. "Why do you ask?"

"After his lessons he went with Kevan and Seamus Kelly to visit Ross and his dogs—ye know how he loves them puppies, Mum." Siannon nodded quickly, silently urging the girl to continue. "When I went to fetch him, Kevan told me Timmy had taken one of the puppies to show it to you. Seamus seemed to think ye'd be making a decision about keeping the puppy today. Having just come from the house, I knew Timmy wasn't there. I had hoped to find him here, knowing this is where ye'd be."

A sudden burst of panic scored Siannon's heart and froze her in place. Her father's determination to have Timothy under his control, her son's unfamiliarity with the island, her own inexcusable distraction of late whirled through her in a turbulent wheel of guilt. Was this the unfocused worry and fear she was sensing? Was it her own son? Mary's hand, warm and steady, slipped into Siannon's cold one and offered a reassuring squeeze.

"Timmy has brought no puppies over to us this morning. But puppies and boys are a wayward mix. I'm sure they've just gotten distracted." Her cousin's words offered a warm ray of comfort. Siannon clung to that slender solace and struggled to control her fears.

"Aye, mum. That was my hope as well. It's just—"

"I'll head over to Uncle Ross's to see if they've turned up back there," Bridget interrupted.

Siannon gave a start. She hadn't realized anyone besides Mary had joined her on the stoop.

"My little brothers often go missing fer hours," Bridget said.

"I'll check and see if Fenella and the other girls tendin' the little ones have spotted them." Nora patted Siannon's shoulder. "He'll not have gotten far without someone seeing him."

"Aye, yer husband's charged all the village with keeping an eye on ye since that visitor from Limerick came a few weeks back." Maeve reached for her shawl.

The visitor from Limerick—Nigel Franklin. *The boy will be returned to Limerick. It is only a matter of time.* The threats her father's solicitor made echoed into the hollow depths of Siannon's soul. Nausea gripped her. *Timmy! Timmy!* she wanted to scream as loudly as she could. Panic would get her nowhere.

"Mayhap he stopped to visit with yer grandda. My Danny's over there. He'll help us look." Maeve stripped off her apron and edged by Siannon and Mary. She gave Caitlin's arm a pat as she passed.

"We'll all go and look fer the lad," Grania offered. Siannon turned around. The entire group had abandoned their work and come forward. Concern lit the face of each woman in turn.

"Don't worry, Siannon. My boy Sean did something like this when he was your Timmy's age. It is one advantage to havin' an island. They don't go far when they go explorin'."

Oh, Timmy—where are you? The fear-laced question repeated itself over and over in Siannon's heart.

"It's not the first time we've had to go look for a wee one."

Sympathy flowed in a wave from the women of Beannacht. Some of Siannon's fear ebbed, washed away by their assurances. She forced herself to rein in her worries. Surely they were right and she was making more of the situation than there was, although she would be telling Timothy in no uncertain terms he could not wander off again.

"Thank you."

"That's it, then, ladies." Mary undid her apron with a brisk, businesslike attitude. "Let's set these aside. We've a lad to find."

The women nodded and echoed Mary's movements, unhesitating in their resolve to help Siannon find her son. With the efficiency of a born military leader, Mary organized their small group of plate painters into search parties of two, each with their own section of Beannacht to investigate.

"Caitlin, find Father Dunnavan and ask if he's seen the lad or knows a place he talks of going hereabouts," Mary said. The nurse nodded and took off at a run for St. Bridgid's.

"Nora, will you go ask Dan Kelly Sr. if he's seen anything untoward today? He'll know what ye're askin."

Another nod. "Shall I take yer Davey over to Fenella?" Nora asked. "It's a good thing ye only jest fed him. She can keep him for quite a while afore he'll need his mama again."

Did Timmy need his mama? Was he off playing with no thought, or was he the reason behind the swelling unease that nipped at Siannon? And how would he fare if the storm that had threatened since last night finally broke? Siannon had no answers, and her newfound store of hope was rapidly draining as her questions rose.

"Don't worry, Cousin. We'll find him." Mary squeezed Siannon's hand again after she handed Davey and his basket over to Nora with a final kiss.

Siannon couldn't answer as she fought the tears that threatened at the edges of her eyes. She'd been so absorbed in her own problems, so absorbed by Quin's, she hadn't even seen her son today.

Bridget came back from her uncle's with no more information save that Maeve's boys had seen Timmy a little more than an hour before, complete with puppy. He'd gone off toward Beannacht's broad hills.

"Then we'll spread out like a sail caught in the wind." She spread her fingers wide to illustrate. "And stay no more than thirty to forty paces apart. That way we'll be within shouting distance, so we'll all know when he's been found."

"Agreed."

"Let's be off, then."

"Thank you, Mary." Siannon caught her cousin's hand as the group began an exodus from Mary's cottage.

"No thanks are needed, Siannon Reilly." Mary winked in reassurance. "Ye're family. And they all know it. Shall we send young Dan Kelly to tell Quintin we're off lookin' for his son?"

His son? The question rocked Siannon and brought her thoughts back to her fears of that morning. Quin felt responsible for Timmy. He'd told her that in just those words more than once. She had no doubt Quin took that responsibility very seriously, but his and Timmy's relationship was far from that of father and son. And after last night, Siannon had no wish to ask for anything more from her husband. She had managed on her own before she married him. She would manage now.

"Nay." She shook her head. "We can tell Quin after Timmy is found."

Skepticism chased over Mary's features, but she nodded and squeezed Siannon's shoulder, holding her thoughts to herself. "As ye like, Siannon. Though the menfolk can certainly be of some use if the storm hits."

Was she wrong? She thought of Quin's ruling that women should provide no distractions in the shipyard. And they were already pressed enough for time to complete the ship. But Timmy's safety should come first.

"As you, or someone, said, Beannacht is small enough—if we run into trouble or can't find him, then we'll ask the shipwrights for help. We'll all be better off if we can locate Timmy on our own.''

Was she being pridefully foolish? And would Timmy be the one to pay for the mistake she might be making now? She prayed not, but she could not bear Timmy to be the cause of further goading to Quin's displeasure with his new family ties.

Sharp breezes ruffled the high grass and tugged Siannon's hair, carrying the salt-fresh scent of the sea to cut through the rich, dark scent of Beannacht's hills. Breaks in the clouds sent warming sunshine down to them as they trekked upward into the hollows. Thank heaven it looked to be clearing—not at all reminiscent of the storm-racked search she partook in once when Bryan and Devin went missing. Storms blew up around Beannacht with a speed to catch one's breath. The reminder sent a fresh ripple of unease through her middle.

If only she could feel Timmy. *Where are you, my son?* For the first time in his young life she found herself wishing that he had received a portion of the Mc-Manus Gift, even though it was usually reserved for the female side of the family. Perhaps then, though she could not feel him, he might sense her seeking him.

"It's not like him to wander so far away from everything, especially alone. In Limerick, he never stepped out of the room, let alone outside without someone to accompany him." She voiced her concerns, looking at Mary as they continued to walk up the narrow dirt path.

"Ah, but don't ye think that ta his mind, yer Timmy views the puppy as company?" Mary paused to listen, her head cocked to the side for a moment. "Father

Dunnavan's ta ring the church bell if—when—they find him. I guess I just caught a noise from the shipyard."

The shipyard. Guilt sluiced through Siannon. Should she have told Quin? She shook her head. She didn't have time to second-guess herself. She glanced downward, ostensibly watching her steps as they continued but inwardly trying to push her ability to sense Timmy. To find her son by willpower alone. Even with the puppy, if he wandered too far, surely she would sense his fear.

Pain shot straight through her temples, but she could sense nothing beyond that niggling disquiet rippling through her all day.

Timothy, where are you?

No answer save the distant calls of the other women searching for him and a bracing measure of Mary's determination not to worry. They topped a rise, gaining a vista of the small valley below and the sloping rise of farther hills beyond. Nothing stirred beyond the dance of the deep green grass and the beckoning branches from the trees on the hills.

Siannon's heart sank and twisted. There were no signs of either a small boy or a boisterous puppy. She couldn't hold back the fear that Timothy was no longer here at all. That her father had somehow managed to snatch him and even now Timmy was on his way back to Limerick.

She reached for Mary's certainty and clung.

"Oh, Mary—" she choked out.

"He's here somewhere, Siannon." Mary didn't wait for her to finish, her brown gaze holding the conviction Siannon needed. "It's just a matter of finding him."

Siannon nodded and then shivered as a sudden shock of cold scurried by them, carrying the heavy promise of rain. Another shiver racked her, and suddenly it was not Timothy they were looking for, it was Devin and Bryan, and she was but a girl, trying desperately to convince someone, anyone, that the two youngest Reilly brothers were in danger. And no one would listen.

"Siannon?"

She shook the memory away with an effort. "Aye, Mary. You are right. He's must be close by. Let's go."

They walked on, beginning the downward slope into the valley below as the clouds gathered overhead. Siannon's heart twisted with worry the farther away from the village they got. Perhaps she should not have held so hard to her pride. Perhaps they should have told Quin right away. More searchers would surely mean they'd find Timmy that much faster.

Echoes from deep in her memories continued to ripple through her despite her best efforts to keep them at bay. She could taste the storm from so long ago on her tongue as the clouds overhead darkened and swelled. She could still taste Bryan's despair and the deep wound dealt his pride when he knew he had lost his place at sea and that he would be sent to Limerick to learn how to lead his family through the tangle of English laws. And poor Devin, her friend and ever-ready confidant. His confusion and fear had lanced her almost as clearly as the guilt-shrouded relief that had poured from Quin.

But those dark thoughts had not been the feelings that had pulled at her young heart all day, demanding satisfaction. It had been the underlying certainty about terrible impulses and impending consequences that had forced her to nag her mother, Grandda, Gran—anyone she could get to stand still long enough to listen.

Eventually Gran had set aside her insistence that Siannon was overwrought, perhaps far too involved with the Reilly boys to truly know anything was amiss. She had looked at Siannon then, in that way she had—really looked. Finally, knowledge and acceptance had grown in Gran's eyes with her own alarm swiftly rising there.

A terrible relief had swelled in Siannon even as her fears were realized. Gran took the burden and the two of them had gone immediately to James Reilly. The entire shipyard was called out to search for the boys when they realized Quin's ship was no longer in its special berth in the harbor.

The agony in Quin's eyes as they stood on the docks and watched the storm blow in kept her still. She understood his despair at this moment far deeper than she had even then. For to his core, Quin Reilly believed he had lost his brothers that day through his own arrogance.

It was Siannon who had clung to hope then, as Mary was doing now. Standing on the docks as the rain pelted them and the seas churned. Racked with cold, numb with fear, the torn and broken emotions of Bryan and Devin Reilly roiled through her without mercy. But at least she knew they were alive.

If only she could feel Timmy as she had felt the boys back then. Their emotions had drawn her as surely as beacons in deepest dark. She had known just where they would be, known which direction to send her uncle Michael and Quin when the other searchers had set out in the opposite way.

She had clung to the docks as the rain whipped her, waiting for them to come home, while the conflicted emotions of all the Reilly males tore her heart to pieces. But at least she had been able to feel them.

Timmy, where are you?

Chapter Eleven

"Diabhal." Up to this point they had been lucky with the weather, too lucky considering everything else that had gone awry recently.

Quin's lips twisted over the thought. Rain had threatened several times and then held clear. But the taste was in the air today, and he couldn't help thinking their good fortune had just about run out. That certainly seemed to be the case with every other facet of the business. And every aspect of his life, for that matter.

He sighed and rubbed the back of his neck. A useless gesture that didn't begin to ease the tension wound tight between his shoulder blades and down his spine. Damning and frustrating—and just out of reach—like the answers he sought. Each parcel of information he'd unearthed from the correspondence and invoices in his father's files added fuel to the indignation burning within him. A fire he'd be only too happy to direct toward Eustace Rhodes, given the opportunity.

Backed by the distant rhythms of work in the yard, the papers spread over the desk crackled as he sifted through them yet again, calling his attention to the mounting problems they evidenced—delays from suppliers who had always been on time and whose history of dealing with Reilly Ship Works went back for generations, differing prices on invoices from original quotes, and letter upon letter that had been sent inquiring into the mounting problems, all with no reply.

If he was looking at things aright, the venomous pattern in this morass was only just rising to the surface. If he was not drifting off course. He was a sea captain—a man used to reading the waves and currents, to judging the winds and charting the stars—not some clerk. His temples pounded and his eyes blurred from scrutinizing all the text. Not for the first time, he wished Bryan could come and help him piece the puzzle together or that he had not been so hasty in sending Devin back to Dublin.

No wonder Da had become ill handling this on his own. Quin shook his head. How had his father managed to keep all of this to himself? What had stopped him from reaching out for assistance in dealing with or investigating what amounted to systematic subversion? Pride alone? The question echoed within Quin, stirring something uneasy and far too familiar for comfort.

He couldn't escape his own acquaintance with the self-reliant ego. If James Reilly had shared only a small portion of that worry with his sons instead of allowing it to deepen and fester with each new setback, would they have been able to avoid some of the problems they now faced?

Futility lay in these waters. Second-guessing Da did little to help the immediate problems the shipyard still faced. Or to resolve his father's health issues. Quin could only hope the time in Italy's warmer climes would provide a solution to the latter problem while he did his best with the former. That had been the gist of his mother's latest missive, at least, warning him to take care of himself while he wrestled with the demons that had bested his father.

There's no shame in sharing troubles, my son. Do not let foolish pride keep you from seeking the counsel and assistance you may need, she'd written. There had still been no word from Devin. Bryan was dealing with his own tangle if the message he'd sent via Gill O'Brien was true. Quin was on his own to untangle this mess.

The sooner he got started, the better. He'd leave tomorrow and face his vendors and his nemesis at one and the same time. Face-to-face inquiry and confrontation should suit him better than following this trail of paper and dust. Why, then, did the prospect of departing from Beannacht render him so empty?

He glanced out the window at the clouds darkening overhead. A tug of the selfsame pride that had helped hide the problem for too long twisted his lips.

Despite mounting delays and supply snags, the barque was almost done. She would be a fine ship. Clean and proud and worthy of any name chosen for her. Each day, every bit of progress, had come at the cost of unnecessary struggle. Sending out his own ships and men to hunt down materials had become an almost weekly routine, counterproductive in every way with too much lost time and frustration he'd gladly have done without. All bringing him back to what had started him on this trail of investigation in the first place, Eustace Rhodes and his smug claims.

The time and obvious effort Rhodes had spent to disrupt all progress at the shipyard would have required massive amounts of funds and cold patience. The depths of his resentment over what little interference they had managed when he had chosen to condemn his wife as insane was inconceivable.

Uncertainty chilled Quin's spine and settled a cold stone of worry in his gut. Just what kind of mind would conceive of such a plan and then carry it through? The hostility and commitment inherent in a decade-long course was staggering—filled with the kind of evil and malice Quin had thought existed only in Granny's old tales. Each new piece of the puzzle moved the entire scheme into a larger circle, like ripples in a pond spreading wider until one lost all perception.

If this was Eustace Rhodes's retribution for the futile interference in matters with his wife, how far would he go to regain the grandson he prized so highly? At least this time, Quin would be forewarned. He would not let Siannon down in that regard. He had promised her protection for herself and the boy, and by heaven they would have it. It was the least he owed her.

He shoved away the memory of the devastation in her gaze last night after he practically ravaged her in his mother's kitchen. He definitely owed Siannon much, but he had no time to dwell on her problems—their problems. Finishing the barque—her father's machinations be damned—must come first. All else would have to wait.

Like a hawk gliding over the hills, one clashing notion circled back on him again and again with relentless intensity. Had Siannon known of her father's sabotage? Despite her denials?

I am not your enemy, Quin. I never have been. Yet she was the daughter of his enemy as surely as she lived and breathed. Siannon carried Rhodes blood just as she did that of her McManus forebears. With her ability to sense the feelings of those around her, could she truly have been without knowledge of her father's connivance? How could such raw animosity escape her notice completely?

Doubt stabbed again and again with each question he couldn't answer. She had claimed she couldn't read family, couldn't read anyone close to her. Only strong basic emotions could get through. Not much was more basic than hatred. How could she not have known?

He scraped back his chair and paced the office confines, tempted to join the men in the yard for some mind-numbing physical exertion. It was this cycle of suspicion and mistrust, coupled with his physical hungers for her, that had set off the chain of anger and frustration that had led to last night's disaster.

Perhaps this trip would put things in a better light for the two of them. Let them regain the safe personal distances that would prevent another such occurrence. Why did that prospect not appeal more?

The black satisfaction of taking Siannon in his arms and claiming her angry lips with his own slammed him anew. She had greeted his assault with a raging passion to match his own, to twist a man's soul and rip his good intentions to shreds. It jolted him to realize there had been no surprise in her embrace, no gasp of shock when he had claimed her with such fury. Had she known what he was thinking and feeling?

A more insidious, more glacial cold slithered through him. There could be nothing more basic between a man and a woman than the feelings he had succumbed to last night. Had those base instincts been as clear to her? That possibility galled more than anything else. To be so open to someone, anyone, at a time when he had lost control seemed the ultimate invasion.

"Damnation," he swore, and raked his hands through his hair, trying to clear his thoughts.

Instead, more images of the prior evening twisted through his gut. The gleam of candlelight on her breasts, the feel of her thighs as she clinched his sides and he drove himself into her, their cries of mutual satisfaction echoing through the darkness inside him, and the lonely traces of their passion mingled with her lavender and lilac scent long after he'd sent her away.

She had goaded him to share with her all the things that had been torturing him. He'd shared all right, but his sharing had swelled from a desire so strong as to burn through a man's soul. She had shared with him too—the taste of longing and forever on her soft lips held a fire to match his own. The woman who had trembled at the thought of sharing his bed on their wedding day had vanished in the searing demands they had ignited within each other. Still, he was not truly satisfied.

What would become of them when the passion burned out? When the Siannon who had always looked at him with anticipation and trust, the Siannon who had met and matched his lust and then elicited still more, came face-to-face with the man she had really married. When she saw him at last, not as a boyhood hero or her current savior, but as he truly was. How quickly would those flames of desire be extinguished and the light in her eyes dim. He did not want to think about that.

"Enough." He scrubbed a hand over his face. Allowing his thoughts to drift in this direction would surely drive him mad, if he weren't halfway there already. Hungering after Siannon was even more counterproductive than endlessly contemplating the problems he faced in the shipyard. It mattered very little that her pale skin was softer than freshwater, warm and sweet. That making love to her completed something inside him that he didn't want to face. There were enough questions and uncertainties between them to guarantee a lifetime of conflict, a lifetime of reasons to direct his attention elsewhere.

The office door slammed open without preamble, putting paid to Quin's questions for the moment as Declan strode in, his shoulders squared beneath some invisible weight. The ex-seaman's brows were drawn together in a single line, and even his one empty sleeve seemed to snap with tension.

Alarm jolted through Quin.

"What is it?" He gripped his hands into fists, anticipating some report about the barque in the yard. "More delays? Trouble with supplies?"

"None of that, Quin." Declan shook his head. "It's your son."

Son? What was he talking about? The word made no sense for the measure of several heartbeats.

"What?" Everything Quin had been trying to wrap

his mind around for the last hour contorted as he leveled his gaze on Declan.

"Nora Doyle sent word. They've gone to look for your lad."

"My son?" Quin repeated stupidly, and then slowly it dawned on him. "Siannon's son." *Timothy*—with his hand clamped on his cap and his back braced against Quin's leg as he watched the shipyard activities while they sailed home to Beannacht.

Siannon's son. His now. He could have kicked himself for the condemnation spreading like a shadow over Declan's face. "He's missing?"

"Aye." Declan's nod was short. His gaze glimmered censure that weighed Quintin Reilly as a parent and found him lacking. Guilt pierced Quin's gut and wrenched deep, tearing open old wounds.

In a flash, all the intervening years disappeared and he was again the young man he had been the day of his brothers' sailing mishap, so concerned with his own life he'd put no thought into the effect on anyone else. Declan had been there at the office when Devin and Bryan had turned up missing, and Quin's new skiff as well. James Reilly's anger and Quin's misgivings returned afresh, roaring in on a tidal wave of guilt and recrimination. Memory writhed and he was again in the empty rooms Marie had abandoned.

He struggled to shake the darkness off and keep his attention on the present. "How long?"

Declan shrugged, his lips pressed in a hard line. "She wasn't sure, an hour or two, maybe more. There's no real way of knowing. He'd gone to Ross McGee's for puppies and then disappeared after that. And they've been scouring the village for him for a while."

Timothy was unfamiliar with the island. And whose

fault was that? Fresh guilt churned. Quin could lay the blame only at this own feet. He'd made no effort with the boy once they'd landed safely on Beannacht. His own concerns had claimed his attention. He'd taken no time to make certain the lad felt at home or knew the lay of the land. His own concerns—his thoughts snagged on the certainty that once again another would pay the price for his inattention.

"What of his mother?" Siannon must be beside herself. "Where is she now?"

"All the women are searching for the lad. The village and the hills. Tiomoid and his lads are set to search the harbor area. The old man would let no other take that grim task."

Oh, God, suppose the boy had drowned. That possibility had not occurred to Quin. That possibility could not have occurred. He did not even know if the boy could swim.

"What of Dan—"

"Dan Kelly Sr. swears there've been only a few sails sighted this day, and none have turned our way. He's certain Rhodes is not behind this," Declan answered before Quin could voice Siannon's worst fear.

"Did they check with Ross?" Even as this question left his lips, he knew the answer.

"Aye, but you know how he is."

"Aye." Quin shook his head, feeling the tension inside him wind tighter and tighter. Though gentle-hearted, old Ross McGee had always been a bit vague. As he got older, the problem had increased by several degrees. He might remember the visit, but he would have no idea where a small boy and a puppy would have gone off to.

"Who went to look for him?" Declan had already told him who, but he needed to hear it again.

"The women, all of them. My Mary and your Siannon and the rest of them who have been congregating at Maeve Kelly's."

"How long ago did you learn of this?"

"Only moments ago, Quin." Declan hesitated for a fraction of a second. "Nora sent her son James to tell us when young Timmy did not turn up readily to hand."

Nora Doyle sent word. What Declan was telling him sunk in finally as he repeated it a second time. Knowing Siannon had not sent for him sawed against Quin's soul. History repeated itself. Wasn't that what Devin said he learned from his professors? Wasn't that the truth behind all of Granny's tales? Here he was, continuing to repeat his own errors. Mistakes he had made with Marie he now made with Siannon, for she had not called on him for help. Pain twisted deep inside him, and he shoved such thoughts away. Dwelling on his misdeeds was a luxury he didn't have time for now. Later, after Timmy had been found, he would ascertain what had kept his wife from coming to him. And he would endeavor to fix whatever he could. If he could.

"What did you say about Siannon and Mary?" he asked.

"They're together, Quin."

"Aye." He shoved his guilt and misgivings aside. "What direction?"

"Up into the hills behind Ross's cottage. That's the last anyone saw of him."

A fresh shudder tore through Quin. *The last.* The words had far too final a ring to them. Less than a month into this debacle, and he was already a failure as a father. That would have to change. He couldn't sacrifice his family to save the shipyard.

With a shock he recognized the direction of his own thoughts as he reached for his jacket. Siannon and Timothy were indeed his family, not merely his responsibility. His wife. His son. His family. Just as any Reilly, and just as important. The idea streaked through him straight to his core. When had that happened? His wife and son. And he had let them both down. Blame and guilt raced through him, slamming him like fisted blows.

"You're following them?" Declan read him with the ease of long friendship.

"Aye." Quin nodded.

"I thought as much. I'm going with you."

Declan's declaration didn't surprise Quin.

"Who else can we spare?"

The foreman angled a single brow and then braced a hand on Quin's shoulder. "We can spare them all, Quin. There's none who wouldn't help. You've only to ask."

"Aye. So be it." Quin nodded. Asking for favors was not his strong suit. But that didn't matter at the moment. All that mattered was finding Timmy and preventing further disaster.

Declan disappeared back through the open doorway. Quin followed almost on his heels. In moments they had a crowd of shipwrights assembled. Almost all had grown up on this island just as he had. Tools still clutched in their fists, they thronged forward to meet the need. His men, his crew, just as if they ran the waves and chartered the sea instead of building the ships to go there. Pride tightened Quin's throat for a moment and then loosened his tongue.

"My son, Timothy, is lost in the hills. I've not shown him where he should and should not go." His throat clogged over the admission, and he cleared it. "I'll need the help of every man here to find him."

"Aye." The chorus of agreements came almost before he had finished speaking. Tools clattered into a pile, freely abandoned to search for one missing boy.

"Let's to it, then, lads. Time's awastin'." Declan motioned as clouds gathered overhead and momentarily darkened the earnest expressions on the faces before him. Each man knew the island weather well. There was no need to explain the deepened concern brought by the brewing storm.

As one they headed out of the shipyard and across the village toward Beannacht's hills. Quin watched the clouds swelling dark and heavy above them. So very familiar. Was it only the similarity to the weather and the time of day that tightened the unease edging through him?

Worry sharpened Quin's thoughts as memories rolled in dark and heavy like the clouds and just as unstoppable. Siannon's young face, pinched with fear. Her grandmother's certainty that they needed to act. He could almost feel the heavy pelting of cold rain and see the swells slashing the shipyard docks with dark and heavy seas. If they had not gone when they did, if the search had not been so all-consuming and urgent, Devin and Bryan might both have died. And he would have been at fault for taking such pride in his ship and the assurance it had given so that he had not wanted to face his brother's pain.

He struggled to push the memories away. A storm might be brewing, but that did not equate Timmy's situation with the accident from so long ago that had torn a rift in his family. Timothy Crofton was a young boy off playing with a dog somewhere, far from the mercurial moods of the sea.

They would find him. They had to.

Cold wind, moist and heavy with the storm to come, brushed the deep grasses and whipped up over the rise. In the distance he could hear the cries of the women as they called for Timmy. The echoing calls coiled the fears within him instead of shoring up his certainty.

"*Diabhal*. The storm will hit before we catch him up."

"We'll find him, Quin." Declan's reply came without hesitation.

"Aye." But he could not quell the doubts lurking deep inside him or erase the fears of another search, another storm, and boys who nearly died. His brothers. The emptiness that had torn through him when Bryan left to pursue law ripped fresh currents of guilt and added speed to his steps.

His lips tightened and he shook his head. There was no time for that now. Heaven knew he'd long ago come to terms with the decisions his father had made. And the empty rooms he'd returned to after Marie's death.

Under Declan's direction the men fanned out over the valley and advanced as the first fat drops of rain fell. Crisp and full, the rain spat at them for almost an hour as he and Declan worked their way upward. They passed Grania Keane and Maeve Kelly, who only shook their heads while worry set their lips into solemn lines and clogged their eyes. Water dripped from the shawls they had clutched over their heads. "You'd best head back," Quin insisted after they outlined where they'd already searched. Both shook their heads and set off along fresh paths.

Finally Quin and Declan caught up with Siannon and Mary.

"Quin?" The surprise on Siannon's rain-spattered face underscored the fact that she had not sent for him.

"Aye." He nodded. "Any sign?"

"Thank heaven you are here; the rain has made things so much slower." Mary greeted her husband with a hug. Declan dropped a kiss to his wife's dark head. "How did you know?"

"Nora Doyle sent word, although I think some time had passed before James made his way to us. All the crew are out here as well." Quin kept his gaze fixed on Siannon while he answered her cousin.

Siannon's gaze did not leave Quin's. Pain lurked there, along with worry. Rain ran in rivulets down her cheeks and hair, but she held silent. He remembered her insistence, her persistence in pushing Michael and himself to go and search for Devin and Bryan in the direction exactly opposite the one all the other vessels had struck off in. She'd known right where they were and how desperate and precarious their state. Did she feel anything now? Would she tell him if she did?

Quin's gut twisted again. She had not sent for him because she didn't think he would care enough to come. Just as Marie had not. And ultimately the fault for those assumptions lay with him and his own inability to give them what they needed.

"We'll find the lad, Siannon." Declan favored her with a reassuring smile. "Most of us were boys who played in these hills in our days. No one could hide any lad well enough to escape the lot of us."

"Where is he, Siannon? Do you know?" Quin couldn't stop the questions as he stepped forward and gripped her frozen fingers in his.

She glanced at him sharply, her lips parted in surprise, her eyes dark and unreadable. For the span of several heartbeats her gaze skimmed his face and then she shook her head.

"I told you before I cannot sense close members of my family." Her answer came low and husky. "I only wish I could."

Only strong basic emotions. The rest of her earlier declaration echoed unspoken.

"Quin." She breathed his name—part cry, part question. "My father—"

"No." His turn to be emphatic. The penalty for his failures could not be that large. "I've had men watching every day, Siannon. No one has come to Beannacht for our son."

Thunder slammed almost overhead, threatening to shake the earth beneath their feet as stark lightning pierced the sky and the storm began in earnest. The fat raindrops thinned and came at a faster pace. If the storm held true, those drops would soon become shooting darts of cold. Surely Timmy would know enough to get out of the rain?

But where could he go?

"Damnation." Quin couldn't hold the curse back. Siannon's gaze locked with his through the rain. "We won't have much luck finding him if the storm unloads full blast."

"We cannot stop now." She shook her head, and a slender lock of red clung to her wet cheek. "He's got to be close by. He's so little. How far could he walk?"

A boy and a puppy? Playing? Lost? Quin hadn't the heart to answer her. Perhaps the pair sheltered even now under a tree or within the ruins of ancient stone circles or dolmans scattered nearby. He fanned that hope.

"I'll keep looking. You go back to the house." He guided her toward Declan and Mary. "Declan will take you—"

"No." Siannon gripped his arms.

He looked into her eyes, gray and dark and as stormy as the heavens above them. He could read every bit of love and fear she held for Timmy plain for all the world to see.

"He's my son, Quin. I've got to find him."

Her words tightened some invisible bond inside him, one he had been trying so very hard to ignore.

"He's mine, too," he told her, the echoes rippling inside him. "We'll find him together." She nodded, then shivered , the rain and worry taking their toll. He pulled off his jacket and put it around her shoulders.

Thunder rumbled again overhead, followed by an echo sharp and high, almost like a bark. Siannon gasped.

"Quin, did ye hear that?" Declan urged.

"Aye." Quin waved for silence. Off in the distance a small, enthusiastic yip echoed against the hillside.

"Come on." He grabbed Siannnon's arm and hurried them across the meadow, slipping and sliding through the wet grass. She did not protest, keeping his pace without question.

They rounded a bend, and there in a small out-cropping of rocks sat Timothy Michael Rhodes Crofton, clutching a squirmy, wet bundle of white and black fur.

Relief sluiced through Quin, tinged with the kind of annoyance he used to be on the receiving end of when he was a child. A smile tugged at his lips.

"Hullo, Mama. Hullo, Captain Reilly." The lad beamed down at them both as though he'd been expecting them all along. "I told you they'd be here soon, Lucy."

"Timmy." All of Siannon's fears and hopes shivered out of her along with his name. Quin squeezed her hand and released her. She rushed to the rocks, reaching her arms toward her son. His jacket dropped from her into the muck, and he couldn't have cared less.

"Quin?" Declan shouted from behind them. "You've found him, then? Mary says we're to let Father Dunnavan know and he'll ring the church bell so everyone can come in."

"Aye, call off the search and get back to the yard, Declan. Our wanderer is found. We left all the tools out in the rain." Quin felt only relief and profound joy as he watched Siannon scoop their son into her embrace and hold him tight. "Then send everyone home to their families."

"Will do." Declan's tone was laced with a satisfied I-told-you-so, but Quin ignored it as he watched Siannon. She loved Timothy with everything in her. He could see the emotion fairly streaming out of her, almost a glow of sunlight amid the rain-soaked shadows. Yet she didn't smother the boy, as she obviously longed to do.

He couldn't help wondering what it would feel like to be the recipient of that kind of affection from Siannon Rhodes Crofton Reilly. A pang shot through him, bittersweet and inescapable as the thought twined through him. Disquieting to say the least.

"Declan?" he called again.

"Aye." His answer echoed from far away.

"Make sure Tiomoid McManus knows his granddaughter and great-grandson are safe with me."

"Aye."

Needle-sharp shards of rain started as the last sounds from the impromptu troupe of searchers trailed away in the distance. They had lingered long enough.

"Siannon." His call drew her bright gaze. "We cannot stay here."

"Aye." She stood and put a protective arm around Timmy, ready for anything Quin proposed now that her son had been restored to her. Still, he noticed that she shivered in the rain, and her face seemed overly pale in some parts, too flushed in others.

"It's been a long time, but if I'm right, Granny's cottage is not too far over the next rise. I think we can make a run for it." He locked gazes with Timmy. "Are you game for it, boy-o? We've got to get your mother out of this weather."

"Aye-aye, Captain, I'm ready when you are." Timmy saluted awkwardly around the bundle of wet black and white that was still struggling to lick his face. "And Lucy too."

"Aye, and Lucy too." Quin hid a smile. "Let's go, then."

He spread his arms and gestured to both of them without thinking. They came toward him immedi-

ately. The sight loosed something strange and powerful in his chest that welled out like an invisible force
to encompass them and yet tightened his very core.
His family—wet and bedraggled and be-dogged, but
his just the same.

Now was not the time for maudlin musings and
confusion. He'd very likely lose both of them if they
took a chill from being out in a storm. When they
reached him, he swung Timmy up in one arm, tucked
Siannon's hand into his, and headed for Granny's.

Chapter Twelve

There. He saw it before he spoke.

"Just up ahead." He quickened his pace.

Through the deepening gloom and spitting rain Quin finally made out a familiar shape. Down in a small valley with rich green grass and the smell of dark earth everywhere lay the home Granny had shared with her husband long ago. Smoky purple shadows etched the jagged remnants of a nearby druid circle and draped the mountainous cradle surrounding the dark gray stones that had once housed so many hopes and dreams as they raised their family here.

"We're almost there, Siannon." He squeezed her hand and led her toward their sanctuary as the very heavens seemed to crack open up over their heads. "I'll have you both safe and dry in no time."

Timmy's fingers gripped Quin's neck all the tighter

as he hurried them forward. "Who lives here, Captain Reilly?"

"No one, lad. Not now at least," he answered as they reached the outlying overhang of the thatched roof.

"Are you sure there is nobody home?" Timmy asked Quin.

Quin stifled the chuckle that rose in his chest and shook his head to fling back the hair that dripped in his eyes. "Nay, boy-o. There's been no one home here in a very long time, although I've often felt like my granny waited for us all here."

"Your granny? Here?" Timmy shimmied out of Quin's arms, still clutching the puppy. "Oh, so that is who she is."

Before Quin could hazard a guess what the boy meant, Timmy scampered around the corner to explore with his puppy nipping at his heels. "Don't wander far, son," he cautioned.

Siannon's gasp drew Quin's attention.

"What is it, Siannon?"

"Oh, Quin." She turned toward him, a strange look lighting her eyes. "What a wonderful place this still is."

That strange tightening and twisting sensation passed through his chest again as he watched Siannon close her eyes and tilt her head back ever so slightly. He could almost see her opening herself to whatever might yet linger near Granny's small abode. For a moment he envied her the ability. There were times when he'd have traded his soul to see his grandmother again, to feel her calm reassurance and gain strength from her resolute faith. To seek her guidance.

When Siannon opened her eyes and focused on him again, her gaze was like a physical touch. He shuddered beneath it, struck dumb by the contact.

"She loved you very much." Siannon's voice came musical and soft, as though carried over a long distance.

"Aye. I know that." The pang of homesickness for all he had lost so long ago welled, and he barely got the words out though the stricture that used to be his throat. "How did you—"

"It's here, Quin. She is here. All her feelings and emotions. Clear as sunlight and warm as a hearth fire at the end of the day. I remember her and how she felt about her family. Your granny was a remarkable woman."

All he could do was nod his agreement. He looked around the humble cottage with its stone walls and packed floors. The furniture was simple but glowed with years of care polished into it.

A fresh crack of thunder and flash of lightning caused the puppy to yelp nearby. Siannon shivered. "Shall we go inside?"

Again he simply nodded, as though he had completely lost his capacity for speech. If only his shipboard crew could see him now, at a complete loss for words. In his haste to get her to shelter, he'd left his jacket lying where she'd dropped it when they found Timmy. And now he kept her hovering outside the shelter he'd promised her.

Siannon smiled and preceded him to the doorway. The old oak portal, still stalwart though weathered by time, held shut as she pushed at it.

"Is it barred?" she asked over her shoulder as she continued pushing.

"Probably just stubborn." He leaned his shoulder into the door to help her.

"Like the rest of you Reillys," she tossed at him with a unrepentant gleam in her eye.

"Aye." He grunted and shoved harder, punctuating his momentum as he spoke. "But let us not forget, my lass, you are a Reilly too."

The door gave on his last word, spilling them both into the darkened interior. Siannon gasped as they pitched forward into nothingness. Years on rolling decks enabled Quin to brace himself and catch her to him, pulling them both to an abrupt halt. Shadows filled the room that still smelled of ginger and herbs and echoed with the mingled sounds of Granny's old tales and Siannon's breathing.

Holding her enveloped him in the scent of lavender and lilac and Siannon. With his wife pressed against him and the rhythmic sound of the rain soaking the earth outside, all he wanted to do was press her closer still and cover her parted lips with his own. To drink from her all she had to give.

"Quin—"

"There you are." Timmy's voice sounded from farther inside the cottage. "I came around the back." Quin could just about make out the lad's small figure as he gestured toward the dim outline of another doorway.

As much as Quin wished to continue holding Siannon, he no longer had an excuse to do so. He released her and turned toward her son.

"Indeed?"

"You are a very resourceful young man." Siannon praised him. "And where is the puppy?"

"She's off smelling in one of the corners."

"Smelling?" Quin raised a dubious eyebrow.

"Sniffing," Siannon told him in a soft tone.

"Ah." Quin looked around. It had been years since his last visit—too many years at sea, too much turmoil to feel worthy of this sanctuary. Everything was just as Granny had left it the day her son James had come to escort her to the new house he'd built overlooking the harbor. She'd never been back, but Quin's mother had kept her promise and seen to it that the cottage was kept at the ready against the day her mother-in-law might choose to return to living under her own roof. She never had, but the promise had been made and kept, satisfying both women.

Timmy chased after the puppy, who was busy sniffing at the legs of the chairs and benches in the homey kitchen and beyond to the area by the large hearth in the center of the house. His granny's parlor. The first cottage on the island to boast one—he remembered the pride in her voice when she described the room.

Pride. And what would you think of the mess I've made of things, Granny? What indeed. If only he knew.

A long-ago echo seemed to whisk by on the breeze from the door as Siannon moved to shut it. *"The knowing is one thing, the doin' another part."*

"Too true, Granny," he chuckled. "Right now I do know I've more to do than brood."

He turned his attention to the boy. "Timothy, lad, we'd best light some candles and get a fire started. Have you ever started a fire?"

"No." Timothy's eyes grew wide.

"Quin—" Maternal caution sharpened the edges of Siannon's voice. He'd heard his own mother use that same voice many times when she feared his father was giving his sons more leeway than he should.

"It'll be all right, Siannon."

She sighed behind him but let them be. "I'll look for candles," she volunteered as she walked over to the cupboard.

Quin knelt by Granny's hearth, remembering all the times he and his brothers had spent there. How they'd all loved trekking off into the hills to spend a few days away from the bustling shipyard, steeped in Granny's magical tales. He adjusted the kindling and logs that stood to the ready and found the flint where he remembered it should be.

It had been an unspoken pact with his brothers for years that they would always keep Granny's hearth stocked. He couldn't remember when he'd been here last and who would have been the last to lay the kindling, but he was glad it was there.

"When I was your age, it was my own da who taught me how to light a hearth fire, right here in this very cottage."

"Oh." Timmy's eyes widened still further, as though he could not imagine Quin ever being his age.

He handed the flint to young Timothy. "Strike this way, lad, and hold it close to the kindling."

Timmy bit his lip with concentration and mimicked Quin's example. Once. Twice. On the third, a small spark shot out and licked at the kindling. The lad held his ground without shrinking, though from the working over his lip was receiving, Quin had to wonder what it cost him.

"Well done."

"Aye, Captain Reilly." Timmy smiled up at him.

If they were truly to be a family, it had better start now. He stayed crouched by the hearth as the flames licked the kindling and looked his son in the eye. "I've a matter or two to discuss with you. But first, you needn't address me quite so formally."

"How should I address you, Captain?" Timmy's gray eyes took on a speculative gleam very much like his mother's.

Quin heard the rustle of Siannon's skirts as she stepped closer but held her peace. "What do you think might be appropriate?

"You are my father now, are you not? At least since my papa has gone to his reward?" Timmy wore a thoughtful look.

"Aye," Quin agreed.

"If I were to call you Quin, and you and Mama have a baby like Davey, he be might confused as to what to call you, wouldn't he?"

"True." Quin nodded, intrigued to watch the unfolding of so much logic in one so young.

"Then, with your permission"—Timmy looked up at his mother—"and with yours, Mama—"

Quin turned in time to see her nod before Timmy finished. "Then I'd like to call you Da. I'd like to have a da like Kevan and Seamus. And you and my new uncles."

The rush of warmth that spread through Quin surprised him with its depth. "I'd like that too, Timmy. I'd like to be your da, and I can do that without taking anything away from your papa."

Siannon's hand on his shoulder and Timmy's smile showed they were all in perfect accord on this matter. Now for the more difficult ones.

"Have a seat in the rocker and warm yourself, Siannon. We'll light the candles in a bit and look for something to eat too. You're both soaked through, but I wish to set a few things straight."

With a speculative look so close to her son's, their son's, he nearly laughed. She drew the well-worn rocker, twin to Granny's one at home, closer to the fire's glow as the rain intensified again outside. But she continued to hold her peace.

"What led you out into the hills today?" Quin asked.

"Lucy," Timmy replied as though that answered any questions Quin might have.

"Aye. I got that part, laddie. But did you tell anyone where you were going?"

"Well . . . " Timmy looked from the fire beginning now in earnest toward the hearthstones. "Not really."

"Not really?"

"No, sir. I didn't."

"Then I've some things to tell you, boy-o, and I need you to listen well."

Timmy nodded and Siannon leaned forward in the rocker, the light of the flames dancing over her face.

"The first is a tale of three boys—"

"You and my uncles," Timmy piped up.

"Don't interrupt the captain . . . your da," Siannon reminded the boy, but her smile was aimed at the man.

"Yes, it was me and your . . . uncles, Bryan and Devin, playing Viking raiders."

"Me and Kevan and Seamus play that game some—" Timmy caught himself. "Sorry."

"Your uncles and I were playing, and Devin, who was not much bigger than you that summer, got bored and decided to go off on his own. He got all turned around and lost and couldn't find us or the way home."

Timmy's eyes were round as he listened, and he settled Lucy into his lap, scratching her ears so she'd lie still.

"We looked for him for hours—circling through the grass and hills—afraid we'd never find him, afraid to head for home without him. Bryan and I thought for sure something terrible had happened to him."

Timmy nodded and looked at his mother as the import of the story began to sink in.

"Now, you were a wee bit smarter than him, smart enough to stop and wait in a likely spot where we could find you."

"I was never so glad to see anyone as I was to see you," Siannon said.

"Even though I worried you and had everyone out looking?" Wonder filled Timmy's voice. Siannon nodded.

"You must learn from this and not let it happen again," Quin cautioned. "Bryan and I knew about where to look, in that we were lucky. In the next tale I have to share, I was not so fortunate. It was only through your mother's help I ever found my brothers."

He recounted to Timmy the day his father had announced that Bryan was to clerk at Gill O'Brien's law firm in Limerick instead of following his ambitions to captain his own Reilly vessel, an ambition Quin shared. He explained how Bryan's disappointment and anger had driven him to take the skiff in order to prove he was the better sailor. How he and Devin had set out without a word, and even when the storm blew in and the alarm was raised, the searchers had all cast off in the wrong direction—all save Quin and Michael McManus, who had heeded a frantic girl's pleading and headed to the spot she directed.

"So my mama helped you find your brothers?"

"Aye. But you see, lad, if Devin and Bryan had told someone where they were going, it would not have been left to your mother to help us find them. And they would not have nearly drowned in the process."

"But sometimes a man has to think on his own."

"Aye, lad. That's true, but a man is responsible to more than just himself. If he has a family, then that responsibility stretches to cover them as well."

"Aye, sir." Timmy offered another of his off-balance salutes as the puppy settled onto his knee for a nap.

Quin straightened and turned to find Siannon's gaze on him, dark and glittering in the uncertain light filtering through the cottage. She stood up from the rocker and went to the nearest window, drawing the shutter farther open to the damp greenery beyond.

"Are you all right, Siannon?" He followed her to the window.

"Aye." She didn't look at him. There was silence for a moment, broken only by Timothy's soft conversation to the dog and the splattering of the rain outside. "Is that why you asked me if I knew where Timothy was?"

"Aye."

She blew out a long breath to mingle with the dampness in the air. "Quin, I cannot feel anything . . . reliable where people I love are concerned. I used to try, when Timmy was a baby, to sense him before he woke up at night. Then I would have been able to get to him before the nurse could. When he was really little I tried to understand what he needed when he cried. It never worked. My own emotions got in the way. All I ended up with was a terrible headache."

She offered him a lopsided smile and then turned her gaze away from him again. "I would have given anything to be able to sense Timmy while we were out there looking. I was so afraid. All I ever get from the people close to me are the strongest emotions, the most basic. It is not something I can turn on and off at will. It is not something I can count on."

Strong, basic emotions. Just as she had told him previously. The memory of all that had passed between them the night before returned to hover in the air around them.

"With me?" The question came from deep inside. Lord knew he hadn't intended to voice it, and yet there it was, bald and unrefined.

She smiled again but didn't look at him. "I've known you for most of my life, Quintin Reilly. Most of the time I cannot read you at all. When we were children it was different."

"How so?"

"Children are more open to things. Their feelings are more fluid and flowing. I could read you then. You and Bryan and Devin, but you were the strongest, and so I concentrated on you." Her tone grew husky with the admission, and he wondered what she was thinking.

"Now?"

She turned her gaze back to his. "I cannot read you now."

"Not even strong basic emotions?"

She closed her eyes and a tremor racked her. She rubbed her arms. "How long do you think the rain will last?"

Diabhal. She was wet and cold and he was interrogating her like Bryan would one of his clients. "There's no way of knowing. Let's get you and Timmy warm."

He took her arm in his and tried to ignore the sweet frisson of desire that sizzled through him as he touched her and urged her toward the hearth. He may have settled some things with Timmy, but there was much still to be resolved between Siannon and him.

"I'm all right," she told him.

"Siannon Reilly, you are far more stubborn than I remember. And you get more so every day." He uttered the last under his breath as he crossed the confines of the cottage, passing Timmy and Lucy, who lay curled before the hearth together, fast asleep.

Quin rummaged through one of Granny's old chests before pulling out a couple of thick old quilts. They smelled of herbs and lavender and home. Dropping one over Timmy's shoulders, he carried the other back to Siannon and draped it around her, sliding his fingers along the wet skin at the back of her neck to free the long, damp length of her hair.

"Thank you," she whispered, her gaze fixed on the mesmerizing play of rain on the leaves and grass outside.

"Aye." He turned back to check on the fire.

"Quin?" His name came laced with determination.

"Aye?" Something in her tone slowed his steps.

"I can almost always feel strong basic emotions."

Her words froze him in place and thundered unexpectedly inside him. He could feel her gaze against the back of his skull, waiting for him to turn back to her. And all he could think about were the wild black things that had roared through him the night before. All the raw guilt he hadn't been able to hold back from the deep, unspeakable places within his soul.

All pouring forth for her to absorb and decipher for herself.

Siannon could feel his hesitation as a palpable force. Her heartbeat thumped in her ears as he stood motionless. Now that she had spoken, she wished the words back. Surely goading him with her abilities was not a good thing. But too much, too many unspoken, things lay between them, and they would never have a future together if they did not begin to address them.

He moved toward the hearth and the two innocents now curled asleep on the rug before it for warmth. He knelt and stirred the fire, his motions slow and deliberate as her nerves stretched to the breaking point, waiting for his reaction to the knowledge she had thrown so blatantly between them.

The fire hissed and crackled, consuming the fuel he provided just as the silence threatened to swallow up whatever reserves of energy and courage Siannon had managed to dredge in order to reveal such a bald truth. He coaxed the flames higher and turned back to face her.

"What do you feel from me now, Siannon?"

There. The question he had every right to ask— one she had been asked many times in the past by people who discovered her secret. She released the breath she hadn't realized she was holding as the tempo of her heart quickened. The rain continued its steady rhythm through the ever-darkening air as she searched for the words to explain.

"Most of the time you are like a solid stone wall. There is nothing that comes through, even when I try." A nervous laugh escaped her as she twisted her hands together and pulled the blanket closer around her shoulders.

"Try?"

"Aye. What I feel from people can be a flowing river, a current that could easily sweep me up and carry me away. But over time I have learned to close the floodgates, to keep myself as protected as possible from the things I cannot control and that other people don't really wish me to know. But I can also push it, just a little. It hurts when I do, like when I used to try so hard when Timmy was a baby."

"And am I one more ripple in the river?" He sounded as if that would be a relief.

"No, Quin." She caught back a sigh. *More like a distant ocean I cannot reach.* "As I told you, most of the time I get nothing from you except a distinct and stubborn mantle of pride."

He laughed shortly, as though she had touched a nerve. "Most of the time."

Not a question, just a repetition of her own words, and yet she could feel the inquiry hovering behind them.

She bit her lip and then forced herself to continue. "But there are times when more comes through."

Thunder rumbled, and a distant shard of lightning split the inky sky outside.

"Siannon—"

"Let me finish." She cut off the warning in his tone. If he told her to stop now, if he was determined to keep hidden the mysteries between them, she might never get them out into the open. And she could not live with that. With the questions and the wondering. With half a marriage. She'd protected herself for too long already.

"I have felt pride and fear and guilt from you. Along with something dark and painful lurking deep inside your heart. Some of it has to do with Devin and Bryan and the choices your father made. I understood that part. But the other, the dark thing in your soul, that part I do not understand. There was a woman who was a part of your life. . . . You made choices you have bitterly regretted. And somehow it all has to do with me. It comes back to me and why you will not let me be truly your wife."

"No—" There was anguish in the gaze she could barely discern in the shadows. Anguish and the light of truth glittering in the gloom.

"Aye." She held up a hand to halt his protest as her throat clogged. "I have felt her, Quin. Last night when you . . . made love to me. I could feel her, feel your grief and recriminations as they tore at you. As they tore at me."

A harsh bark of laughter came from him, but it was edged with pain. "Is that what I did to you last night, Siannon?"

A question she sensed he truly did not want her to answer.

"Somehow I doubt that love had anything to do with what went on between us last night."

That statement, so bold and open, spliced pain through her heart and skewered her hopes. His honesty was what she had silently asked for when she'd pressed this matter. She shuddered and closed her eyes, remembering the feel of him inside her and the dark, unspeakable emotions rippling within him.

"Who is Marie, Quin?" The question flowed out of her on a low groan as tears pricked her eyes.

He sucked in a breath. "Marie?" Wariness emanated from him like a shield. She could feel him stiffening, bracing himself for the pain they both knew would come with the telling.

She pushed it aside. "Aye. Tell me about her."

"No." Raw misery husked his voice.

"Aye."

"What is in my past is in my past. It has nothing to do with you." Protective walls rose between them. "Do not ask questions about things you'd just as soon not know, Siannon."

Who was he attempting to shield more, himself or her?

"Your past has everything to do with me. As does your present and your future. I am your wife, Quin. And I—" She stopped, struck by something that had come through as clearly as if he had spoken the words aloud.

"Oh, Quin." She stepped toward him as her heart lurched.

"No." He shook his head.

"She was your wife too." A painful emptiness gripped her, though her own or Quin's she couldn't say. Perhaps it was both. "Your first wife."

Lightning and thunder crackled and sizzled together above the thatched roof of Granny Reilly's cottage, but all Siannon could focus on was the stark aspect of grief on Quin's face. Grief and punishing guilt.

"Aye, she was my wife. For a short time. Too short."

He scrubbed a hand over his face but did not change his expression. "I married her a long time ago. A lifetime ago. She was the daughter of a friend in the Maritimes. Pretty, fragile, alone—she needed me. And I needed to take care of her. I promised that I would."

Images flowed along with the emotions that surged from him. Siannon steadied herself against the windowsill, clinging to the damp stones and the cold feel of the rain against her fingers as she absorbed from him what he needed to tell her.

"But I was a ship's captain and she could not go with me when I went to sea. She didn't like that, wanted me to stay ashore. To find another way to make my living."

He shook his head. His voice was flat and distant. "But I am Reilly born and Reilly bred. Bryan lost his dreams because of me. There was more than just my responsibility to my wife riding my shoulders. I could not give that up for her, for anyone."

He sighed. "I believed she would adjust. Other captains have wives and Halifax was a port city. In my arrogance I believed eventually she would understand. She was so young. So much younger than I realized."

Tears dripped over Siannon's cheeks as he continued.

"She tried to tell me"—Quin's words thickened— "that she couldn't be left alone for so long. But I didn't listen. She was pregnant when I left for Boston the last time. I thought maybe that would help. A baby. She would have someone else to care about, to think about."

Waves of invisible pain radiated from him, filling

the cottage, filling Siannon's soul as she wept for him.
For his lost wife and child. Longing to hold him to
her and heal the awful void inside him choked her,
but that wasn't what he wanted. Not now. He needed
to tell her all of it.

He continued to stare outward, past and through
her as the rest of the tale poured out of him. "She
killed herself while I was away that last time. Threw
herself from the rocks at Mauntauk, shattering herself
and our unborn child in the sea."

"Oh, Quin." Siannon's breath lurched out of her.

His gaze caught hers. Telltale moisture sparkled
there, marked by events he could never change. "Her
family has never forgiven me. I have never forgiven
myself. I vowed then I would never marry again. I
would never be responsible for anyone else's happiness. All I've done all through my life is let people
down. I am a prime example of a cursed Reilly."

"No, Quin—"

"It's the truth, Siannon. I have never been there
for anyone when they truly needed me." He shook
his head, self-loathing lacing his tone as he vented
all the latent, unreachable pain from the dark void
inside himself. She let him pour it all out.

"I failed Bryan when I was the one chosen to stay
with the shipyard." He paced away from her as though
the feelings gushing from him would not let him rest.
"He was sent off to study the law, and all I felt was
relief. I turned my back on Devin when he wanted
to help with the problems that are going on right
now. He was here ahead of me and doing a fine job
at it. I sent him back to school as if he were still a
lad in short pants."

He stopped to face her again. "Both of them were

so offended by our father's decision and my smug acceptance of it, they nearly killed themselves in an effort to be accepted as every bit the Reilly seaman I am. And when Marie needed me the most, I was not there."

Silence held as his words echoed around them. *I have never been there for anyone when they truly needed me.*

"You are here now, Quin. In this cottage, with us, because we needed you."

"Nay, *mo ceile,* I failed you too."

"But—"

"If I had allowed you to trust me, you would not have raced off to look for our son without me. You could have seen him just as much my responsibility as yours. But you did not. You could not. I cannot blame you for that. I am not the kind of man you should have married, Siannon. Not the man you thought I'd grow up to be. You deserve better. Had I the choice to make over again, I would find another way to help you."

His words tore into her, scraping against her heart. Pain tightened her throat and sparked fresh tears in her eyes. How easily he hurt her, even when that was not his intent. She swallowed hard and forced the tears away. There had been no revelation here. It should not ache so much to hear him say aloud what she knew he had been thinking all along.

"You cannot change the past, Quin."

"A concept I am more than familiar with, I assure you." Already the barriers were going up again. She could feel them as surely as if they were made of stone and mortar. He regretted all that he had just told her as he buried his yearning for acceptance and understanding. Later he would flail himself for not just brushing off her questions and keeping his past to himself.

She could not let him hide behind the walls of his regrets again, not after tearing them down. She would not let him protect her by keeping her at a distance. Even if getting closer, growing together meant sharing pain. They would never truly have a marriage, a shared life, if they stayed at safe distances from each other. Gran always said it was the women who did more of the bending because they are the ones built to carry the pain. Perhaps it was time to rend away her own barriers and risk her heart completely.

She stepped toward him and dropped the protective coverlet to the floor. "I would not take back anything that has passed between us."

"Siannon—"

She reached out a hand and stopped him from turning away. "Nothing. You have been here for me. You saved my son for me. You offered protection without question or hesitation and asked for very little in return. You did come to find our son today as soon as you heard and despite my mistake in not alerting you myself."

He stared at her hard, obviously struggling to come to terms with all that she was pouring out to him. "You are my husband, Quin. You are my friend. You are my lover. We have both made mistakes. Nothing in life is perfect, and often it is not pretty.

"We must take the good things we can, grasp them with both hands, and hang on for dear life." She took another step, closing the distance between them as her skirts brushed against his legs. He gripped her fingers on his arm and concentrated on what she was saying.

She smiled, putting all her sincerity into the gesture. "I am your wife and your partner, just as I always wanted. I will share with you all that you are and all that you hope to be. Together we can heal whatever pain lies in the past, for both of us."

Chapter Thirteen

Siannon's pledge tore into him, rasping over his skin, cutting through his conflicted needs to hold her at a distance and pull her ever closer.

I am your wife and your partner, just as I always wanted. I will share with you all that you are and all that you hope to be. Together we can heal whatever pain lies in the past, for both of us.

He gritted his teeth against the fresh wheels of pain rebounding from deep inside him. Why was it this one woman could shred his resolve like this? How did she manage to break open the places buried deep inside him and draw out his pain, scraping her very soul against his as she offered what he couldn't accept. Her hand on his arm seemed to burn clear through his flesh, searing a path into the darkness inside him, offering to be his companion and light the way out for him.

At this moment, it felt far worse to stand there and want her—to crave the acceptance she offered so softly than to carry the burdens he'd borne alone for the past decade.

His pride demanded he reject her outright to salvage what he could of himself. This was not the bargain he had made, had not been his goal when he had marched into the courthouse to rescue an old friend. But standing so close to her in the sanctuary of his granny's cottage, tasting Siannon's breath on his tongue and wanting to taste all of her, pride was a hollow shell that echoed with empty foolishness. The words to set her from him would not come.

"Quin?" She prodded him ever so softly and yet laced with that underlying strength that made her the woman she was. He winced deep inside himself, torn with longing and filled with an ache so profound, he couldn't fathom where it began and ended.

"Siannon." Her name rasped out of him as he cupped her cheek in his palm, wet with tears for him. He knew that without the benefit of any special abilities. And the knowledge twisted through his gut. He traced her soft lips with his thumb, ignoring the hot burn blurring his vision. "There are some wounds that cannot be healed."

"Nay, Quin," she denied on a shuddering breath. "There are some wounds we have not even begun to address. But we could heal them, heal them all if we would but try. The choice is ours. If we make the right decisions, we can forge the life we want together."

Logs hissed in the hearth fire as her promise reached inside him, slipping past the barriers he'd guarded for so long and past his need to raise them up again. Straight into his reluctant heart like balm, a true blessing to echo Granny's words.

The choice once made cannot be undone. The decision once forged cannot be altered.

He slid his fingers into her hair and watched the dark red tresses glide over the backs of his hands as her rumpled coiffure released beneath his touch. She felt so fragile in his hands and yet so solid. What had happened to the desperate woman who greeted him in Limerick or the gangly girl who used to trail after him?

"Who are you, Siannon Reilly? What makes you think you can heal my past? That I deserve this future you would have us forge."

"I am your wife," she told him simply. She turned her mouth into the palm of his hand and pressed a small kiss there. Her breath was warm on his skin, waves of reassurance rippled through him from the quiet heat of her lips and the wealth of unspoken meaning behind her statement.

Defenses crumbled within him as her words thrummed through his objections, snaring his soul. From deep inside himself he felt again the crashing rhythms of the sea and heard the beat of waves against solid timber in the distance, just as he had on their wedding day. *The Blessing.* The smell of fresh salt riding white water mixed with Siannon's heady lavender and lilac scent, creating a seductive siren call and pulling him toward her. He brushed his lips across hers. A sudden blinding wave of heat rolled, demanding everything he had to give and more.

"So be it, then. Blessing or curse for all time." He threaded her hair—cool, damp silk—between his fingers and pulled her closer and then closer still.

She leaned into him, her hands sliding over his ribs and up across his shoulder blades. "So be it, my wife."

He covered her lips with his, and a groan wrenched from deep inside him, wrenched and twisted and coiled out of him, tearing open old half-healed scars as he tasted her softness and the promise welling from her like sunlight and soft summer grass.

She clung to him, accepting the raw passion of his kisses and the needs he couldn't hold back from her as he molded her against him. Heaven and hell, torment and salvation, she was everything he wanted and everything he had feared. But he could not stop. Not now.

The choice once made cannot be undone.

The Blessing roared through his soul and back again, rippling waves against the sandy shore—the pitch and toss of an unseen sea along with the taste of fresh salt spray and freedom. Why giving himself over to her would make him feel free made no sense, but he could not escape that truth as her tongue slid seductively against his own and she shivered in his arms. His groin tightened in response, eager in anticipation of the delights to come if they but continued this course.

The black void inside him rose up in protest, slamming against his heart as he drank acceptance from her lips. He turned from the pain, shoved it aside as if it didn't matter. Nothing mattered but the incredible rightness of his wife in his arms and his desperate need to make love to her.

"Siannon." He released her lips, tilting her head back with his hands to taste the fragrant skin below her ear. "My Siannon. How foolish you've been to trust your future to such a blackguard."

"No blackguard, Quin." She laughed, and the sound, breathless and seductive, sent a hot thrill through his blood as she quivered against him. "You were the hero of my every fantasy. You still are."

Desire surged in his belly, molten and liquid and undeniable.

"Fantasies?" He laved her ear, whorling his tongue over the tender tip.

"Aye." She shivered again, a delicious set of movements that skimmed her breasts over his chest.

"What fantasies were those, sweet Siannon?" He nibbled her earlobe, grazing her with his teeth. His hands sought the softness of her waist, pulling her against the swelling of his very real need for her.

"I . . . I used to dream of you coming home to me . . . holding me and . . . oh, Quin." Her fingers dug into his shoulders.

"Aye?"

"I never thought of you touching me the way you do."

Satisfaction curled in his stomach and then twisted through him in hot longing. "What way is that?"

"As though you cannot get enough of me."

"I cannot." He panted his answer, breathless with wanting her. "I'm beginning to realize I never will. But I'm willing to try. Again. And again. And again."

"Oh."

He swallowed her soft gasp as he claimed her lips, sipping the passion he'd kindled within her just holding her in his arms while his desires raged hotter and higher. Their tongues danced and their lips pulled even more from each other. He could kiss her like this for hours, ragged and yearning, but kisses were only the beginning.

He pressed her back toward the cool stones lining the cottage walls, cradling her with his arms. He released her lips, stopping for a moment to gaze down at her. Pale firelight flickered over her face and gleamed in the red depths of her hair. Gray eyes stormy with passionate need glittered up at him.

"Mo chroi, mo ceile." His heart, his wife, one and the same, a blessing in itself. He stroked a hand over her throat and down across the bodice of her gown. She sighed and closed her eyes at his touch as he outlined the full roundness of her tempting breasts against the fabric. When she opened her eyes again, they were slitted, her lids heavy as he stroked her, feeling her nipples pebble into hardened points beneath the damp fabric of her gown.

"Again and again," she whispered, firing his blood still further as she echoed his sentiments.

"Aye." He tugged at the buttons, freeing them, freeing her until the gown parted to reveal the upswept curves he longed to taste and savor beneath the sheer clinging softness of her chemise.

"Timmy." A breathy protest as he bent to her lips again. Slowly and languidly he kissed her, determined to torture her every bit as much as she tortured him.

"Aye, Timmy." He pulled away from her and crossed to the hearth to scoop up child and dog in one quick bundle. The puppy blinked, but the lad snoozed on as Quin carried him to the small bedroom that had once been his own father's. He took the boy's shoes off and snuggled his son securely under the blanket. Poor lad, tired out from his adventuring.

"Keep an eye on him, Lucy." He patted the pup, who licked his fingers and settled herself comfortably atop the blanket.

Siannon had shrugged off the outer jacket of her dress and hung her skirt to dry on the rocker by the fire along with her hose and shoes, leaving her in her pale lawn chemise and petticoats. She stood by the window, where he had left her, a vision of white and spun red-gold that made his blood pound with desire. The rain had stopped and a soft glow of waning sunlight bathed her. Her petticoats emphasized the trimness of her waist without benefit or need of a corset. Her breasts were starkly outlined against the soft sheer covering of her chemise. High and proud and firm, her nipples pushed tight against the fabric.

"Mo chroi." He strode over to her and she turned into his arms, all soft woman and solid determination.

Her arms slid around his neck, silken and warm, her fingers threading his hair. "Make love to me, Quin."

"Aye." He nibbled her lips, teasing her with quick kisses as he traced his hands over her arms and down over her ribs and then slowly up over her breasts, teasing them both with his leisurely touch. He cupped and weighed her softness, thumbing her taut nipples in tighter circles. "There is no question of that between us. Again and again."

Bending to nip each tender tip with his lips and his teeth, he sucked her through the sheer fabric. The thin barrier goaded him and teased him as he continued his attentions. She shivered and shrugged her shoulders out of the chemise. The garment sluiced down over her bare skin to drape in casual elegance over the fullness of her breasts. He tugged it down, baring her to the waist.

"So beautiful," he managed to say on a groan as

he bent to taste the softness of her flesh with nothing between them.

Her fingers threaded his hair as she cupped him to her. He sucked her again, laving the soft nipple he'd captured as he cupped her other breast and caught the second peak tight between his fingers.

She shuddered and arched against him. He sucked her farther into his mouth, drawing hard upon her succulent flesh as though he could derive her very essence from her and make her part of him forever.

She moaned as he released the first nipple and transferred his attention to the other, all the while busying his fingers with the fastenings to her petticoats, needing to lay her bare to his every attention. The coverings sighed to the floor, leaving her naught but her own sensuality.

He stood back and admired her, his breath hitching and his desire pounding as she stood before him without shame, her breasts high and full, nipples tight and glistening from his passionate concentration. He'd never seen her look more beautiful. And she was his. His, no matter the reason.

His because she chose to be.

"You are perfect, *mo ceile.*" The praise came huskily from him, breathlessly, the hot need swirling inside him.

Wordlessly she reached for the buttons on his shirt, undoing them and spreading the edges open, sliding her hands over his flesh.

"I would see you as well, husband," she boldly told him as she coaxed the shirt from his shoulders and then applied her attention to the fastenings of his trousers. He groaned as she released him from the constrictions of his clothing. The air caressed the painful length of his erection.

And then it was not the air, but Siannon, so swiftly was she there. Her soft lips whispered over his skin. Seductive. Mesmerizing. He watched in fascination as she flicked her tongue over the thick tip of him. He reached behind him to brace himself against the rough-hewn stone wall and then hissed in his breath as she parted her lips and took him fully in her mouth.

"Sweet heaven, Siannon." He groaned as the hot, wet velvet sensation surrounded him and she sucked him boldly deep into her mouth, laving him with her tongue as she drew on his length. He shuddered, awash in sensation as she ministered to him, her fingers sliding over his buttocks, caressing him, teasing him, sucking him deeper and deeper. Giving him more than he had asked for, returning in full measure each touch he had given her.

Surely he would go mad from this exquisite torture. He shuddered as she swirled her tongue again and again over his swollen, sensitive head.

"Siannon, dear sweet God." He was incoherent, beyond speech as his orgasm ripped through him, wave upon unutterable wave of pleasure exploding every nerve in his body.

He grasped her shoulders and pulled her to her feet. Fire and triumph glowed together in the depths of her eyes.

"Beloved witch," he growled at her, overwhelmed by what she had done and just as determined to have her experience her own fulfillment at his hands.

He hauled her up against him, covered her lips with his own, and kissed her deeply, sliding his tongue intimately against hers. Tasting the essence of her gift, the essence of himself, still lingering as he pulled her fully against him. All satiny skin and smooth, fluid warmth.

And his. All his.

Fierce, possessive pride rived him and splintered any lingering resistance to the love she would claim from him. He scooped her against him and carried her the short distance to the hearth, setting her bare feet atop the hearthstones so that the fire gently warmed their calves.

"Stand here, Siannon." He ground the words out, backing up just a bit to observe her silhouetted against the glowing fire. "I want to see you, all of you. That is my fantasy."

She lifted her chin and arched her shoulders back, anticipation and the light of a challenge in her eyes. He knelt before her on the rug and stroked his hands over her feet, her ankles, and slowly up her calves, then to her thighs, nudging them apart as he stroked her, wider and wider, until she stood with her legs akimbo, firelight licking every inch of her body in a golden radiance.

Between her thighs her silken folds glistened with arousal, surging pure male triumph through him. He continued to stroke her, slow and teasing, closer and closer to those moist, sensitive areas awaiting his touch.

"Quin." A plea escaped her as he teased her, almost touching and yet not.

"What is it, *mo chroi?*"

"I want you, all of you." She told him, her voice raw with need. "Past, present, future. All."

"Aye." He slid his hands around to cup her rounded buttocks and nuzzled his lips to the parted apex of her thighs, drawing a cry from her as he applied his expertise where she needed him the most.

He tongued her fast, slow, fast, tasting her salty-slick heat as she groaned and clutched him to her, sliding her fingers into his hair and arching her hips forward to grant him better access.

He complied, cupping her closer to him, kneading her lush, tender curves as he supped from her, sucking, licking, darting into her with his tongue again and again as his own desires responded to hers and arched his erection hard and painful and more than ready for her.

Siannon reached out to clutch the cold stone mantelpiece for support, her mind a whirl of sensation as he laved her so intimately. Her back, her bottom, her legs were warm from the hearth behind her, and cool air wisped her from head to toe in the front, tightening her already sensitive nipples to hard nubs of flesh, and between her outstretched thighs Quin brought a different, all-consuming fire to drive her wild.

She shuddered as he arched her farther forward, raising her onto the balls of her feet as he darted his tongue into her again and again, alternately sucking her into his mouth, grazing her with his teeth, biting, then sucking. She could stand no more.

"Oh, Quin, oh." Release poured through her in hot, wild torrents, racking her body, undulating within her, until her knees gave out and she would have fallen if he had not supported her.

Her breathing was ragged and overloud against a distant patter as the rain began again and the fire hissed softly behind her.

"Come, Siannon." Quin urged her with his arms,

and she released her trembling hold of the mantel-piece to seek shelter in his arms as he stood to catch her to him. She felt boneless, weightless, and sated.

"I don't think I'll ever walk again." A breathless laugh escaped her.

"There's no need, darlin'. Not yet." His laugh joined hers, husky and low and intimate.

"Not yet?"

"Aye."

"But—"

"I'm not through with you yet, wife."

She felt the bold press of his hot flesh against her.

"Oh, Quin, I'm not sure I can take any more." Heat washed over her cheeks as she met his gaze, a glittering, deepest, darkest green, the color of passion.

"Aye, you can. We both can. Lie here, Siannon." He stretched her onto the blanket and rolled her to her stomach. Then he stroked her again. From her shoulders down to the balls of her feet. His hands cool against her fire-heated skin.

"Mmm," she sighed. "That feels so good."

"I like to touch you, Siannon." He spoke softly, his voice a caress to match the strokes of his fingers. "Every bit of you. I like to watch you move and respond just for me. It is passion and pleasure and intimacy rolled into one."

He stroked his fingers over her sides, slow and teasing up the sides of her breasts. Already the hot tingle had begun to curl insistently inside her again. For him. She wondered if he planned to make love to her all night, just as he had said. Over and over and over again. And she smiled into the blanket.

He parted her legs and she made a move to turn toward him. "Nay, Siannon, stay as you are."

"But I want to take all of you."

"And so you shall." He kissed the back of her neck and the side, sucking gently on her flesh, drawing a groan of pleasure from her.

And then she felt him against her from behind, the hot hard thickness of him pressing intimately. She drew in a breath as he almost entered her but not quite. He slid the heat of him back and forth and then around, teasing her.

"Quin," she protested, hearing the pleading in her own voice.

"Aye." Rough and tight and filled with determination. He did it again, teasing her, sliding against her, so velvety smooth and thick and hot.

She arched upward, eager to sheath him inside her. He laughed, but the sound was shaken and breathless. Then he slid an arm beneath her hips, keeping her arched up to him as his fingers unerringly found the slippery flesh he had sated such a short time before. And now he teased her with both his fingers and the hard, pulsing flesh she ached for. Waves of color and heat shot through her.

"Oh, Quin. Please."

"Soon, beloved." He continued the torment as she clutched the blanket beneath her for what seemed an exquisite eternity. At last he pushed himself into her, parting her and sliding his hard length inside ever so slowly as his fingers continued to stroke her. All she could do was groan and clutch the blanket tighter as sensations swamped her.

He filled her farther, deeper, stretching her to

accommodate his length. "Take all of me, Siannon. Heaven and hell, make of us what we will."

His arm around her hips pulled her closer still, and she welcomed him, rising on her elbows to take the last of him. He gasped his pleasure.

She knew it was more than his sex he spoke of as he began to move inside her, in and out, the rhythm a wildfire in her blood as he rode her deeper and deeper, pressing to her womb with each hard thrust. Her breasts swayed into his hands. He pulled at them and circled her nipples with his thumbs, increasing the whorls of color and pleasure spiraling through her. He quickened his pace, harder, faster, their breathing simultaneous. Pleasure exploded inside her again and again, until at last he followed her over the edge, filling her with a hot spurt of wet heat.

"Siannon." Only her name, but it shuddered through her. His pain still undulated around them, a ghostly behemoth eager to grind their future into the dirt before it began. But they had a chance now too. She could feel that rippling tenuously beneath the rest of the tangled emotions inside him. And that was all she could ask for at the moment.

Curled in her husband's arms, damp and replete from their lovemaking, Siannon slept, uncaring of anything beyond the confines of Granny Reilly's cottage.

The earliest bands of morning sunlight brought renewed tension to Quin as they crept across the well-worn floor. He awoke long before Siannon and Timmy and lay there staring up at the rafters and debating his course. He would have to tell Siannon his plans. He couldn't risk the tentative peace between them by leaving her in the dark. And if

Eustace Rhodes was even half as determined as the evidence Quin had uncovered seemed to suggest, it would be just as well that she remain alert and aware.

Especially when he would not be there to protect them. A pang shot through him on the heels of that thought. He was equally torn in both directions. Logically, staying here would provide him only with the veneer of accomplishment. He would be satisfying the niggling voice inside him that demanded he keep a close watch on all he held dear—the shipyard, the island, his wife, their son. He tilted his head and watched as warm light streaked Siannon's hair to burnished copper.

But he would not be addressing the root of the problem, a decade-long wound that had festered and decayed. If he did not put an end to this once and for all, no amount of money and no fresh source of supplies would provide them a way out of the pit Rhodes had so determinedly dug for them.

Siannon sighed and snuggled closer against him in her sleep. Warmth curled in his chest and blossomed outward as her hair spilled over his fingers. There would be no escaping the newfound closeness between them, another unsettling thought. And yet he realized he didn't really want to escape, that somehow in the dark of night she had taken part of the burden he had always carried away from him and replaced it with something he wasn't yet ready to name. He wasn't sure how she had done that. Had it been in the thorough openness of their lovemaking? Or the tenderness of her touch? Or the open trust with which she slept against his side?

There was no sense in ignoring what transpired between them any more than he'd been able to ignore having her as his wife or the invisible bond that had somehow developed between them. Developed? Or had it always been there, a silent, intangible force underlying everything? Whatever the reason, things were different this morning. Far different from what they had been the day before or even the previous night, when he had tried so hard to resist her. Now he could only wonder what on earth he had been trying to resist. And why.

She shifted against him and opened her eyes.

He lay still, watching her and wondering what went on inside her as she slowly perused their surroundings. When she turned to look at him, hesitation lurked in the depths of her eyes.

"Hullo, Quin." Color spread over her face and neck.

"Hullo, wife." His greeting came thick with the emotions churning through him.

She smiled, but the hesitation didn't fade.

"What do you feel from me now, Siannon?" He hadn't meant to voice the question, but there it was, bold and unadorned and basic.

"Quin—"

"Tell me." He cut off her protest, unwilling to go back into the guarded stance they had each held before.

"I . . . don't know." A fresh wash of color addressed her soft skin, and he fought the urge to kiss every inch of her.

"Tell me," he repeated.

She sighed and closed her eyes. Silence thumped by on the slow beat of his heart. And then she opened her eyes and looked at him. Hesitation still lurked, but it had shifted from what it had been only a moment before.

Lust bolted through him, hot and unexpected. He held it back with an effort, confining himself to tracing the line of her collarbone with his fingers.

"I feel pride," she offered with a lift of one silky eyebrow.

Her skin was so smooth and soft.

"Aye?" He trailed his fingers over the upper swells of her breasts, hidden beneath the edges of the blanket he had wrapped them both in.

"Aye. That deep Reilly pride that has always been a part of you."

The gray of her eyes seemed to lighten and sparkle.

Why had he never noticed how truly lovely she was?

"And what else?" He loved the play of her lips as she spoke.

"Passion." She told him on a shaky breath as a third wave of color washed her skin. "You want me."

"Aye, I do." He bent and tasted the soft warmth behind her ear. She tasted of morning and promises, early dew on grass and sunlight gleaming on the waves. "Very much so. But I don't think you needed any special abilities to tell you that."

"Nay." She shivered in his arms and twined her own around his neck to pull him closer. "Nay, I did not."

So close to her, with her silken warmth pressed against every inch of him, he could no longer remember his questions. Only the need to love every inch of her, until neither one of them could move. He took her lips in a long, slow, drugging kiss. Thorough and leisurely as their tongue slid together, mating and matching the need building inside him.

He rolled her beneath him and she welcomed him as he settled against the warm valley between her thighs.

"Siannon—"

"Lucy, wait, come back!" Timmy's cry was followed almost immediately by the zealous invasion of a squirming bundle of black and white. For one small dog she seemed to have come equipped with enough tongues for ten.

Irritation flared in Quin, but Siannon dissolved into giggles beneath him as the dog switched rapidly back and forth, lavishing wet kisses on both of them. Timmy skidded to a halt beside them and then knelt, trying to retrieve the excited puppy. She finally relented, and after thoroughly kissing his face as well, disappeared to inspect the corners of Granny's cottage.

Quin hoped she confined her inspection to smelling only.

"Hullo, Mama. Hullo, Da." Timmy cocked his head to one side. "Did you sleep good? I'm famished."

Quin caught back a sigh.

Siannon smiled up at them both, her warmth spreading through him until he smiled back.

"Good morning, boy-o." He reached out to tousle the boy's hair as Siannon clutched the blanket closer. "We'd best get ourselves together and get your mother back home."

"Home?" Timmy transferred a worried gaze to his mother.

"Home, here," she tendered quietly.

"Oh. All right." He brightened. "Caitlin can fix me breakfast. I'm ready when you are."

"Then you'd best take Lucy outside before she does

more than smelling in the corners. Stay within sight of the cottage, boy-o and . . ."

"Aye, sir?"

"Beannacht is your home forever now."

"Aye, sir." A simple answer, yet the smile beaming from his young face made it worth the effort.

Quin turned back to Siannon to find himself snared in a glowing gaze of silky gray. He'd tell her of his trip once he'd gotten her home and settled. "Come, wife, a new day awaits."

"Aye, husband. But they'll be occupied for a few minutes. Leaving can wait just a bit. We've unfinished business to attend." She pulled him down for a lingering kiss.

Chapter Fourteen

The crisp ocean breeze nipped at Siannon's cheeks and whipped her hair into wild disarray behind her. In her haste to leave the house, she hadn't bothered to put it up. She hadn't bothered with much at all save knowing she could not bear to remain there and wait while her husband prepared to leave her.

Her body still thrummed with the aches and twinges of the lovemaking they had just shared during their night spent in Granny Reilly's cottage. Her heart still swelled with the joy of listening to their son peppering his new da with questions as they trekked home in the bright promise of a new day and the possibilities inherent in the new accord between them.

And then he had told her he was sailing away almost immediately.

She stood on the bluff above the Reilly house overlooking Beannacht Harbor and the shipyard. Morning sunlight sparkled on the water, shimmering against the rising tide that would carry her husband away on the ship making ready at the docks below before it ebbed.

A crisp breeze rose from the waves beyond the point behind St. Bridgid's, the air scrubbed clean from the rain the previous day and carrying the pensive scent of the sea twined with a deceptive pledge of good things to come, carrying the prospect of a day that stretched out before her, barren and empty. Followed by more days just the same, empty and barren because Quin would not be there to fill them.

She hugged her shawl around her shoulders. How is it that she had allowed him to fill so much of her thoughts, her plans, so that the prospect of a short separation left her feeling so hollow? She had Timmy. She had her own business venture to occupy her days. She had friends and family close by for company— yesterday's search for her son had certainly proved that.

Even after Quin had explained his very real and urgent need to leave today to attend business for both of them—and even offered to take her with him when she could not bring herself to enthusiastically endorse his plans—even then she had not been able to contain the keening loss and desperation welling from deep inside her.

The screech of gulls fighting for scraps being thrown to them by a tiny dark figure at the harbor's shoreline, the sounds of hammers and saws ringing at work on the barque in the shipyard, the occasional sounds rising from the village in between, even the rustle of the grass around her prickled her senses like tiny needle points stabbing her and repeating the refrain—gone, gone, gone.

She sighed and chewed her lip, seeking the source of her turmoil. Yesterday the worry stinging her had held a close and immediate warning. The gray void threatening to swallow her today carried an insidious, twisted allure, tempting her to release her cares and fears and surrender to the cloying embrace of despair. She'd never felt anything quite like it. It was almost seductive in its appeal.

Perhaps the devastation and loneliness stemmed from disappointment after the very real progress she had thought they made last night in bridging the distance between them. Sharing their secrets had surely given them new ground to tread together. Would the weeks Quin spent away enable him to rebuild the barriers they had broken? Would she have to begin all over again when he returned?

Her thoughts snagged . . . sharing their secrets . . . Quin's face in the shadows, twisting with the anguish and guilt he felt over the death of his first wife.

Marie.

The truth rushed into Siannon with a wrenching gasp that threatened to knock her to the ground as the breeze whipped up around her. All the horror of his return home to barren rooms and unspoken accusations of neglect from Marie's family clawed Siannon with fresh talons. Quin's sorrow for the wife he felt he failed, the wife he never truly accepted. His grief for the child he would never hold. His self-recriminations and blame for putting his work before familial obligations poured through Siannon far sharper than before.

These were the stones that built the barricade they

had dismantled between them only yesterday. The basis for his belief that if he did not let his new wife care for him, he could not hurt her and in the process rip himself apart ever again. It humbled Siannon to realize just how much trust he had placed in her to let her know that side of him. The whole of him.

Tears streamed unchecked down Siannon's cheeks. Not for herself. Not for Quin. From a distance, beneath the stark wreckage of guilt she had absorbed from their husband, lay another person's cry. A gentle, fragile soul who offered forgiveness and yearned for her own absolution. Siannon could almost feel the shattering of her own heart under the weight of regret and repentance surging from the past.

Here was the source of her reluctance to say farewell to her husband, even for a short trip. Why she couldn't bear the thought, the sight, of watching him sail away. Her mind's eye caught on another coastline, a distant vista and a set of sails disappearing over the horizon for the last time. Her breath hitched and she let the tears flow, bathing the hurt and grief that had festered and become unbearable so long ago.

A movement at the corner of her eye drew her attention and anchored her once more on Beannacht. She inhaled a deep breath of granite and grasslands, salt and home.

Quin was climbing the path toward the bluff. He was dressed in his dark gray business suit, the one that set off the deep sparkle in his green eyes and made the tiny dent in his chin seem more pronounced. The suit he had worn the day they married on his last trip to Limerick. He moved quickly with a grim set to his shoulders and determined stiffness in his spine.

She looked at him striding toward her and saw him with fresh eyes. Not as the hero of her childhood or the embodiment of her fantasies, but as a man she could love with her whole heart to a depth she could never have imagined possible in all her years of daydreaming combined.

Her Reilly Blessing in the flesh.

The urge to shout her revelation to the hills shot through her. She wanted to run to him and tell him, to pour out all the wondrous freedom of her discovery and the promise of the lifetime stretching before them, a lifetime in which they could heal and grow and support each another as man and wife. Together.

Could she? Should she? She caught herself back as she started forward to meet him. Not now. They had a lifetime. Now was not the time, with his departure imminent and the need for his attention to be focused on uncovering her father's schemes and answering his latest legal maneuverings regarding her son—*their* son—and his inheritance. She would wait—wait right here if need be—until his return.

Then they could begin their future. Then she would tell him that she loved him, and that she knew one day he would love her too.

He was in love with his wife. And she was scaring the hell out of him.

The twin truths ripped through Quin with a ferocity that would quail most sailors who had seen and beaten the Horn as he spied Siannon, at last, at the top of the bluff.

He loved her.

That knowledge added a following wind to his need to reach her and reassure himself that she would be all right while he attended his business on the mainland.

She had turned so pale when he first told her of his need to follow the evidence he'd uncovered in his father's papers and visit some of Reilly Ship Works' oldest and most reliable suppliers—those who still did business with them and those who did not. Kiernan Rogers and the *Achanaich* were scheduled to depart that morning, and he intended to be on board and on his way to Limerick so he could accomplish his investigations as quickly as possible.

She had only nodded absently when he had added the news that he intended to consult with Gill O'Brien over the latest correspondence from her father and his own solicitor. He'd chalked it up to exhaustion stemming from their activities during the night when she failed to ask for details of her father's latest tactics to regain his grandson, going upstairs instead to change her dress.

She disappeared from the house while he packed his kit for his brief voyage. She had not been on the docks waiting to bid him farewell as he hoped, nor was she with the other women gathered at Maeve Kelly's—at least not according to Kiernan, who had just come from there.

Disappointment stronger than he cared to acknowledge had flashed through him, along with swift, unsettling anger. Why would his wife not want to bid him farewell?

Panic clutched him then, fear born from experience, especially when he had spied her on the edge of the bluff above his parents' house. Her slender figure with her hair flowing free in the breezes looked so eerily familiar, an agonizing ghost of memory he'd begun to exorcise only a few hours before. He couldn't leave until he knew how things stood between them, knew Siannon would be all right until he returned.

He passed the house and took the path toward the summit as quickly as he could without breaking into a run that might alarm her.

Dressed in a turquoise gown the shade of the Caribbean seas he'd once sailed, Siannon turned toward him. She stepped forward, a strange light glowing in her eyes, then she hesitated. Her cheeks glistened in the sunlight, wet with tears. He'd thought last night had brought them so much closer, the intimacies they shared an expression of their growing trust. What had changed between their departure from Granny's cottage at daybreak and now?

He was leaving, his answer roared forth in accusation. Loose in the wind, her fire-gold hair streamed around her. The whiteness of her gown's collar highlighted the pale luster of her skin. She was still far too close to the edge.

Siannon has the look of her mother, with that fey red hair and pale white skin. In the end you'll find you'd have been much better off if you'd never crossed her path, Rhodes's taunts rose from the depths as Quin topped the bluff. Blessing or curse? It no longer mattered as long as she was his.

He ran.

He pulled her close as he reached her, planting his lips on hers while a mind-numbing tumble of all that he'd feared, all that he'd realized, churned through him. He kissed her fiercely, feverishly, striving to tell her all that he could not yet put voice to. Demanding the comfort he needed from her.

Her arms slid around him and she mercifully kissed him back, filling the void that had yawed before him at the thought of losing her. The salt of her tears lashed him, but he knew he needed to taste them, to make them his own.

He laced his fingers through the wild tangle of her windblown hair and cupped her face. Her gaze searched his with total acceptance, devoid of any trace of hesitation or wary expectations.

"What—" she started to say.

"Nothing matters as long as you are mine," he managed to choke out before kissing her again.

This time he brushed her lips gently, savoring their softness, tasting the sunlight she hid within them, the sunlight that warmed him to his depths. A lover's tribute. He kept the kiss soft and easy, letting the essence of Siannon and all that she meant to him fill his heart.

He loved her, but he could not tell her so and say farewell in the same breath. Pulling her against his shoulder so that her cheek rested next to his restored heart, he stroked her hair and pressed small kisses into the shining tresses while he searched for the right thing to say.

The gulls crying in the distance—the sun's rays dappling the hills—the sounds of the shipyard. All blended together into the beating of his heart. He was home. He was content. And no matter what he'd told himself before, he would never put to sea again. He'd found his true berth in the arms of his wife.

"Tell me you will be all right while I am gone, Siannon. Tell me you will still be here when I return." If only he could tell her just how important her pledge was to him—would be to him while he was away. How he would treasure it and count on it. But he wanted her answer to be freely and honestly given.

"I will wait for you, Quin. Right on this spot if this is where you want me to be. Or any other place you choose."

Her assurance flowed through him. Her voice was calm and in control, not at all like the specter of his past leave-takings. A portion of the tension twisting his gut eased.

"You could still come with me, *mo ceile.*" He brushed the hair away from her cheeks and traced her jawline with his fingers before tilting her face up to his. "We've a little time left. We could pack a trunk for your needs quickly before Kiernan must sail if he's to catch the tide."

His breath caught on the sparkle in her eyes when she looked at him. She smiled and squeezed her arms tighter around his waist. "I have no wish to go back there, Quin. Everything I need, save you, will be here with me. The last time I left Beannacht I did not make it back for over ten years. I'm home now, and this is where I want to stay, waiting for you."

Her face grew serious. "I've waited for you my whole life, Quintin Reilly. I am not about to stop now."

She stretched up on tiptoe then and cupped his chin, bringing her lips to his. Her turbulent, storm-tossed gaze remained locked with his as she reached up to him. Impossibly, he could hear the sounds of children laughing in the distance, smell the fresh scent of bread baking, feel the enveloping warmth of arriving home after a long day to find Siannon waiting for him, a strange and seductive image pulling him toward her.

She brushed her lips across his. A sudden blinding

wave of heat rolled through him, carrying the pitch and toss of an unseen sea, demanding everything he had to give and more.

The Blessing.

'Tis a sound once heard that lingers on. A sight once seen and never forgotten. A feeling once felt, always remembered.

Granny Reilly's teachings roared across the years, promising the formidable appreciation that was his right. No, more than that, his duty. He felt powerless as the maelstrom exploded within him, an echo of the onslaught he'd felt that first time in Limerick's courthouse.

He pulled Siannon to him, ravishing her mouth, molding her body thoroughly against his. She was so incredibly, bewitchingly, soft. Her hands clutched the small of his back as he anchored his fingers in the coppery length of her hair and tilted her head to more openly accommodate him.

The drugging smell of sun-warmed lavender and lilacs rose from her to envelop him. No woman had ever felt so in his arms, never threatened to tear his soul from him with the touch of her lips or rend to shreds any measure of self-possession he laid claim to. He reveled in her siren's call. His wife.

His tongue slid against hers, tasting her. Sunshine and deep summer grass, the fiery heat would surely burn them both to cinders. She moaned against his lips and met his tongue with her own in a dance that ignited the fire in his blood. He had never wanted a woman more swiftly or completely than he wanted Siannon Reilly, over and over, for all eternity.

Siannon's hands slid down until they rested on his buttocks. She kneaded the flesh and pulled him closer until the raging evidence of his desire for her pressed into the softness of her belly. Fierce possession exploded through him. He could make love to her right there, damn the consequences and the ebbing tide.

The tide. The tide and a full ship's compliment of sailors likely looking toward this very bluff as they awaited the signal to cast off.

Reaching desperately for any tattered shreds of sanity he might yet possess, he pulled back. Her cheeks and lips were flushed, her gaze wide and filled with a sultry mix of confusion and passion that stabbed fresh desire through his gut as he stepped back and held her at arm's length, breathless.

Everything Granny had crooned about The Blessing proved truer than he could have guessed and more overwhelming than anything he had anticipated. It threaded inexorably through his love for his wife.

"I . . . would . . . take you—" He halted his stammer when she arched a delicate eyebrow and smiled, eyeing the eager protrusion at the front of his trousers.

He squeezed her hands and returned her smile. "I would take you with me always, but I understand your reasons for staying on Beannacht. I find I am loath to go myself."

"Indeed?" Her smile grew. "Do we have time—"

He shook his head and drew her to him again, turning her this time so that her back rested against his chest and her womanly softness cradled the hardness of his desires.

He wrapped his arms around her waist and pulled her close. "Soon Kiernan will unfurl his sails. He is, no doubt, even now pacing the deck impatiently against my return. We'll have many nights and days to enjoy together once I return. But for now this last embrace will have to do us both."

"How long?" she asked after a moment while they watched a gull careen by. Father Dunnavan must be done with his daily feeding ritual for his flock down at the harbor shoreline in front of St. Bridgid's.

"Five minutes and not much more, then we shall have to fly down the slopes if the *Achanaich* has a prayer of making it past the point before the waters recede." He could still make the priest's dark figure out along the rocky shore. Often he'd stand there for some time, lost in prayer or quiet contemplation.

Siannon nodded and crossed her arms in front of her to rest them atop his. "You'll be careful, won't you? You'll take Kiernan or Seamus Keane with you wherever you go?" Worry laced her tone. "You may be a fine sea captain used to the currents and backwaters of the world, but my father was born in the city. His domain is the shaded offices and back alleys."

Quin chuckled deep in his chest. "As you command, Admiral. I would not have you worrying needlessly while I am away. I will hold my own and young Seamus can hold my hat, if that will make you feel better."

"See that you do, Captain Reilly," she answered primly enough, but the humor was back in her voice and she relaxed against him. She felt so good in his arms, so right.

"And how will you fill all your days, wife, with no husband to occupy your time?" He nestled his chin over her head and never thought he had felt more content than at that moment, bantering with his wife. He took a deep breath of her scent, willing it to linger in his nostrils until he returned.

She turned her head to the side, nudging his shoulder with her forehead, her fingers tightened on his forearms. "It is the nights I will find . . . difficult to fill, Quin. My days will likely remain as they have these past weeks. Together with the other women, painting at Maeve Kelly's."

"Ah, yes. That crockery business—"

"We're painting china plates and cups," she corrected him. "For the American market."

"China . . . crockery." He shrugged. "My point, Siannon, is when were you planning to enlighten me about this scheme?"

"I am doing only what you asked me, Quin."

"What I asked?" Her simple, almost offhand explanation astounded him. "And just when did I ask you to send all the shipwrights up into their rigging over the preoccupation of their wives?"

She sighed, an exaggerated breath that wound through him with simple joy. "I do hope you are clearer in your orders when you are in command of your vessel, Captain. Else it would be no wonder if you wandered the seven seas for ages."

"What are you saying, Mrs. Reilly?" He was puzzled by her reference but tickled by her joking with him.

"It was your idea for me to find a diversion for the wives, to deter their discontent over the long hours your shipwrights are spending at the yard." She wiggled her back indignantly, at the same time sending delicious sensations cascading through his lower body, still pressed intimately against her bottom.

"Now," she continued, "you dare to upbraid me, telling me it is the shipwrights who are discontent. I do not think I can solve their problems earning extra coins by painting china. Somehow, I cannot picture

Dermot Keane swathed in an apron, painting delicate flowers and leaves on dessert plates and saucers for American inns and hostelries."

He chuckled and kissed the edge of her ear, giving it a little nip for her impudence. "Neither can I, *mo ceile*. But could you do something about the starch in his collar? I cannot recall if he suffers from too much or too little, but I do know that the problem vexes him sorely."

They both laughed then, enjoying these last precious moments that seemed more like a beginning than an end. He stifled the urge to turn her in his arms and sink into the tall grass with her. To bare her for the sun and gulls and make love to her in the fresh air. Another day. The first day such as this upon his return.

He sighed. "In all seriousness, Siannon. I hope that you are not all wasting your time in this pursuit. That you are not simply filling yourselves with false hopes of riches to come. These unwise schemes seldom pay off as easily or as well as they are promised. You might as soon send our people scavenging the hills to catch one of the wee folk and his pot of gold."

That sounded too close to his ill-spoken comment to Devin when last they'd met. He hoped Gill would have some word on his younger brother since the barrister's son attended school with Dev.

Siannon pulled away and turned, leveling a serious gaze upon him. "I do not make unwise bargains, husband, as well you know. Soon you'll see, we'll reap a handsome profit for our efforts when Mr. Cartwright pays us. And all you naysayers will be gladder of it than you know."

He pulled her into his arms. "I do not seek an

argument here at the last, Siannon. I only looked to counsel you to be wary. Would you like me to check on this Cartwright fellow while I am in Limerick?"

She shook her head. "Kiernan will handle the barrels we send and the payment. You have enough to deal with between your visits to your business contacts, the matters you must look at with Gill, and did you not mention some news from Bryan?"

"Aye. . . ." What was that acrid smell? Had Declan deemed it necessary to heat the pitch and re-do any of the hull seams? They had inspected those more than a week ago and found everything in good order, had they not? He surveyed the shipyard below. Nothing seemed out of the ordinary—there was no activity near the vats. What, then?

Smoke, definitely smoke. The bane of seamen and shipwrights.

"Quin?" Siannon pushed her hands on his chest to regain his attention. "Bryan's news?"

"Aye, lass, there's interesting news from Bryan, at least according to Gill. I'll know more—" He looked along the docks, trying to make out if all was well there. Right on schedule, Kiernan was unfurling his sails. "Time to go."

Siannon froze. "What's that smell?"

He spied a figure on the rocks below, arms waving wildly. Then Father Dunnavan's figure answered and took off at a run for the church door, disappearing inside. With alarming speed the bell at St. Bridgid's began a frantic tolling.

"Fire," Quin growled.

"Where?" Siannon spun to search the source with him.

"There." He pointed to the village, an icy vise tightening around his gut.

He grabbed Siannon's hand and was already beginning to run, when the realization hit her and she cried out.

"Oh, Quin, it's Grandda's house."

Chapter Fifteen

The bucket line was already forming by the time they made it to the village. Flames licked hungrily at the sky from her grandparents' roof. Gasping for breath as she ran behind Quin, Siannon's lungs felt as if they were burning too, but she refused to stop.

Black smoke choked the paths and narrow roadways of Beannacht as worry choked her heart. Thick spirals of acrid smoke poured from the windows in Grandda's workroom. Had he gotten out?

The people of Beannacht village—shipwrights, sailors, wives, and children—flocked to help. She searched their grim faces and peered through the bitter fog, no sign even when they stopped on the path just before the gate. No sign of Grandda at all.

"Grandda," she gasped as she clutched Quin's arm.

He put his hand over her fingers and squeezed, his face set in a harsh line as he fought to catch his breath. The worry in his gaze stabbed fresh alarm through her. "We'll see." His voice held all too little hope.

Grandda. What good was her Gift if she could not use it to warn those she loved best? She tried to catch her own breath without choking on the fear and smoke surrounding her.

"You men, knock the fence down over there." Dan Kelly Sr. seemed to be directing the confusion of anxious people with willing hands into a semblance of order. "We'll get the buckets over that much sooner and leave the path clear for the lads running the empties."

With a mighty heave the three seamen pushed over a section of the picketing twined with Granny's ivy. Dan turned his head and saw them then. He strode over to Quin and Siannon. Harsh lines etched with soot and agony screamed his concern. "Captain, Missus," he greeted them.

"Tiomoid?" Quin shouted over the din.

Dan shook his head. "He was at the shipyard with young Jimmy Doyle and the horses when we first caught a whiff of smoke. My grandson Danny was here."

Sympathy for the pain and worry that must be riving the older man swept through Siannon along with ever swelling worry for her grandfather. She admired Dan's control faced with the horror they both must have shared at that moment. Dan's hands were clenched into fists. Quin's fingers tightened over hers as Dan continued. "Tiomoid went in after him. We've yet to see either one."

They all looked up at the flames and smoke pouring from her grandda's house. Siannon's heart dropped out of her. Dan drew in a long breath and coughed. "Declan Rogers and his brother went in right after them. I won't let anyone else go. It's been too long already."

Quin sucked his breath in through his teeth.

Oh, sweet God, so many. Were they all lost? That could not be. Panic and disbelief numbed her to the thought.

She spied her cousin standing a few feet away, trying to comfort a sobbing Bridget McGee. Next to them stood Maeve Kelly, her hands clasping her mother-in-law's as they waited for word of her son.

"Mary." She pulled her hand out from under Quin's. His gaze roved her face for a moment, and then he nodded his understanding. She turned and ran to Mary.

"They'll be out any second, Bridget. Ye'll see." Mary was soothing the girl as Siannon reached them. Mary's voice was calm and reassuring, but her eyes held all the horror of Siannon's own fears as she stared toward the house being devoured by flames before them. "Ye cannot stop a Rogers bent on being a hero, Bridgie. They'll come out in jest a moment and Kiernan will not like ta see yer tears."

Siannon slipped an arm around both young women's shoulders and hugged them. Tears welled at the corners of Mary's eyes as her gaze locked with Siannon's for a moment, and Mary shook her head. She pulled one hand free from Bridget and clutched Siannon's arm. So little hope remained in her eyes as she returned to staring at the fire, Siannon thought her heart would crack for Mary and Davey alone.

What of Grandda? How much hope could be mustered for him?

The smoke was too thick. Too many minutes had passed. If hearty young men like Declan and Kiernan Rogers were overcome, what chance had her grandfather? Sorrow and loss threatened to sink her to her knees. She looked at Maeve and her mother-in-law, staring at the fire in grim vigil, holding on to hope by an ever thinning thread.

Just then a shout went up from the villagers manning the bucket line. "What is it?" Bridget gasped. "What's happening?"

Two figures loomed in Grandda's doorway, silhouetted against the smoke. They staggered out, and two of the impromptu firefighters rushed forward to pull them clear of the building. It was so hard to see through the smoke, to hear above the confusion.

Almost as one, the women with the most at stake remained frozen, stiff and still, holding their breath and waiting for any clear sight of their loved one.

The cluster of rescuers deposited their burdens on the grass. They stepped back to let the men roll free and choke out their need for fresh air. Siannon was afraid to hope Grandda was there. And afraid for whoever was still inside.

Quin and Dan Kelly Sr. turned from directing the bucket crew to stride over to the figures as they sputtered and heaved.

"Not my Danny," Maeve gasped, and turned away to sob her fear and disappointment into her apron while Mrs. Kelly Sr. rubbed her back, her own struggles to keep her grief in check etched on her face.

"Keirnan," Bridget cried and pulled free to race to her betrothed as he took off the handkerchief tied about his mouth. The man lying beside Kiernan was too small, too round, to be Declan. Quin thumped him on his back to help clear his lungs as he sat up.

"Oh, Mary," Siannon managed to say as she realized Grandda was the second man. Grandda had come out with Kiernan, not Mary's husband.

Mary's grip on her arm tightened. "Go on, Siannon. Go to him."

"I can't leave you." Siannon's heart felt as if it would shatter.

Mary took a breath and let it out slowly. "I'll join ye in a minute. I am the healer. Yer grandda and Kiernan may need me. Declan would not want them to suffer because . . . because—" She could not finish. Her gaze returned to the fire even as she pushed Siannon to go.

"Oh, Grandda," Siannon cried as she hugged him, then pulled back to check him for any injuries beyond the smoke he had swallowed. He coughed and sputtered as he swiped at his blackened face, but his eyes twinkled at her and she knew he was as glad to see her as she was to see him.

She smiled up at Quin, then turned to Kiernan, who held a weeping Bridget in one arm while he, too, tried to wipe the soot from his brow and catch his breath.

"Thank you," she told him, grateful for whatever providence had led him to find her grandfather and guide him to safety.

Kiernan shook his head and caught Quin's eye. "He found me and dragged me to the door. The smoke is so thick. I lost Declan almost as soon as we entered," he managed to get out between gasps for air and Bridget's sobs.

A sharp intake of breath was all the reaction Mary

gave as she bent over her brother-in-law. "Let's have a look, shall we?"

Quin's lips were pressed together as he gazed at the house. "Where?" he asked Grandda.

"Found him in the front room," Grandda choked out, "while looking fer young Danny Kelly. Think there was someone nearby, but couldn't reach both. Figured it was better to save at least one."

Quin nodded and stripped off his jacket. Alarm bells tolled in Siannon's stomach. He pulled his handkerchief out of his pocket and twisted it around before tying it over his nose.

Oh, no!

"What are you doing?" she cried, but she already knew before he turned to her—before he reached over and caressed her cheek with the backs of his fingers, his green eyes dark with determination and a promise that he would be back.

He was going in after Declan. He was going to find Danny. He was not going to let his friends down. Not waiting for her reaction, for her to scream the denial that welled from her depths, he grabbed his jacket and raced to the line to douse the wool garment with water before he flung it over his head.

And then he disappeared into the billowing smoke.

If ever there was a time that she needed to master her Gift, to put her version of The Sight to use, it was now—when her husband's very life might depend on it. When other lives depended on him. She had seen Devin and Bryan when they needed her. She would find Quin.

She rocked back on her heels and closed her eyes. Grandda took her hand in his as she willed herself to seek Quin in the flow of emotions around her—

fear, grief, determination, and sympathy steamed around her from the islanders, from herself.

She sensed rather than heard Mary come over to kneel beside her. Reaching out for her cousin, their hands connected, and she felt the soft white illumination of Mary's healing trickle into her along with Grandda's quiet strength and faith in her. Three McManuses united in a quest. She moved out into the river of feelings surrounding her.

There. There in the dark shoals ahead she sensed the flicker of Quintin Reilly's soul, of the piece of herself he carried in his heart to match the piece of him she carried in hers. He was moving slowly, circling the floor with his feet, trying not to breathe and not to panic in the dark. Counting his steps and changes of direction so he could find his way back. Their way to fresh air.

She wanted to let him know that she was there, that she was with him, but she had never tried to send someone her emotions. She didn't want to alarm him. She thought of him the day he strode into the magistrate's chambers in Limerick. She'd been so nervous, and then just the sight of him, so straight and tall and handsome, she'd been so proud to know that she was marrying him.

She concentrated on letting him know how she had felt that day. The flicker of his soul burned brighter, and she turned her attention to the wisp of emotion she sensed near the doorway and the second, fainter pulsing of fear in the corner.

The corner. Danny Kelly was hiding in the corner.

Overcome with panic and the certainty he was going to die, Danny Kelly had huddled in the corner. Even now his life force was waning.

"The corner, Quin. Check the corner," she whispered, her throat raspy with smoke.

Nausea spread through her belly, and the beginnings of a headache threatened. The noises of the firefighters threatened distraction around her for a moment; the connection with Quin thinned.

No, she would not lose him. She could not let that happen. She battled back, past her reactions and past the intrusions of the real world, finding him triumphant. He had both Danny and Declan and was dragging them toward the air.

She opened her eyes in time to see the three of them crawl out the door. Then all that she'd held at bay for Quin's sake rushed in on her like a black curtain, and she collapsed.

When she came to, she was cradled in her husband's lap. She knew it was Quin without opening her eyes. He felt solid and warm and smelled of heavy smoke. She could not have been happier, content to lie there and bask in having him near, until she heard the concern in his voice. "She has been like this for too long, Tiomoid."

"What she did cost her dear, but she'll be all right," Grandda answered. "She is unused to the manner in which she worked this day. Some Gifts come with a terrible price. She'll wake up when she's paid her due and not until."

"Spoken like a true McManus," she ventured to say before her husband cut off further speech in the muffling embrace he pressed on her as he gathered her into his arms and kissed her forehead.

When Quin eased his clasp enough, she tilted her head and looked at him. Soot streaked his face and collar, and concern dug deep lines around his mouth, but he looked to have come out of his rescue unscathed.

She inhaled a satisfied breath and swiveled to look at Grandda. He sat on the grass with a ruffled patchwork coverlet wrapped around his shoulders and a steaming mug in his hand. The wrinkles in his weathered skin showed white against the soot, but otherwise he looked well enough for a man whose house had gone up in flames.

"I'll do, *reannag bheag*, I'll do." He answered her concern before she could voice it. "And I'll make do."

"But your house. Your work—" she started to say.

"Aye, but the fire did not take anything of value. At least, not that I value above the lives saved. And our neighbors managed to quench the flames in time so that not as much is lost as ye might suppose."

"Then Danny will be all right?" Relief for Maeve sluiced through her.

"Mary says he'll be coughing black for a few days and his mother will have to make him sit up and watch for signs of pneumonia," Quin told her as he continued to cradle her in his arms. "He's young. He should recover right enough."

"And Declan." She searched her husband's dear face. "How is Mary's husband?"

"I've been better," a hoarse voice just over Quin's shoulder answered. "And I've been far worse. Though it's my ears that bother me most at the moment."

Quin kept one arm around her still as he turned to look up at his foreman and friend who stood over them, soot streaked and wrapped in his own coverlet.

"Your ears?" Quin drew his brows together in mock

consternation. "Now, if it were your arm paining you, boy-o, I'd have to shoulder the blame, seeing's I stepped on it on my way to find Danny."

"Mary boxed my years once she knew I'd be all right." A coughing fit nearly doubled Declan for a moment. He flexed his arm and looked at them with his own brow raised. "Have a care next time, will you, Quin? It's one of a kind and it has to last me." His broad smile invited all to share in his joke.

"Have a care yerself and thank Quin for going in to fetch ye, Declan Rogers, or I'll box them twice next time ye go racing into a burning building." Mary slipped her arm around her husband's waist. "I sent Danny home with his mother and I intend to do the same with you."

"I like your cooking better than Danny's mother's," Declan teased. "If I promise to be good, will you let me come home with you? I feel the urge to give my son a kiss."

It felt good to laugh now that the worst of the fright was over, though the sounds of their chuckles seemed at odds with the activity still bustling around them. The inhabitants of Beannacht village were still hard at work, tending the smoldering ruins of Grandda's workroom, cleaning up, and tending to one another as good neighbors should.

"Fenella Doyle and that Caitlin O'Brien have all the little ones tucked in safe in the church narthex, where they have their lessons," Mary said when she caught her breath. "I'll get you settled, then go to fetch Davey."

Another coughing fit doubled Declan over, so he just waved his farewell and moved off through the thinning wisps of smoke.

Nora Doyle and Grania Keane handed out hot mugs of tea despite being waterlogged and dirt-streaked from their efforts in the bucket line. The shipwrights and seamen sorted the buckets, sending them off with some of the older lads back to ship and storerooms against another day. The whole village seemed abuzz with the activity and banter of busy people.

Dan Kelly Sr. approached with Benen McManus and several other men loaded down with some of Grandda's salvaged belongings.

"Yer workroom and the attic above are gone, Tiomoid," the dry-goods-store owner said without preamble. "It was too close when we got here. From what little Danny could manage, seems he knocked a lamp over on some wood shavings, then tried to put the flames out himself before turning his attention to yer drawings and models."

"We found these under yer wife's lilac bushes." Dermot Keane placed a roll of diagrams and Grandda's latest models on the ground beside him.

The men deposited the rest of their loads on the grass. Much of it was damp or smoke-streaked. Some things were scorched outright. More must be just gone. Tears prickled Siannon's eyes at the sight. Quin gave her arm a reassuring squeeze.

Grandda's shoulders sagged under his coverlet while he eyed the mess. "Not much to show fer a lifetime of work and a lifetime of marriage."

Dan Kelly nodded in sympathy, then turned his attention to Quin. "I can't thank you enough, Captain Reilly, fer findin' me grandson like ye did, when we'd given him up fer lost. I don't know how ye did it, but I'm in yer debt."

"I had help." Quin looked at Siannon with a blaze

of light that lit his green eyes and made her heart forget to beat.

"You heard me?" she gasped.

"Aye, you were just as your grandfather described you, *reannag bheag,* a little star that lit the way for me. For us all."

Ridiculously pleased that he had felt her with him in the smoke, Siannon fixed her gaze on the trunk Benen carried, her mother's trunk, the one that held all her mother's suffering and secrets. The one she hadn't been able to bring herself to open even after her grandfather had transferred the trunks to the keeping room.

She explored all the rest during her visits to Grandda. Fingering her christening robe and laughing over the pictures she had scribbled for her mother, so like the ones from Timmy she herself treasured. Smelling again the comfort of her mother's sage and verbena scent. Yet, she still had not been able to bring herself to even touch this one.

"Put that all on the cart, Benen," Quin directed. "We'll store things up at the house until you get things squared away, Tiomoid."

"No," Siannon heard herself saying.

Now. Like a warm summer breeze wafting through her, Siannon felt her mother's bidding. It was time to open the trunk and unlock the secrets.

Not here. Not in the open for all to see. Whatever lurked inside was dark and frightening, not something to be shared.

Here. The breeze puffed encouragement.

Still, she could not bring herself to so much as move her hand toward the clasp. Reaching out to Quin during his rescue had both exhilarated and drained her. Remembering all that had jolted through her in the attic when Grandda had first sent her up there, she didn't think she could stand any further use of her Gift just now.

"Little star?" Grandda's worry reached her from far away.

"Siannon?" Quin's voice sounded oddly at a distance. Wasn't he still kneeling right beside her?

"What is it, *reannag bheag*?" Firmer now, The McManus asserted his right to an answer.

"The trunk," she managed to say. *Hurry*.

She could not put this off, too much rode on it. "I must open it, now."

Quin let her go so that she could rise to her knees. She looked over her shoulders at the two men she loved so dearly. Concern laced their expressions, but what gave her the strength to face her fears and turn back to the trunk was the underlying trust and faith she saw in both their faces. They believed that she knew what she was doing, and that gave her the strength to face whatever lay inside.

She placed her hands on the timeworn lid and waited for the frisson of white-hot energy to sizzle through her as it had the first time. Nothing. Pain and fear still lingered inside. Entreaty and warning. But not for her.

She raised the lid. Verbena and sage flowed through her. Her mother. There were shawls and several pairs of gloves on the first layer. Paper crackled as she reached beneath several lovingly wrapped silk nightdresses. Sorrow flowed from these things, dreams that had died long before they'd been packed. What danger could possibly lurk here? Where was all the horror she had sensed before?

Patience.

And then her fingers touched hard leather. A book. She drew it out with both hands. Triumph scoured her as the heavy tome landed on her lap. Larger than a diary, thicker than a ledger, the book had several papers wedged in its pages. It also had a lock.

Her mother's love poured from this book, love for her daughter, love for Beannacht, and under that a keening love for the husband she had lost to greed and ambition.

Heedless of the crowd gathering around in curiosity save to feel their sympathy, tears welled in Siannon's eyes. Her mother's tears, unshed for so long. Her breath hitched and her soul ached for her mother's lost dreams. Quin placed a consoling arm around her shoulders.

"Would you like me to cut the clasp now, Siannon?" Quin offered. The crowd murmured their approval. "Or would you like to wait until I get you home and settled in some privacy."

The villagers did not take the hint. They leaned in for a closer look. Siannon managed a watery smile. "When you live as close as we all do, there's no use in trying to keep secrets; that's what my gran would say. Let's see this through now."

He sliced the clasp with the small dagger Benen offered him. And the loose papers fluttered out into the open.

Wildness ripped through her, grief, agonizing worry, and a despair so strong, it tore jagged holes in her heart. Pain exploded at her temples. This time she was prepared. This time she was stronger. She battled back the darkness.

The proof.

Quin gathered up the papers and held them out to her. She shook her head. She wasn't up to reading just then. The ragged grief and jarring emotions were still too raw.

"You read them."

"What is it, Captain?" Dermot Keane craned his neck.

"What did your mother send here so carefully hidden, child?" Grandda asked.

"Whatever it is," she said, "my mother thought it was enough to buy our freedom. To make my father let us go."

"If only she'd told me." Grandda let the old grief, the old wounds, dangle in the air.

"She couldn't, Grandda. It's a very dark thing, and she wasn't sure enough of what to do to tell about it."

"Diabhal," Quin cursed through gritted teeth.

"Until now," Grandda supplied.

"Until now," Siannon agreed. She looked at Quin scowling at the papers.

"More's the pity," he growled. "We could have put paid to your father long since if only we'd known. The blackguard."

"What is it, Quintin?" Grandda stood then, as did Quin. He looked so fierce—anger and indignation rippled from him for all to see.

"Seems Rhodes was engaged in slavery in the Caribbean long after the Slavery Abolition Act was passed." He spoke to Grandda, but he kept his gaze fixed on Siannon. "Somehow, Mary got a hold of these papers proving his wealth was based on criminal profits. Profits based on human suffering." He practically spit out the last.

Grandda closed his eyes. "She must have thought to use this to make him stop. To make him let her come home."

Look.

Siannon looked at the page that she clutched in her hand. Her mother's handwriting leapt at her. "When I knew what kind of man he was, the depths he would sink to, to gain his ends, I knew I had to give up once and for all my dream of the man I'd once thought Eustace to be." She read the words quietly aloud. "I had to get Siannon away before he used her too."

"Oh, Quin. Oh, Grandda."

Quin held her close and kissed her temple as her tears flowed.

"There is still good to be wrung from this. We can force your father to cease, to give up his claims to Timmy and to leave us in peace. A man such as he would not favor prison. Your mother will have her retribution."

"But what of all the people who have suffered because of him? All that he has cost them?"

"Retribution comes in many ways, *reannag bheag.*" Grandda spoke with a harsh edge to his voice. "For some it is swift, for others slow and painful."

"I'll set Gill to this investigation." Quin gripped her shoulders. "He'll know what to do to ensure your father is stopped. In the meantime, since Kiernan is out of commission for the time being, I've a ship to ready to catch the next tide."

Chapter Sixteen

Sunlight glimmered over familiar blue water as a fresh salt-tipped wind whipped into the rigging and teased the sails awaiting their first time at sea.

Quin strode down the quay, his boots ringing loud against the docking. His time away from the island had felt more like months than weeks. A more exquisite welcome home he couldn't imagine save the one he planned in Siannon's arms this night.

The barque, *Julianna's Dream* after her new owner's wife, finished and fine, tasted the water with a resounding splash, ending the long struggle to build her as a cheer burgeoned up from the shipwrights gathered around.

Slowly easing out of her dry dock and slicing into the water with an eagerness that more than fit her name and the Reilly heritage she represented, the *Dream* was ready for the journey around the Cape and

over to Bristol, England, her new home port and to
receive her official christening. They'd brought her
in with time to spare, thanks to Declan and all the
men who'd put in extra hours over the past month
to make it so.

James Reilly had always said there was nothing to
compare with the sight and sound of ship meeting
water for the first time. How many family dinners had
Quin spent expounding that very perception with his
father? He shook his head and grinned.

As the barque's virgin keel sliced cleanly into the
water, fierce pride raced through Quin, and he finally
tasted an inkling of his sire's meaning. How right
he'd been.

Quin was glad he'd been able to conclude his business with Rhodes, and with Gill and Bryan as well,
on the mainland, and return in time to witness the
launch. Despite Rhodes's recalcitrant manner and
the evil pall that had hung over the shipyard for the
past decade, they had triumphed. The struggle had
been more than worthwhile, and there was no deny-
ing the deep satisfaction to be seen on the faces of
the men gathered around.

"Good job, Declan." Quin thumped the shipyard's
foreman on the back as another cheer rose up from
the gathered crowd, nearly drowning him out.

All raised their mugs in salute, a tradition at Reilly
Ship Works to christen and toast all the vessels
wrought there with good Irish ale to ensure safe passage for the ship and good health to all who had a
hand in her creation.

"Thanks for keeping things moving despite the
odds, boy-o." Quin spoke this last for Declan alone.
"All's well that ends well."

"Welcome back!" Declan raised his mug to Quin. "If I'd known you were due back this day, I'd have waited the launching for you. But it's not me ye need to thank, Quintin Reilly, although the praise is much appreciated."

Declan drained his ale and essayed a mock bow. "It's the women who managed the final bit and tied our parcel together."

"The women?"

"Aye." Declan nodded and directed his gaze off into the crowd. There were more women there than usual for all save a Reilly boat launching. He searched the crowd for a familiar flash of red-gold, unable to contain his disappointment that Siannon was nowhere in sight.

Nora Doyle and her brood stood stiffly in a cluster by the shipwrights, dressed in their Sunday best, including new shoes. At the front of the crowd, Grania Keane held her husband's arm and beamed a broad smile as her eyes followed the *Dream*'s masts skyward. Beside her, Dermot tugged at a collar that to Quin's eye looked as if it had more than enough starch.

Out of the corner of his eye, Quin saw Mary cuddling young Davey and whispering to Bridget McGee. Maeve Kelly was there with her boys. All the village women—wives, mothers, and sisters—stood with their menfolk, pride beaming from each and every one of them as they gazed at the ship.

Where were Siannon and Timmy? "I don't understand."

"All their work paid off, Quin. With more benefit than any of us imagined." Declan lifted a brow and studied him as Quin shook his head, at a loss.

Declan nudged Quin with his elbow. "Do you not

remember your wife organizing the others into painting barrels upon barrels of pottery?"

"I remember," Kiernan Rogers inserted with a wry grin from where he stood beside his brother. "I remember each and every barrel I escorted to Limerick with all of them warnin' me to be careful as if I were a lad at Sunday tea sure to break our gran's best cup." He rolled his eyes.

"Ah, yes." Quin rubbed his jaw. Where was his wife? He was eager to see her, although crockery had little to do with his thoughts of her. The trip had held him too long away. "I remember the numerous complaints I heard from their husbands. What about it?"

Declan laughed. "Well, they painted enough pottery to supply the canvas for the *Dream,* there. No sooner had you set foot in Limerick than we received a missive from the sailmaker in Tralee insisting we must make payment in full before they'd deliver. Much as I hate to admit it, without the payment our women supplied, we mightn't have made our deadline."

"Aye, he's right there, Captain." Kiernan echoed his brother. "And there'll be no turning them away from it now. My Bridget's already asking me to build a special room with extra windows onto our cottage."

"Indeed?" Another thing he had to be thankful for. When he'd first asked Siannon to help him with the wives of the shipwrights, he'd had no idea of the benefit gained in such an unexpected way.

"Indeed."

"They don't intend to stop that infernal nonsense anytime in the near future." Dermot leaned forward to complain in a dissatisfied undertone. "Pardon,

Captain Reilly, I overheard ye. They've been a help, I'll admit that. But it looks like I've got to resign meself to too much starch and not enough socks.'' A forlorn sigh accompanied the last even while a glow of pride lit his face as he looked toward Grania.

Quin smothered a laugh as he realized that many of the faces of his men bore similar expressions of pride and perturbation mixed together. It made for an odd and somewhat painful combination.

"Speaking of Siannon—" His question to Declan was interrupted by parting of the crowd.

"Well done, Reilly." Jonathan Carruthers, the *Dream*'s owner, approached, his hand extended. He was a rugged man, a former ship's captain himself, now establishing a wine-importing business in Bristol. The *Dream* would run from Bristol to Marseilles if his plans held.

"Aye, Mr. Carruthers." Quin shook his hand.

"I must say, I had my doubts there for a while. Reports of delays and problems have been coming my way for some time now. And with your father's absence, I had begun to wonder if my ship would be ready at all."

The man's comments raised the hackles on Quin's neck, and he struggled to keep the ire from showing on his face. This man couldn't know the battle they had faced in order to fulfill his contract and deliver the vessel.

"But I can see," Carruthers continued, admiration rife in the gaze he ran over the ship, "my information was incorrect. Your shipyard appears to be all I was told originally by your father. I am more than pleased with *Julianna's Dream*."

Declan's gaze caught Quin's, and the foreman

offered a shrug as he stepped away to let the discussion continue in the relative privacy the celebration afforded.

Obviously the man might know ships, but he was not yet polished in his business dealings. Quin recognized this failing and his hackles lowered as Carruthers continued. "I can foresee the need for at least two more such vessels in the near future. Perhaps even a third on a larger scale, depending on how profitable my new ventures prove to be. I gather you are now in charge of Reilly Ship Works. Do you think you'll be able to handle the demand?"

"Aye." Quin nodded. Fresh pride welled through him, tugging his shoulders straight. *You're in charge of Reilly Ship Works now.* Something in the way Carruthers put it made him realize that he truly had become a part of the Ship Works in a way he never had been before. Part of the struggle and the labor and the innate self-respect that went along with every nail pounded through and every plank set. A ship's captain put to shore, but for the first time the thought didn't wrench conflicted needs in his heart. How odd.

And then again not, as he thought of his wife, wherever she might be. Siannon in his arms, kissing him, that was where she should be.

He shook off the temptation to stride up the hill looking for her and tended to business. "Would you like to spend some time going over the specifics now?"

"I've already spoken with the other fellow, the one who lost his arm?" Carruthers motioned toward Declan and Kiernan.

"Declan Rogers."

"Yes, he was very helpful and more than happy to

discuss details with me when I gave him the bank draft to pay off the remainder of *Julianna's Dream*." Carruthers let loose a hearty laugh that rippled out over the water. "I've left my specifications with him. If you can turn those out as timely and skillfully as you have this one, I have a number of friends I can direct your way."

"That would be much appreciated."

Carruthers nodded and offered his hand again. "Not at all. Happy to do it. I like a man who can keep to his schedule and meet his promises. The legal firm that sees to my affairs will forward the contracts as before. Willard Jefferies is my man's name."

With a firm shake on the deal, Quin thought back to Siannon. There were other promises he had yet to keep both to himself and to Siannon and Timmy. But there would be time for that now.

"Quin." Only his name, soft and quick, and yet it set Quin's heart to thumping faster in his chest.

He turned to find Siannon standing next to him in the pale turquoise gown she had worn before he left. The image he had carried in his mind, along with so many others as he waited his chance to return to her. Memories were etched in the depths of her eyes, their time in Granny's cottage, the fire, and their farewell. His chest tightened.

"Siannon." For a moment he forgot time and place and could only remember his need to hold her.

"Ahem." Carruthers cleared his throat. "Your wife, I presume? I understand you just returned."

"Aye." Quin couldn't seem to keep the smile from his face, so he gave up the struggle. "My wife, Siannon Reilly. Siannon, this is Jonathan Carruthers."

"How do you do?" Siannon nodded politely and then transferred her gaze back to Quin's.

"Fine indeed, ma'am. Your pardon, but you seem familiar to me. Do I know you, Mrs. Reilly?"

Siannon paled slightly and stared at Carruthers for a moment without answering. Then she smiled and her tone held firm. "I believe we met in Limerick once. I was formerly Mrs. Percival Crofton."

"Ah, yes. I remember Mr. Crofton. An excellent man of business. A shame. Belated condolences, my dear."

Siannon nodded. "Thank you, but none are necessary. Percy lived a full life and had no regrets. I am very happy here on Beannacht."

Pride surged through Quin again. He wished they were away from the crowd and prying eyes so that he might show her just how pleased he was with her answer.

Carruthers nodded and returned his gaze to Quin. "If there is nothing else you require from me, Mr. Reilly, I will bid you good day and depart with my new vessel. I don't want to miss the tide."

"Good luck with her, Carruthers. May the wind be always at your back."

"Jefferies will be in touch." The man tipped his bowler and disappeared into the swirling throngs along Beannacht's small quay.

Jefferies, the name had a familiar ring to it that Quin could not quite place. Later. He turned to Siannon. The all-too-familiar burn started again way down deep inside him. He linked his hands with hers and pulled her nearer, rewarded with the wonderful scents of lavender, lilac, and Siannon.

"Hullo, wife."

"Hullo, husband."

The glow in her eyes turned the flame inside him up a notch. Damn the crowds. He pulled her closer and kissed her softly, banking the raw hunger that welled up at the taste of her.

"I have much to tell you, Siannon. Where is Timothy?"

"He's gone with Kevan and Seamus, closer to the water. They promised to keep an eye on him."

Quin followed her direction to find Timmy standing as proud as the other boys did with their gazes glued to the new barque.

"Come then, there is much to discuss." He linked her arm through his and made his way through the congratulatory crowd with her at his side. Spying Declan with his arm around Mary, Quin caught the foreman's eye and nodded toward the office.

Declan nodded back, catching the unspoken message.

In moments they had reached the office. Declan was not far behind them.

"Hullo, Siannon. What's up, Captain?" He nodded to Siannon and perched himself comfortably on the edge of Quin's desk.

"I've much news from my travels. First, we've an investor coming on board in the not too distant future. I saw Bryan in Dublin."

"Dublin?"

"Aye, Siannon, a long tale. Suffice it to say I had a delivery for him that he was more than pleased to receive. And the financing he went in search of has turned up in the most unexpected place."

"Unexpected?"

Behind Quin's words lurked deep satisfaction and

the knowledge that perhaps an old wound had begun to heal. Along with that, Siannon caught something murky about a woman with pale white-gold hair and how foolishly proud Bryan had looked standing next to her.

"Aye. They'll be along sometime soon, I'm sure. And I'll give you all the details." His green eyes shone with satisfaction. "More important, I believe we have finally put an end to the sabotage that has hounded us for far longer than we realized."

Declan raised a brow in question at the bend in the conversation. Siannon sighed. "My father."

"Ah." Declan's brow cleared, but his look hardened to match Quin's.

"I met with Eustace almost as soon as I reached Limerick. He wasn't a bit happy to find me perched on his doorstep and fixed for battle. But the evidence in my hand and my connections through Gill's office made him much more amenable to discussion than he might otherwise have been.

"He capitulated completely, Siannon." Quin rapped his knuckles on the desk. "Even Nigel Franklin has washed his hands of the matter. Gill has the papers now and will hold them until such time as they may be needed."

Declan chuckled. "Ye threatened him, then?"

"Aye, boy-o. Flat out. Rhodes is a man all too accustomed to getting his way. Our discussion was not pretty and not at all gentlemanly." Quin rubbed his jaw. "But there are some things even he could not argue with. In the end he was backed into a corner by his own machinations.

"Either he saw reason and released his determination to work against us or he faced ending his life in

prison, paying for the dastardly trade he engaged in."
His gaze fixed on Siannon, who worried her lips with
her teeth.

"Are you sure, Quin?" Doubt edged through her.
"My father is not given to seeing reason, especially
when it is not *his* reason. I cannot believe he would
easily give up his quest after all this time to destroy
you or control Timmy."

"I know." Quin laced his fingers with hers and
drew her nearer. "But he knows that I can set the
torch to his destruction any time. For once in this
whole sorry debacle we hold the upper hand. I only
wish we could have done the same for your mother.
I made it clear that it was only for your sake and for
the sake of our son that I was not pursuing his long-
needed retribution. He is angry, but he is not mad."

Siannon could only hope Quin was correct, but she
remembered too well her father's anger and the cold,
empty places inside him where his heart and soul
should have been. Only his love for Timmy had made
him really human. His love for Timmy was warm and
caring and true. Quin squeezed her fingers and she
squeezed his in return, feeling the rippling confidence underlying his words.

"He's leaving, Siannon," Quin told her. "Leaving
Limerick, leaving Ireland. He's going to pursue his
interests in the islands and won't be back. Listening
to him, I got the feeling that this was not a spur-of-
the-moment decision accomplished only because I
was there to confront him. He's been planning this
for a long while. Perhaps he always suspected his
misdeeds would catch up with him eventually."

"Aye, I hope you're right."

That news twisted a sharp pang of unease inside

her. She wished she could dislodge it and cling only to Quin's certainty. But the memory of all that bolted through her when she finally opened her mother's trunks and touched the papers that bore evidence against her father still mantled her heart.

"Good riddance." Declan offered his own insight. "It's a good thing you didn't take me along with ye. One arm or two, I'd have had enough to scuttle his hide for ye."

Quin laughed. "I was tempted to scuttle him once or twice myself, but I managed not to. He knows the situation he's placed himself in. There is far more gain open to him in his choice to place himself on the other side of the world from us than to remain where his past can only serve to do him injury."

Declan scowled, obviously spoiling for a fight. "At any rate, it's done now, you say? And where does that leave us with our suppliers and the problems we've been facing?"

"Good question. It will take us months at the very least to begin repairing the damage Rhodes has spent so many years manipulating. Possibly longer than that. But that does not concern me." Quin slipped his arm around Siannon's shoulders and gave her a reassuring squeeze as she continued to fight the waves of unease rippling through her.

"We've a long history here on Beannacht, and despite what Rhodes has done, he cannot take away from the work we do here and the ships we build. Though it will still be an uphill struggle, we will eventually overcome this. Reilly Ship Works will be all that my family intended it to be."

"Aye." Declan sighed and offered a lopsided smile. "There is nothing worth havin' that comes easy, as my old mum used to say. Pity there's so darn much truth in that statement."

"Indeed."

"And yon client was quite please with the *Dream*."

"And we have the promise of at least two more."

Siannon hid a smile as Declan and Quin locked gazes with the kind of wide grins she hadn't seen on either of them since they were children. Their pleasure overrode the nagging in her heart. Nostalgia twirled through her for the boy her husband had been. But she would not wish him back; she loved the man he had become even more.

"Well, that's it, then." Declan capped a hand to Quin's shoulder. "This is a good day. I'd best go share it with the men."

"Do that. And, Declan?"

"Aye."

"Make sure they know that it is due to them that we have this new contract."

"Aye." He nodded to Quin. "Siannon?" He paused in the doorway.

"Yes?"

"Thank you again for doin' what you did." He tilted his head toward the shipyard. "For helpin' the wives with your pottery."

"China," she corrected him with a smile.

"Aye, so Mary tells me." Declan scratched his head, his look skeptical as he continued. "But it all looks like crockery to me."

He winked. "Yer help, their help, got us through."

"You're very welcome." She curtsied. "But they helped me as well, so the bargain was twofold and well worth it."

He disappeared back through the doorway, his footsteps taking the stairs with a quick tattoo.

"Siannon."

She would never become accustomed to the low, intimate way Quin said her name. She turned back to face him.

"I'd like to add my thanks to Declan's and to the rest of the men I saw out there caught between pride and chagrin. They are a proud lot, not given to charity. They have seen that their wives are just as capable of contributing as they are and that the shipyard is every bit as important to every member of their families."

"They are very like their employer in that respect."

"Aye. I think you're right." He crossed the distance separating them. "I missed you, wife."

Four little words, but it was the closest he had ever come to saying what she really wanted to hear. Her throat tightened. "And I you, husband."

He pulled her toward him for a thoroughly satisfying kiss that left her in no doubt as to just how much he had missed her. "A few short weeks ago, Siannon Reilly, I wouldn't have believed one woman could make such a difference in my life."

"And now?" she asked, leaning back in his arms to watch his face.

"Right now I've had enough talking to last a lifetime." His eyes, that deep green she'd missed so much while he was gone, darkened slightly as he bent his head to hers. And deep inside him rippled the edges of feelings that warmed Siannon through and through. "I need a thorough welcome home, *mo ceile*, one to fill the empty days since we parted."

He pulled her against him and laced his fingers up

into her hair, pulling loose the pins until it showered down her back. Everything inside her flowed toward him.

"Lock the door," she managed to say as he released her lips to nuzzle her neck.

"Aye."

An hour later she was straightening her skirts and trying to redo her coiffure without benefit of a mirror, but it was more than worth it. He'd made love to here in the office, as she had suspected he wanted to do once before—the only other time she had entered this sacred portal.

Sacred. Heat washed her cheeks as she watched him button his shirt. She could still feel his muscled chest pressed against hers as he loved her in the full light of day. Her knees were still weak from his attentions, which were all the more exciting with the noise of celebration continuing just outside and the risk of discovery imminent. The whole interlude had been every bit as warming and satisfying as she suspected it would be.

Her husband was well and truly home.

She turned away from him as his gaze caught hers. If they didn't turn their minds to other pursuits, they would likely spend the rest of the day in occupations that had nothing to do with shipbuilding.

"Quin, there's a letter here."

"Aye?" He peered over her shoulder at the contents on his desk, pulling her back against him as he did so, to softly nuzzle her neck.

"It's from America."

That piqued his interest. He retrieved the envelope she had picked up from the desk.

"It's from Maine. From Devin." He tore it open.

"What on earth is that pup doing in Maine?" He scanned the contents in silence for a moment before letting out a low chuckle. "Stubborn and determined. So much for him going back to the university. That'll teach me to misjudge one of my brothers."

"What is it?"

"Devin is indeed in America and he seems to think he's come up with a new supplier for lumber. 'Direct from the forest to the shipyard' is how he's put it."

He scooped her into his arms and twirled her around without further explanation. A frantic knock at the door halted him just before his lips reached hers.

"Come."

"Quin."

Both words fell at the same time, Quin's filled with curiosity and annoyance, Siannon's with black dread. The knock seemed to echo inside her like loud claps of thunder rolling over the ocean as she watched the doorknob turn ever so slowly.

"Unlock the door, Quin," she whispered, her voice choked with fear.

He swung the door inward. Her heartbeat drummed in her ears far too fast as Caitlin stumbled breathless in to the office. The young nurse's face was bright red and streaked with tears, as though she had been slapped repeatedly.

"*Diabhal.*" Quin crossed back to Siannon in two long strides. "What happened."

"Where is Timmy?"

"They've taken him, ma'am," she gasped. "Them men. I tried to stop them, but they hit me."

Her words shot through Siannon, and she didn't need to ask who or why.

"My father." She turned to Quin as Caitlin wept into her apron, trembling and overwrought.

Quin helped Caitlin into the nearest chair and knelt before her. "Tell us the whole of it, Caitlin, and quickly. How long ago?"

"Not long, sir. We were on our way back to the house. Timmy was so excited and we were going to make a . . . a special tea to celebrate. Then these blokes just swarmed over us and took the lad up like he was a sack of flour. There were so many of them."

"I tried to stop them." She turned a tearful plea toward Siannon. "I tried, Missus, but they struck me down and ran off with him."

Siannon longed to comfort the girl, to commend her for trying and for running here right away, but there was no time. She needed to get the whole story first.

"Which way?" Urgency rammed Quin's question home and rippled through Siannon.

Caitlin swallowed, hiccoughed, and took a breath. "They headed off toward St. Bridgid's. I watched them disappear down the path, and then I came straight here."

"Good lass."

"Oh, Missus, I'm so sorry." Caitlin cried into her apron again. Siannon stroked Caitlin's hair, but she wished it were Timmy she was soothing, and hoped her son was not suffering the same kind of fear as his nurse must be experiencing.

Her father loved him. Surely he would not harm his grandson. But the thought offered little comfort when juxtaposed with all she knew about her father, both from her own experiences and from her mother's pain.

"Quin?"

"Aye, darlin', the cove beyond St. Bridgid's. It's the only place he could have put to shore without us knowing. But because of the hills, it's also the slowest spot to put out to sea. Eustace wouldn't know that. We've a chance to catch him still."

"Caitlin, can you go and find Declan and Kiernan Rogers and tell them what's happened?" Quin's question was more a command. "Send them to the cove, and quickly—along with any other men they can bring."

The nurse nodded, accepting Quin's commands as she wiped the tears from her face. She looked glad for the direction. "Aye, sir."

"Quin?"

He turned to Siannon. "I was too lenient with your father, too willing to believe he would drop his malevolent course. I should have known better. I won't make that mistake again."

Dead certainty echoed behind his words and shuddered through her.

"Stay here, I'll bring Timmy back to you. I swear it."

"No, Quin." She shook her head. "They are my son and my father. I cannot stay here and wait. I can hold my own on the way to the cove. It won't be the first time I've trailed after you."

"Aye." He stroked her face, his mouth a grim line. "Come on, then, Siannon. Let's go get our son."

Chapter Seventeen

Caitlin gathered her skirts and hurried out the door ahead of them, scurrying as fast as she could.

Quin sent a swift prayer after her that she would find Declan and Kiernan quickly. From her descriptions of the men who attacked her and took Timmy, he could use all the help he could get to retrieve the boy unharmed.

He turned toward the cabinets behind the desk, where he'd unearthed all of his father's correspondence over the last few months. Inside one cabinet lay something that had surprised him at the time but now held possibilities he'd never thought to face.

He pulled open the door and reached inside to retrieve his gun. It felt cold and deadly in his grasp. Siannon's worried gaze snared his as he turned with the pistol in his hand.

"Siannon—"

"I know." Her face was pale but determined, not refuting his need to bring the weapon along.

She swallowed. "I hope you don't have to use it either."

"Come on, then." Rhodes had too much of a head start on them already. There was no time to debate their course.

The choice once made cannot be undone.

The thought echoed through him as they ran, affixing a new and sinister ring to Granny's old tales.

How unbounded of Rhodes to agree to all of Quin's demands and then undermine them by coming to Beannacht on Quin's heels. The timing of it could not have been worse. With everyone gathered at the shipyard to watch the barque's launch, there was no one left on guard, no one to ring the bells at St. Bridgid's to announce an intruder.

Siannon ran beside him, keeping his pace with a determination he admired. He could imagine what she was feeling. Her mother had passed along all of her horror at what Rhodes had done to her and all of his misdeeds to others. Quin damned himself for not following his gut in his dealings with the man. Now his overconfidence had put Timmy in danger.

They raced down the path toward St. Bridgid's as the bells sounded high against the early evening sky, skidding them to a halt.

"He's there, he's got to be." Siannon panted, holding her side. "I can feel it."

"Aye." Quin nodded, reaching out a hand to steady her. "Father Dunnavan would know how to ring the bell to announce an unknown ship."

"Oh, Quin."

"We'll get him." He squeezed her shoulders for

emphasis, as much a vow as an attempt at reassurance. "We'll get him."

St. Bridgid's rose before them. An old, dark gray stone edifice that had withstood the repeated and sometimes virulent pounding of Beannacht's winter storms and the passage of time. It had been there almost since the time of the Druids. It had lasted through Viking raids and the ever changing political climate through the centuries. Praise heaven it would see them through this as well and still be standing when Timmy is a very old man.

The bell was still swinging back and forth as they reached the steps and the archway that led into the cool, darkened interior.

"Father? Father Dunnavan?" Quin called into the church, hoping to gain some information. If the priest had seen Timmy and Rhodes, he would be able to direct them.

"Father." Behind him, Siannon's gasp sent chills up his spine.

"Hello, daughter." Rhodes's cold greeting rippled toward them from within the sanctuary. "I see you have completed your journey into your mother's mindlessness. I am not surprised."

As Quin's eyes adjusted to the interior of the church, he could make out the crumpled form of Father Dunnavan on the stone steps at Eustace's feet. Eustace stood before the simple granite altar, his self-satisfied smirk a sacrilege all its own.

"What have you done?" Anger roiled through Quin. "Where is my son?"

"Da!" A shrill squeak of protest came from beside the altar, just beyond Father Dunnavan's still form.

"*Your* son." Rhodes laughed, the sound tinged with

indignant disbelief. "Percy would probably disagree with that. Wouldn't he, Siannon? After all the work he did to accomplish the task of getting you with child."

"Father—"

"Oh, don't worry, the meddlesome priest is not dead." Rhodes cut off Siannon's distress and waved a dismissive hand. "At least not yet. He came upon me as we awaited my ship's departure. I chose to remain hidden here when your latest venture rounded the point lest you be on board for her maiden voyage, Reilly. Your island tides have provided some difficulties. Timothy and I will be on our way to our new home soon enough, however."

"No." Siannon breathed the word. "Please."

"Come to me, Timothy," Rhodes directed over his shoulder.

Quin watched as Timmy, pale and frightened, crept forward to stand near his grandfather. Loyalty and trepidation warred on his young face. Siannon moaned softly as her father placed his arm around the lad's shoulders and pulled him closer.

Quin's fingers itched for the weight of the gun in his pocket, but he dared not pull it out until he had further gauged Rhodes's stance. Quin edged slowly down the aisle between the darkly polished pews with Siannon behind him, wondering where the thugs Caitlin described had gone to, and hoping the young nurse had delivered his message.

"This is the one thing you did right in your life, daughter." Rhodes patted the lad's shoulder approvingly. "Beyond Timothy you have been a severe disappointment. But then, I should have expected nothing less, given your mother's temperament."

"There was nothing wrong with my mother." Siannon's voice shook. "You know that better than anyone."

"Indeed?" Rhodes laughed again. "The doctors didn't agree with you."

"Doctors that you paid to commit her."

"I did what I had to." Rhodes shrugged.

"You did what you have always done, Father, exactly what you wanted to do. And you tortured her with her love for you."

Rhodes narrowed his gaze. "Insolence was ever your strong suit, Siannon. Shut your mouth before you anger me further."

"Stop where you are, Captain Reilly." He lifted a brow at Quin and continued without pausing for breath. "Or you will suffer the full consequences of your ill-advised actions. I am not alone here. I have come more than prepared to reclaim what is mine."

Timmy uttered a single sob as his grandfather squeezed his shoulders. "My wife saw fit to gift me with one puling daughter. Percival fulfilled his bargain with me by seeing to it that I had a grandson, and I intend to see that the lad is raised as he should be. Fully cognizant of his place in society and all that is owed to him."

"You cannot stay in Ireland. I thought you understood that." Quin stopped, close enough to see the worry on Timmy's face, the calculating determination in Rhodes's eyes, and the cold solid black of the pistol in his hand.

"Indeed." Rhodes nodded, unperturbed. "You have managed to make my adopted homeland as well the rest of Her Majesty's dominions unavailable to me. Pity for you. As you have seen, your family paid for past mistakes with your livelihood and your island's miserable future. It may take me longer to achieve my ends from across the world, but I am a patient man. Retribution will come to you in its own sweet time. Never fear."

"You love Timmy. I know you do. Prove it, Father. You're frightening Timmy, not binding him closer to you. Is this the legacy you wish to leave your grandson? Tearing him away from his mother? His home?" Siannon's voice cracked over her words as she entreated her father, "Surely even you can recognize what you do is madness."

"Madness?" Rhodes chuckled coldly. "I think not, my dear. It was madness of Tiomoid and Michael McManus to think they could meddle in my affairs. It was madness of James Reilly to think he could interfere with the judgments of his betters. What I do now is merely fair-minded vengeance for the unwarranted attacks against my person."

"Fair-minded?" Siannon gasped. "I'd hardly call locking your wife away in a mental institution an unwarranted attack."

"She had plans I couldn't allow to come to fruition. Imagine, the trollop thought she could leave me and take the only thing of value she had brought to the marriage. Through you I gained what I truly wanted, an heir to carry on my name and to whom I could leave the fortune of wealth and influence I amassed."

He pulled Timmy closer against his side. "It is Mary's fault. Hers and both your families', that she is dead now. I offered her freedom and a lifetime of security. She had only to relent, to agree to let me keep our daughter, and she would have been re- leased. But she was far too headstrong for that. Headstrong, willful, and obstinate. A true Irish lass. Had I known those traits about her, I'd never have married her. She'd have come easily enough to my bed without benefit of the church's blessing. I could have had my fill of her without all the messy consequences. But I was blinded by my own passion for her. After that, I couldn't release her. She is better off dead."

Siannon shuddered and tears dripped down her cheeks. "How can you say that? She loved you. Even after all you had done. She still loved you."

"Don't you defend her with that," Rhodes snapped, his cheeks flushing a dull and angry red.

"It's true."

"I don't want to hear it. You know nothing of what went on between us. Nothing of her plotting and her threats against me. I was her lawful husband, her master. It was her duty to obey me, to serve me in any way I saw fit. Yet she dared threaten me with exposure."

"I know how she felt."

"You were but a child."

"She sent trunks here," Siannon told him, moving forward slightly. "That's where I found the information about what you had done. It's also where I found out what you did to her and how she felt. It was all locked away inside that trunk, waiting for me. It was the most awful thing I have ever been through."

"Maudlin female hysteria." Rhodes tsked in disgust. "You and your *feelings* disgust me. I should have known you would show no better loyalty than your mother. I cannot fathom how I managed to have a child such as you."

"Rhodes—"

"Ah, ah, ah, Reilly." Rhodes waved the pistol in

Timmy's direction and then back toward Siannon. "Don't tempt me to do something I'd rather not."

"You would threaten the grandson you claim to love?" Siannon whispered the question.

Rhodes shrugged, unconcerned by the cost his scorn exacted on his daughter or the example he set for his grandson, pale and wan at his side. "I know what I want and I know how to get it. There are those of us in life who are like that, my dear. And then there are those who pass through life as victims. It is your choice."

Horror gripped Siannon, burning wheels of pain burrowing down deep and killing off whatever remnants of affection and familial respect she might have once felt toward her father, almost bringing her to her knees. What roiled from him in the quiet confines of the ancient church was so cold and obsidian black, there was no end to it and no hope of redemption. How could any person harbor such emotions and still claim the ability to love anyone? With a shudder she realized that she couldn't even feel that. She couldn't even feel the one thing that had made him reachable. Though he still claimed aloud to love his grandson, there was nothing there, nothing where the emotion used to be inside him.

Everything her mother had felt, her hopes, dreams, and fears, which had flowed into Siannon when she'd finally opened those trunks, echoed inside her. Futility and loss. Even in the end, when her mother had faced her husband's heinous crimes and threats, she had still managed to love him. Siannon covered her mouth with her hand as bile rose in her throat.

Beside her, Quin's anger and determination glowed like a burning lantern. Energy welled inside him, and she could feel him holding himself back from the violence he wanted to vent against her father. But he was waiting, waiting and praying for Declan and Kiernan and the other men from the shipyard. She prayed with all her might that he was right and they were even now approaching St. Bridgid's. Fear held no place in her husband's thoughts, and she clung to that.

"You'll never leave here with my son." Challenge laced Quin's tone as it echoed from the high ceiling of the church.

Siannon bit her lip.

Her father laughed, a cold and virulent sound. "You will not stop me, Reilly. There is no use in trying. I would have no qualms about shooting you dead right now. It is only that I would prefer to have you suffer a slow and humiliating defeat first. You will end the same eventually. But it is what *I* prefer that holds sway here."

"Mr. Rhodes, we're ready when ye are, sir." A burly seaman entered the church through a side chapel door. "The way is clear and the tide is rising at last."

"No." Siannon couldn't stop her horror.

Her father smiled. "Farewell, Siannon. Reilly." He waved the pistol at both of them. "Who knows, we may meet again sometime in the future."

He urged Timothy toward the seaman.

"Mama. Da." Timmy hung back and Siannon's heart twisted inside her.

"Now, Timothy." Cold command laced her father's tone as he all but snarled at Timmy. "There is nothing here for you any longer."

Timmy looked toward her and then toward Quin, his gaze holding for the span of several heartbeats.

After a moment Quin nodded and Timmy turned toward the waiting seaman. Siannon's heart thundered in her ears as she watched him. *No, please, oh, please.*

She watched as her father patted Timmy's shoulder and released him, urging the boy toward the door. As soon as her father's hand left Timmy's shoulder, Quin's command exploded beside her. "Now, Timmy, run!"

As though he'd been expecting Quin's order before it was given, Timmy took off. He ducked between the waiting seaman's legs and disappeared out the chapel door, taking Siannon's heart and soul with him. She rushed forward, uncaring of anything but her son.

"Get him, you dolt!" her father shouted, and the seaman disappeared after Timmy, just as her father closed his hand over Siannon's wrist and dragged her to his side.

She struggled and he leveled the pistol at Quin's chest. "You have proven far more trouble than I anticiapted, Quintin Reilly."

"No."

"Shut up, my dear. I'll deal with you later. First I've your husband to see to. You were more useful to me as a widow anyway."

"Let her go, Rhodes. You've failed."

Her father chuckled, the sound rumbling against her back as his tight clasp dug into her skin. "Hardly. This is merely a small setback. Timothy will be retrieved and we will be on our way. But first I'll deal with you."

"No." Siannon struggled to allay his aim as he tensed his arm to pull the trigger.

"Enough," her father snarled.

She didn't see the blow coming. Stars exploded

behind her eyes as pain knocked her square in the temple. She crumpled at her father's feet, her head spinning and nausea swirling in her stomach.

"Siannon." She heard Quin's rough protest from a distance, and then the sharp report of the gun as her father shot Quin. Once. Twice. The sounds tore her to pieces, echoing inside her heart.

Blackness sucked at her, and she struggled to stay conscious. The church doors thundered open, banging against the stone walls.

"Not this time, Rhodes. Ye'll never hurt my family again." Grandda's voice filled her, vibrating with old anger and a determination not to be denied. She struggled to focus on him, standing in the doorway, framed by ancient stones and looking like a Fian warrior of old. The McManus had arrived with all the strength and fury that was his right, his duty.

Her father's surprise registered briefly before the loud report of a gun rang out.

Death swirled up to meet her, and her strength gave out as she plummeted into darkness.

"Give her a minute; she'll be all right. Won't ye, darlin'?"

"Grandda?" Confusion swirled in Siannon's thoughts. "What? Oh." Pain throbbed in her temples and memory returned, sparking hot tears in her eyes.

A hand smoothed over her forehead. "Shh." Lips pressed to hers, engulfing her in the salt of wild ocean waves and the glow of warm winter fires.

Quin.

She opened her eyes to find herself cradled in her husband's arms. His green-eyed gaze sparkled into her own as he pulled her closer.

"Thank heaven." Rough and tender, his words, as he pressed a kiss to her brow.

"But what happened? Where's Timmy? My father?" She struggled to sit up, ignoring the pain in her head. "I though he shot you."

"He tried, darlin'," her grandfather told her quietly. "But he did not succeed."

"But—"

"He's dead, Siannon," Quin told her. "Your grandfather saved your life, and mine as well."

So he had paid full measure for everything he had done—to her mother, to herself, to the Reillys. She glanced behind her, expecting to see the crumpled heap and empty shell that had been Eustace Rhodes.

"They've taken him out," Quin said gently.

"Good riddance," her grandfather growled, his tone tight with the memory of old pain. "He'll never hurt my family again."

She turned to look at her grandfather's grim face and the old rifle resting next to him against the polished oak of one of St. Bridgid's dark pews.

"Timmy?"

"He's outside with the men—Declan and Kiernan. Tiomoid brought them all."

From her grandfather, old pain and quiet satisfaction radiated. He'd laid to rest his own guilt at not saving his daughter. For that Siannon was grateful.

"Father Dunnavan's gone to fetch Mary. Beyond a headache, he's seems to be in good condition. We were a mite worried about ye though. Ye didn't seem in any hurry to wake up." Grandda leaned down and kissed her on the cheek. "Ye had me worried, little star."

"I'm sorry, Grandda."

"Well." He cleared his throat and winked at her. "Seein' as how ye're all right now, I'll go see about my great-grandson."

He took up the gun and slung it over his shoulder, loose and casual. Tension that he had held for years seemed to have sluiced away. The church doors closed behind him, leaving her and Quin in naught but the gentle eddy of ancient history within St. Bridgid's stalwart walls.

Silence settled around them in the aged church. She could feel the past swirling around her—from the struggles of those early Reillys to protect the Druids who had first brought them their special Blessing, on through the ages. Despite the anger and violence that had just passed here, peace pervaded her.

"Siannon, I'm sorry about your father."

She looked up at her husband, and her love for him welled from deep inside her, washing the fear and sorrow from her soul. "I'm sorry about him too, Quin. He's had nothing but poison inside for as long as I can remember. The only thing that made him human was his love for Timmy. But I couldn't even feel that at the last. Maybe there was a time he loved my mother. She certainly seemed to think so. But if he did, the emotion didn't last."

She sighed and rested her head against Quin's chest, listening to the reassuring beat of his heart. She had so feared she had lost him.

But confusion still twisted inside her as she remembered the look that had passed between her son and her husband. "Quin, how did Timmy know what you were planning?"

"When I told him to run?" His lips curved in a teasing smile. "What makes you think he knew?"

"You looked at him. Just before . . . my father let him go. And then you nodded."

"He's your son, Siannon. He's got good McManus blood in him. I took a chance that he would be able to read what I was thinking. When he looked at me, I knew he understood."

"But, how—"

"He got the same look in his eyes that you do, *mo ceile.*" He stroked a finger over her brows. "The look that tells me you feel everything inside me and accept it without question."

Her heart twisted inside her at his words and the warmth flowing behind them.

"Siannon."

A glow lit the depths of his green eyes. Something wild and sweet tugged at her heart.

"I believed in The Reilly Blessing all my life. I retold the story. I held it to me as a legacy from my grandmother, and I believed."

Tears filled her eyes. "I remember, Quin. I remember the tale and how you felt about it."

He stroked her cheek. "Even when Marie died, I still believed. I merely assumed I had fallen afoul of the curse and would live my life with regrets forever after. And then I walked into that courthouse in Limerick and pulled you into my arms."

A shiver coursed over her.

"And in that moment I knew."

"What did you know?"

"That I held my blessing in my arms. That she had hair of burnished red and a fiery pride to match my own."

"Oh, Quin." She pulled him down for a kiss that

set her heartbeat thumping faster, tasting tomorrow
and forever on his lips.

"I love you, Siannon Reilly, with all that is in me
and all that I will ever be."

Around them the memories of long-dead Reillys
seemed to sigh with satisfaction. A gift completed. A
path chosen.

"And I love you," she told him, feeling her heart
swell in her chest.

He covered her mouth with his and their tongues
slid together, mating in a rhythm as ancient as time
itself. In the distance she could feel the echoes of
the pain he had carried with him for the past decade,
but it was faded and muted now, something he would
learn to accept over time as they went forward with
their lives. No more would he flail himself for the
mistakes of the past and the things he couldn't
change.

Truly blessed. He had found all that he had hoped
for.

Pride welled there as it always had and always would.

ABOUT THE AUTHOR

Elizabeth Keys is the pseudonym for the multiaward-winning writing team Susan C. Stevenson, and Mary Lou Frank. As lifelong friends who finished each other's sentences and shared a love of reading romance fiction, it was natural for us to begin the adventure of creating our own stories together.

People frequently ask us how two people manage to write as a team, and the best answer we've been able to come up with is that we cannot imagine writing without each other. It truly helps to have another brain to bounce ideas off or to park characters and thoughts in.

Members of both New Jersey Romance Writers and Romance Writers of America for over seven years, we currently juggle life and beginning our professional writing career with the support of our two husbands, seven children, and assorted pets. Susan is the vice president of a local bank and Mary Lou works part-time as a grant-writing consultant/administrator for local nonprofits.

The Irish Blessing series we are creating for Zebra Ballad Romance highlights our belief in achieving one's heart's desire through love's special magic.

We love hearing from our readers. You can visit us on the Web at http://www.elizabethkeys.com, reach us through E-mail at mail@elizabethkeys.com, or via regular mail at P.O. Box 243, Alloway, NJ 08001.

COMING IN JUNE 2001 FROM
ZEBRA BALLAD ROMANCES

___ENCHANTMENT: Hope Chest #1
  by Pam McCutcheon   0-8217-6906-5 $5.99US/$7.99CAN
Gina Charles checks into the Chesterfield for some solitude, only to discover
that her room is already occupied by a friendly ghost with compelling
eyes. Gina agrees to help Drake Manton uncover the details of his death
in the fire that left the hotel in ruins. Suddenly she is transported back to 1883
and standing face-to-face with the living, breathing Drake.

___THE SECOND VOW: The Mounties #2
  by Kathryn Fox   0-8217-6821-2 $5.99US/$7.99CAN
As a member of the Northwest Mounted Police, Braden Flynn had only
one mission: escort the Sioux across the U.S. border after the battle
of Little Big Horn. And yet he couldn't help but be distracted by Dancing
Bird. Though a fierce desire smoldered between them, Braden feared that
Dancing Bird would never accept the love of a white man.

___MEANT TO BE: The Happily Ever After Co. #3
  by Kate Donovan   0-8217-6820-4 $5.99US/$7.99CAN
Though her father had made a success of the Happily Ever After Co.,
Noelle Braddock wouldn't let him play matchmaker for her. So when
he opened their home to Lieutenant Zachary, Noelle was determined to
show her absolutele disdain. But ignoring Zachary wouldn't be easy,
especially when his seduction threatened to destroy every ounce of willpower she had.

___ONCE AN ANGEL: Jewels Of the Sea #3
  by Tammy Hilz   0-8217-6819-0 $5.99US/$7.99CAN
A turbulent childhood left Grace Fisk longing for a more stable life. The
only man she's ever loved, Jackson Brodie, has been gone for eight
years. So Grace sets sail for Boston where a loveless, but secure marriage
awaits her. But her plans go awry when her ship is raided by pirates
. . . led by none other than Jackson himself.

Call toll free **1-888-345-BOOK** to order by phone or use this coupon to order
by mail. ALL BOOKS AVAILABLE JUNE 1, 2001.
Name _____
Address _____
City _____ State _____ Zip _____
Please send me the books I have checked above.
I am enclosing $ _____
Plus postage and handling* $ _____
Sales tax (+in NY and TN) $ _____
Total amount enclosed $ _____
*Add $2.50 for the first book and $.50 for each additional book. Send check
or money order (no cash or CODS) to **Kensington Publishing Corp., Dept.
C.O., 850 Third Avenue, New York, NY 10022**
Prices and numbers subject to change without notice. Valid only in the U.S.
All orders subject to availabilty. **NO ADVANCE ORDERS.**
Visit our website at **www.kensingtonbooks.com**.

Put a Little Romance in Your Life With
Shannon Drake

Merlin's Legacy

A Series From
Quinn Taylor Evans

__**Daughter of Fire** $5.50US/$7.00CAN
   0-8217-6052-1

__**Daughter of the Mist** $5.50US/$7.00CAN
   0-8217-6050-5

__**Daughter of Light** $5.50US/$7.00CAN
   0-8217-6051-3

__**Dawn of Camelot** $5.50US/$7.00CAN
   0-8217-6028-9

__**Shadows of Camelot** $5.50US/$7.00CAN
   0-8217-5760-1

Call toll free **1-888-345-BOOK** to order by phone or use
this coupon to order by mail.

Name _____
Address _____
City _____ State _____ Zip _____
Please send me the books I have checked above.
I am enclosing $_____
Plus postage and handling* $_____
Sales tax (in New York and Tennessee) $_____
Total amount enclosed $_____
*Add $2.50 for the first book and $.50 for each additional book.
Send check or money order (no cash or CODs) to:
Kensington Publishing Corp., 850 Third Avenue, New York, NY 10022
Prices and Numbers subject to change without notice.
All orders subject to availability.
Check out our website at **www.kensingtonbooks.com**